VIRGIN

A Henchmen MC Novel

--

Jessica Gadziala

Cover image credit: Shutterstock .com/ g-stockstudio

Dedication:

This book is dedicated to the endless string of distractions and the epic case of after-the-holidays-stress-hangover that made it their very mission in life to try to prevent this book from being written. Also, to coffee. I couldn't have done it without you, old friend.

ONE

Freddie

If you're going to be stupid, you've got to be tough.

That was my first hard-won life lesson. And, as with most life lessons, I hadn't learned it willingly.

I had to have my freedom taken away from me to harden me up. I had to spend my days in a cage inside a cage inside a cage.

There was a perpetual chill there, something that burrowed under the skin, whittled away at the bone to settle in the marrow, making you sure that you would never feel warm again.

I still felt it, even clad in my own clothes again for the first time in a decade. Jeans of the boyfriend variety skirted the heel of my open-toe wedge sandals. On top, I had a simple white tee under a lightweight jacket. My aunt would call it a *windbreaker*. And me, well, I didn't know what to call it. And I didn't really even know if it would be in style anymore. Or if I would walk outside and everyone would know where I had been for the past ten years.

The embarrassment - long buried because there was no one around to judge without being considered a hypocrite - welled up stronger than it had been on the day when I had first shuffled shackled feet through the cinderblock walled halls.

I wondered as I accepted my old wallet from a male guard behind the desk - a man wholly disinterested in the enormity of his position, of his daily impact - if it was something I would ever get used to. The prickling, uncomfortable sensation of eyes on me, seeing me for what I was. At least on paper. And on paper was all that really mattered, wasn't it?

A felon.

Ex-con.

Just another part of a debilitating statistic.

"And sign here," the man behind the glass that wasn't glass at all demanded, pushing the paperwork toward me, the pen attached to his side of the desk with a bunch of interconnected rubber bands tied together.

A precaution against pen theft? Or fear that one of us might jab it through the soft of his eye and into his brain?

Like we'd risk our freedom before it was even fully granted to us.

"Hope we don't see you again." It was a phrase that was likely meant to sound hopeful or supportive. But it always came off as condescending. And maybe there was some fairness in that. Seeing as eighty percent of us who walked out these doors as free women would return in the next five years.

And while I never would have thought of myself as someone who would go to jail at all a decade ago, I had a sneaking suspicion that I might very well be shackled and shuffled back in within the next year. Though, next time, rightfully so.

"The bus stop is at the end of the street," he added, a plastic pre-paid debit card to me. On it, I knew I would find the money I had earned from the prison job I had been working for the last few years, minus what I had spent at the commissary. I was crossing my fingers that it would be enough to get me back to my hometown, back to Navesink Bank where my brother would be welcoming me into his life.

I'd never taken a bus - save for the ones that would shuttle me to school when I was younger - in my life. There was going to be a learning curve to figure out how to get from where I was now - in the middle of nowhere Pennsylvania - to the coast of New Jersey. A Google search a week ago had told me it would be over six hours if the drive was straight through. I would likely be getting into Navesink Bank sometime around dinner time.

I could have made my life easier by having one of my brothers pick me up. Guilt was what had me telling them that I didn't know my release day yet, that I would let them know as soon as I did. They already did too much for me. Putting money in my commissary so I could buy extra tampons or pads on heavy months when what the prison supplied as though it was freaking contraband was nowhere near enough to get me through, could get extra socks or panties, soap, toothpaste, shower shoes, deodorant, Tylenol. If there was one thing you learned quickly, it was how important personal care items were in prison.

On top of the generous monetary contributions they made every week without fail, there were the trips they made out to see me. Not as often as when I was first sent away, but at least a couple times a year.

And now I was going to be leaning on them while I got back on my feet as well.

It was too much. I simply couldn't ask for anything else from either of them.

I would merely have to do this on my own.

Worry twisted in my belly as I slipped the card into the clutch that had been mine once upon a time and turned away from the desk, eyeing the door I was supposed to walk through, a guard standing beside it looking bored, his gaze moving over me in a dismissive way I had come to know and accept.

Taking a breath, I pushed my shoulders back and made my way toward him, inwardly hoping my feet wouldn't betray me, wobble on my heels, send me face first to the floor, so unaccustomed they were to heels anymore.

"Don't come back, you hear?" he told me as he opened the door to my freedom.

I forced my feet forward, stepping outside.

Dreary.

That was how one would describe the day.

It was perhaps too much to ask for a bright, sunny day that would warm me, make me think that maybe I did want to do right, act right, get my life on track, never return to the cold halls of the minimum security women's prison that had been my makeshift home since I was eighteen.

A third of my life I had been in those walls.

Somehow, despite the outside world being vast, it felt like it was closing in on me as I forced my legs to carry me out, away, toward the end of the paved drive. My chest tightened. A hand curled around my throat.

It was pure stubbornness that pushed me forward, likely reinforced with the simmering anger that had managed to keep me sane all those years locked up with a revolving door of, well, a mix of nut jobs, general undesirables, and those wrapped up in an endless cycle of incarceration, making them hard and rough around the edges, made them grate on your softer skin.

A horn beeped as I made my way down the street toward the covered bus stop where I knew everyone who saw me board would know I had just been set free, would sit and wonder what I did, would maybe clutch their purses closer, move their children to the inside of the row.

My head turned to find a group of guys giving me knowing eyes and obscene gestures of the oral sex variety, making me sigh out a breath as I turned back away.

Sex - oral or otherwise - was hardly even on my mind. I knew it was different for most of the women inside who sat around and talked about the men they left behind, all the things they planned to do to them the moment they were free. It was a favorite pastime, really. Each tale more sordid and detailed than the last, leaving me a perpetual odd-woman-out.

Which was fine.

Because my plans did involve a man.

But there would be nothing sweet or sexy about it.

It would be rough. Ugly. Violent.

Bloody, even.

Hopefully.

If I had enough rage left.

If I hadn't burned through enough of it while locked up.

And if, well, I had the stomach for it. Which was possibly the most significant factor. I wasn't like the women the other inmates told me about from the medium or maximum security facilities, women who made you afraid to sleep in the bunk with them, women who shaved down their toothbrushes into shivs, women who thirsted for blood like the worst of any men could be known for.

No.

I was the kind of person who felt a bit queasy and had to look away when my big brothers fell out a tree or something and came home bleeding.

But I would harden up.

I had been doing it for years.

I had a feeling I would be doing it for many years to come.

Hard.

And stone cold.

That was what I would need to be to get through this, then through the repercussions afterward.

Eyeing the covered bus stop shelter bench, covered with half decomposed leaves from the past fall - brown and gold and auburn - along with the gritty texture of the salts from the past snow, and a single daddy long legs moving from one end to the other, I moved back outside, leaning against the wall, taking another breath, checking out the schedule, seeing which route I needed to pick from the ticket machine.

It wasn't that I *wanted* to go back to prison, of course. No one who went in actually wanted to go back once they were free. Sometimes - maybe most of the time - it was just the cycle of poverty or addiction. They couldn't survive on the outside without money, without support. They turned back to the drugs. Or they got desperate and went back to crime to make money to keep a roof over their heads, food in their bellies, clothes on their kids' backs.

It wasn't like the food was amazing inside. That the two-inch thick, used mattress was the right kind of firm for my back. That being strip searched was the highlight of my life.

No.

Of course, I didn't want to go back to shitty medical care, horrible choices for hair products, the stink of dozens of people in the same space, the occasional abusive words from the guards, the impossibility of a restful night sleep thanks to others talking, yelling, crying.

It just seemed like there wasn't much of a choice in the matter if I got my hands on that bastard. Really, even if my plan wasn't premeditated like it clearly was, and I just happened upon him one day on the street, yeah, I was pretty sure it would lead to me heading back to a cell.

I heard the chugging, hissing sound - an old, familiar one - looking up to find the rusty silver bus approaching, stopping at my side with a grinding screech. The door squeaked open as I straightened up, checking the bus number against the schedule, making sure it was heading in the right direction.

Reaching for my ticket from the machine, I climbed the grime-covered steps, stopping a few feet from the driver - a man in his fifties with a hangover of a waistline and an impressive handlebar mustache - to slip my ticket into the machine.

I was thankful for the measly smattering of people scattered around me - a middle-aged man in a custodial jumpsuit, an older woman in a waitress uniform, a duo of high school kids clearly ditching class. There were glances, but nothing damning, nothing that said they knew where I had been, what I had done.

It was a comfort of sorts as the bus jolted back to life, taking my belly with it for a moment, and I sat back to watch the world speed by me.

I hadn't been in a bus since the ride into the prison, my wrists and ankles shackled, a female guard standing up by the front with a baton at one hip and a gun at the other. I'd been too sick with fear, with uncertainty, with bone-deep trepidation to notice the world moving past me. And after so long in a standstill place, the way the trees, budding with spring leaves, raced past me was making my chest tight, my stomach queasy.

After the fourth transfer, the queasy feeling was replaced with one of hunger. But I was finally across the border of New Jersey. And I was running short on money on my debit card. So I decided to suffer until I got to my brother's place, knowing he would have something in his fridge I could steal.

Real food, too.

Nothing mushy or unidentifiable. Made with actual spices.

And then I could shower. With hot water. For as long as I wanted. Be allowed to use a razor without worrying about having to return it in a certain amount of time or else I'd get in trouble.

Then, finally, I could get a night's rest a decade in the making. On a comfortable bed. With soft, numerous blankets. A TV on as background noise. And no one yelling or crying to keep me from rest. I could wake up when my body wanted to, not when the lights clicked on and guards started yelling.

Such bliss was worth the churning, angry emptiness in my stomach as the final bus deposited me half a block from the train station in Navesink Bank.

I don't know what I expected.

For things to look different. Or exactly the same. When the reality was somewhere in between. The station was the same as it had always been - a little worn, a little in need of paint or a power washing. But there were new trees planted. The restaurant across the street that used to be a Mexican place was now Italian. The parking meters were covered, replaced with some central ticket system that seemed a lot less efficient.

I chose not to call a cab, knowing the walk would just be about half an hour to the apartment building. Sure, I had to walk through gang territory, and the me I used to be shrank away from the idea. But the woman I was - who had once seen a fellow inmate hold another inmate's hand in a pot of boiling oil - knew there was little that truly scared me anymore.

My brother's apartment building was one that had been a mere debate in the town meetings when I had been in Navesink Bank last - most of the citizens agreeing that it would bring more and more unneeded traffic to the area. Clearly, the taxes outweighed the community uproar.

The building was nice - sand-colored stucco with each apartment getting a wrought iron-lined balcony.

It was pretty.

More upscale than the other buildings that had been in the area.

Luck I never had in the past shined upon me as a woman came to the door with a stroller in front of her and a toddler on her hip, struggling to open the door for it. I rushed up, holding it open, accepting her thanks, inwardly giving her my own as I slipped inside, making my way to the elevator to ride it up to the fourth floor.

Unexpectedly nervous, I stood in front of the door for a long moment, trying to find the guts to knock.

Then I did.

And there he was.

Thaddeus.

In a gold, white, and blue thigh-skirting kimono and a gold sequined turban on his head. Despite the fact that he didn't even have any friggen hair.

"Bitch, you don't tell your brother you're getting out? You make me find out when I call the prison to talk to you? That's how we do things now? Christ, this hair," he said, grimacing as he reached out to stroke the admittedly dry tresses I had pulled back because I had given up on it years back.

Thad and I looked a lot alike. The same deep skin, the same high cheekbones, full lips, sleepy-lidded, golden brown eyes. But where I was only maybe five-five on a day when I was standing up straight, and slim if perhaps a bit thick of thigh and back end, Thaddeus was about six feet of solid muscle, making his black wifebeater look like it was holding on for dear life over his strong chest, leaving his impressive arms on display.

"Come on, get your pretty ass on in here," he demanded, stepping aside to invite me into the apartment.

It was what I would expect from Thad. The walls were a warm golden color, peppered with giant art prints in bright, crazy primary or neon colors. The living room to the left was full of plush, tufted creme furniture, a sleek oversized coffee table with a marble top that matched the countertops in the mostly-white kitchen.

Thad was neat by nature, save for a chair that was undoubtedly still in his bedroom where his discarded wardrobe choices would be piled, awaiting the day some months in the future where he would feel motivated to steam and hang them all back up again.

Everything had a place and was in it.

Except, of course, for the completely out of place black leather hairdresser chair sitting butted up against the kitchen sink.

"Um, Thad, why do you have that?" I asked, waving a hand toward it, watching as his eyes went to my hand, his head shaking as he grabbed my wrist, inspecting my short nails, my overgrown cuticles.

"Girl, I know they have emery boards and nail polish in there. This is a disgrace. And I have the salon chair because when a bitch hears his sister is getting out of federal prison after a decade, he makes sure he gets what she might need when she comes in. Like food in the cabinets. Fresh sheets on the guest bed. And the basic fundamental necessities for a much-needed makeover and pampering day."

Maybe I might have been offended by the idea of him insisting I needed a makeover. But, well, my own reflection had told me as much just that very morning.

"I also have some new clothes on the way."

"On the way? Do they deliver clothes now?" I asked, feeling like I had been under a rock only to reemerge to find an entirely different world had grown around me.

"They? As in the stores? No, angel baby, no," he said with a lip twitch. "But I have friends who love the idea of traipsing around buying pretty girl things. They will also be picking up a new cell for you. Handbags. Some girly shit for your lady business."

"You have friends that would pick up girly shit for my lady business?" I asked, completely unable to wrap my head around such a person.

"Well, boo, my friends don't have lady caves, so there is no embarrassment for them picking up stuff to stick all up in there," he said, waving a hand at my crotch. "Now. Go shower that public transit off of you. Wrap yourself in the spare kimono. Then come back out here for some food and pampering. What?" he asked when I felt my lips tipping up.

"I'm trying to wrap my head around having a single kimono, let alone a guest one."

"Um, Winifred, angel, I know you've been locked up for a long time. But I'm sure there was some lady cave digging or licking or whatever goes on with that whole situation you have down there. And just like there is lady-on-lady lovin' on the inside, there is man-on-fine-ass-man lovin' on the outside. And when one of those fine ass men stays over at my home and hearth, honey, they need to have themselves a kimono."

Since I had never worn a kimono in my life, I couldn't quite agree with the necessity of it in general, let alone for romantic encounters. But, hey, what the hell did I even know about anything anymore?

"Okay. If you say so."

"Oh, and there is a package of hair products on the vanity. You use them as instructed, you hear? Otherwise, I won't be able to do a damn thing with that dried out mess you have going on."

I snorted at that, shaking my head. "I love you too, Thad."

"Girl, you know how we show love in this family," he countered, shrugging.

"With food."

"With food. That's right. Now go get your scrub and shave on. Some private self-loving if you so require. I will be out here with my fine ass, cooking you a four-course meal."

My stomach rumbled in response as I gave him a smile before making my way toward the hall where I found the bathroom behind the first door on the left.

There were some strange things you forgot about when you were on the inside. Fluffy, not stiff blankets. Real glass mirrors. Pretty shower curtains. Shelves where you could put - and keep - personal care products. Of which Thad had about two dozen. Shaving foam, powder, exfoliator, body lotion, facial moisturizer, face masks, eye cream, toner. The list was endless.

I turned on the water to get warm as I read the instructions on the bottles of my specialty hair products before setting them on the edge, sliding off my clothes, then slipping under the hot spray. Without the worry of other women seeing me. Without concern about guards yelling at me.

It was just me.

In a shower.

What a small, yet monumental, luxury.

I was in there until the steam tufted up thick in the room, making the air hard to breathe, until the water ran cool, until every inch had been scrubbed, exfoliated, shaved if it needed it, and pumiced when it came to my feet, knees, elbows.

It wasn't for another half an hour of adding in the products Thad had given me and covering myself in lotion, then sliding in the admittedly amazing feeling of the guest kimono that I emerged from the bathroom to the sounds of Prince coming from the speakers, Thad swaying his hips to a song that talked about *titties bouncing* while he mixed something in a pan.

The air was full of too many smells to place any one dish. Onions danced with garlic who lightly kissed the starchy smell of cooking pasta. Underneath that, a smell I knew only from my aunt who always had a bottle open and breathing on the counter after work, not from any personal experience with it.

Red wine.

Sweet, yet vinegar-like somehow at the same time.

On the long list of things I had never done, tasting alcohol was right there in the middle. Not a taste of wine at Church. Not a vodka cran sucked down at a house party. Not a foul-smelling beer some friend's brother picked up.

Nothing.

Not a sip.

Don't bother. She's a goodie-goodie.

If I had a dime for every time I heard that growing up, well, I'd have had enough money to hire a decent attorney and maybe avoid incarceration as a whole.

"Alright, girl. I didn't know what to make you. So I made you everything. We got mac n' cheese noodles cooking. Creamy tomato soup bubbling. Breaded chicken in the oven with some potatoes, carrots, and onions. Brownie batter just waiting for the chicken to finish. I got all the comfort foods, boo. And if you want takeout later, I got a drawer full of menus."

There was something pulling me across the floor, a string situated in my chest, dragging me toward the one attached to his, making me move up behind him, wrapping my arms around his comfortingly strong frame, resting my head on the jut of his shoulder blade, taking a deep breath of him, and squeezing hard.

"I'm happy to have you here too, boo," he told me, closing his giant hand over my finer boned one.

"I didn't know how to ride a bus," I admitted to his back as though there was anything to be ashamed of in the first place.

"Honey babe, that is because people as *fine* as us shouldn't be taking public transportation," Thad told me, his voice funeral serious, something that made a laugh bubble up and burst out until I could feel something long-buried, something almost foreign, move through my body.

Happiness.

And it was warm. Hot even.

That was why I had been so unbearably cold for so long. Because there was nothing even akin to joy in the world I had been in for so long.

Feeling it there in my brother's kitchen while he made me dinner and talked about how he was planning to chop off most of my hair, I realized that maybe things wouldn't be as easy as I thought.

To go through with my plan.

To, likely, head back to jail.

Possibly for life.

It had been so long. I had forgotten how it felt to love and be loved. Under the daily drudgery of prison life, I had somehow lost these parts of me. The ones that knew humor and food made of love and the touch of affection that wanted nothing but to soothe, to make things better.

As I sat across a little round table loaded down with more food than I had seen in years, made with flavor and familiarity, listening to my brother talk about the men in his 'rotation,' and telling me about all the things he had planned to do with me now that I was home, I wasn't sure how I could do it.

Give it all back.

Give it away.

Willingly, this time.

It wasn't just about me, either. It wasn't about all these soft, warm things I would be refusing for myself. It was about my brothers. It was about what I would be doing to *them*. With purpose. Fully aware of what I was doing to them all over again. Making them worry about me. Knowing they would continue to fill my commissary even if I told them not to. Having to deal with the back flack that would inevitably come from having a family member spending the rest of their lives in jail.

Could I do that to them?

Be that selfish?

As Thaddeus rubbed red lipstick on my lips, fluffed my hair, then moved me in front of the mirror, I was almost sure I couldn't.

The woman who looked back at me was a me I didn't recognize, a me that hadn't looked back at me in a mirror in a decade. This was a woman who had people who loved her, who wanted to spend meals with her, go to movies. This was a woman who had places to go, people to see, a future to make.

Thad was true to his word. He chopped off the shoulder-length, dried-out hair I had been abusing for ten years, shortening it to just under my ears, the tresses falling in bouncy, yet loose curls, giving it the volume it had been needing to set off my cheekbones, he cut somehow making my eyes more of a focal point. Mascara darkened and lengthened my lashes. My brows were perfectly tweezed. And my lips were a bold shade of red that I never would have chosen for myself, but found myself loving.

"And that, beautiful, would be Benny with your clothes," Thad announced when there was a knocking on the door with what seemed like the tip of a shoe.

Benny, as far as I remembered from the somewhat lengthy list, was not part of Thad's rotation. Just a friend. The one who let him borrow the salon chair in the first place.

The next few hours were a whirlwind. I was plied with wine that made me both light and heavy at the same time, making my head feel floaty, but my heart feel slow and sad as I was stripped down to my panties and dressed, undressed, and redressed while being inspected by the keen eyes of both Thaddeus and Benny who debated each piece of wardrobe as if the fate of the country depended on them being the right shade for my skin tone and the right style to accentuate my waist and behind while making it seem like I had more up top than I actually did.

By the time I was shuffled to bed wearing a silk camisole and short set in a sweet soft yellow color that felt buttery soft on my skin, staring up at the white ceiling fan whirling around lazily enough not to even rustle the sheer drapes on the windows, I understood one thing.

If I had to continue this path, if I chose to let the rage simmer and overflow, if I took out long-sought vengeance, my brothers would never forgive me.

I'd have to give them up.

I'd have to be okay with having no family left, never knowing warmth again.

And, quite frankly, I wasn't ready for that yet.

I wondered if I ever would be.

If I could live with myself if I didn't make him pay for what he did to me, what he stole from me. If I could face myself every day for the rest of my life knowing he was out there with a clear conscience, getting off Scot-free. If I could ever truly move on from a youth stolen, trust annihilated, happiness ripped away.

I didn't, as it turned out, get a restful night sleep.

While the world around me might have been silent for the first time in years, the voices in my head screamed louder than anyone else possibly could.

TWO

Virgin

There were, by my count, eight kids running around the compound.

Freeze tag.

Simon Says.

Cops and robbers.

High squeals, gut laughs, end tables toppling to the floor with choruses of *Oooh, you're gonna be in trouuuuble.*

Leaned back against the bar, long-buried memories tugged at the edges of my consciousness.

Eight dropped down to two.

Me and Sugar.

Two kids in a place never meant for squishy, impressionable minds. Boys forced to shoulder the responsibility of manhood far too young, never allowed to cry, to feel affection and love.

Fuck. I didn't even know what those words meant, to be perfectly honest.

I was a product of a clubhouse. Of rough men with sharp edges that didn't hesitate to cut even young flesh if it got too close.

"What's up?" Sugar asked, sidling in at my right, following my line of vision to where one of the smaller kids - head blocked by the edge of the pool table, making them unrecognizable save for solid foundations and light hair - was doing a real shit - so bad it was comical - attempt to hide from the seeker who was counting down from twenty, missing a few numbers here and there.

"They don't belong here," I mumbled.

"Don't be a fuck," Sugar shot back, shaking his head.

"Not like that," I insisted, shrugging my shoulders. "They don't belong here like we didn't belong in a clubhouse."

"Yah, maybe. But this isn't like that," he reminded me. "Look around. No one is getting head in plain sight. Not a single Devil's Triangle to be seen. No heroin powder on the coffee tables. This is different."

That was true enough.

A lifetime - literally - in MCs had given me a full picture of what they had to offer. And, for the most part, it was some none-too-subtle misogyny, oftentimes horrific hazing of probates, addiction, and violence.

Coming to Navesink Bank had been Sugar's idea. The Henchmen had a great reputation of being stable, of having great leadership, and - thanks to an unfortunate incident that culled their numbers - were needing new members. He said it was time to find some roots, a place we could really settle into instead of jumping MCs every few years because the leaders got locked up and things fell apart.

I hadn't been an unwilling tagalong either. I had participated. I had come to the open house. I had met the crew. I had tried to impress Reign and Cash and Wolf so we could get in.

And there had been no shortage of action thanks to the complex underworld in this particular town on the river.

I had even been happy for a long while.

I didn't know what was going on.

Something was bothering me. Some phantom itch under the skin that no scratching could ease.

Maybe it was as simple as Sugar settling down. Though, maybe, 'settling down' was not the right phrase for what he and Peyton were doing. Anyone who knew Peyton knew that the woman would never do something as mundane as settling down. Not her. Not this woman who had turned over the booth in the diner when we had been out to eat after overhearing some young shits talking about making a girl come and demonstrated with her fingers where the G-spot was located and what rhythm to work the clit to.

No.

Peyton would never settle down.

But she had stolen most of Sug's attention and time.

I had to admit, it had been an adjustment.

If there was one thing I could count on from age of four on, it was that Sugar was going to be around, be down for whatever trouble I wanted to get into.

And it seemed as soon as bonds were formed with my new brothers, a woman came crashing into their lives, dragging them away from the club.

Pagan and Kennedy. Cy and Reese. Edison and Lenny. Reeve and Rey. Adler and Lou. Roderick and Liv.

It was just me and Roan and Cam, the latest addition.

Roan spent most of his time swearing some storm was coming. And Cam, well, he was around. He brought donuts every morning. But, yeah, you couldn't exactly get to know the man. He didn't speak.

If ever I was feeling like an outsider, it was here. Now. In this club full of happy couples and contented children.

I had jobs, duties, allegiances.

But I didn't feel like I had a place, not really.

"You know how I hate the touchy-feely shit," Sugar said to my silence. "But Peyt thinks I am being a shitty friend if I don't say something."

"Something about what?"

"About you. Something's going on. And since you aren't exactly a conversationalist, I guess I have to ask."

"Guess I'm just bored," I said, shrugging it off.

"Bored? Here? Christ, wasn't it just like a year back that we took down V and saved the girls. And before that all the uncertainty about who was after us. Think there's been more action here than the other MCs combined. Raids aside."

"Can't argue with that."

I could feel his gaze on the side of my face, trying to burrow in, trying to understand something that I didn't exactly understand myself.

"Maybe you need to go out and get some tail," he suggested. "It's been a while."

Now that he mentioned it, it had been a while. While I was fine going out alone, hitting the bar by myself and waiting for the right woman to walk in was boring as fuck. So I had been spending most of my free time picking up extra guard duties at the compound to give all the guys with better things to do a break.

I did need to get out.

Get laid.

Clear my head.

"Yeah. You're right," I agreed, jerking my head over toward Cam, knowing that Roan was a lost cause. He'd been worse than usual lately. Like the storm wasn't just some *Farmer's Almanac* prediction, but an ache in his bones. "You up for Chaz's?" I asked when he gave me a raised brow.

His nod was all I was going to get.

"Let's go. Tell Peyt I said hey," I told Sugar, knowing that was where he would be when I got back. Peyton wasn't opposed to spending time in the clubhouse. In fact, she got a kick out of it. But she had this circle of friends all around her, ones that crashed at her place all the time, and she - understandably - would take their company over ours.

An hour and four beers later, I was starting to think my luck was going to run out. It was a fight night - some bullshit feud between two men faking bravado when you knew damn well they respected the shit out of each other in real life, but, hell, that didn't make great TV. The place was packed full of people not willing to shell out the cash to watch the fight in the comfort of their own homes. And women, well, they stayed far the fuck away from a bunch of drunk ass men cheering on brutal violence.

Cam was kicked back in a booth, head lulled back, a drink cradled in his hands, staring at one of the TVs, but I got the feeling he was looking through it instead of actually watching it, leaving me to do just about the same.

Cam wasn't a bad wingman.

In fact, in the time he had been with us, he had somehow managed to bag his fair share of women when we went out to the bars. How, when he couldn't talk to the women, I wasn't exactly sure. But it was a level of suave most men could only dream of aspiring to. Because you had to have a fuckload of game to get a modern-day, cautious, suspicious, untrusting - rightfully so - woman to go home with you when she didn't even catch your name.

After a cursory scan of the room once we stepped in, he seemed to abandon the idea of getting laid and set to just about ignoring everything.

Or so I thought until I felt a jab - elbow into my ribcage - making my head jerk over, brows lowered, finding his eyes on me. As soon as I caught his gaze, his chin jerked outward toward the bar I had been sure he'd been all but blind to.

Turning, I saw her.

And there was only a gap between seconds where I was curious as to how Cam had spotted her before me.

Especially because she was a living, breathing version of the perfect woman. Or, at least, my perfect woman.

We all had our preferences. Cam, for example, went for the soft girls. Creamy skin, lighter shades of hair - blondes and strawberries and ashy browns. Tall and willowy. Delicate, almost. The quiet ones who tagged along with their ballsier girlfriends. The introvert that the extroverts adopted and made it their mission to bring them of their shell.

That was his type.

But me? I went for darker skin tones. Shorter girls with curves a man could sink fingers into. And with that extra unspoken *thing*. That attitude that came through from somewhere deep, that clouded up the air around them without even having to hear them speak. A confidence. A hardness.

That was my type.

And this woman?

Fuck.

I caught a side view first, her head turned away, giving me only her short-average body with her thick thighs and ass clad in jeans I had no fucking idea how she got on since they clung like a second skin. A basic white tee, tailored, but not tight, hung out underneath a simple army green bomber jacket. A set of gold hoops peeked out from below her short, curly hair.

Then a noise - two guys yelling at the fight - made her head whip over in my direction.

And fuck if that wasn't the kind of face that could take a man out at the knees.

No one would ever accuse me of being a romantic, but there was no other way to say it.

The soft bone structure.

The light eyes.

The full, bright red lips.

An image of that mouth wrapped around my cock shot through my head, her head tipped up, eyes open, watching me as she sucked me deep. My cock stiffened a bit at the idea.

But it wasn't just the looks. Though let's face it, that was undoubtedly a factor.

No.

There was something in her eyes. Something weighted. Something dark, guarded, but somehow certain. Confident.

A soft and a hard place at the same time, that was what she was.

And that was some intriguing shit, now, wasn't it?

I nodded my chin at Cam, a silent thanks, placing my hand on the table, getting ready to stand. When a man moved into the picture, sliding in front of her, taking up all the space between her and the bar. Close. Too close for a random pickup.

With a sigh, I eased back into my chair, reaching for my beer.

No one could say I was the most moral of men. I'd been in heroin and cocaine dealing MCs. I'd been an enforcer, beating the shit out of people solely for the paycheck. I'd taken up the generous offers of an unknown number of clubwhores. I sold guns to other undesirables.

But I didn't fuck around with women who had men. At least not if I knew they had men. Sometimes shit happened, and drama was inevitable, but I wasn't about to set my sights on a woman who already had a man.

Cam's hand slammed down on the table, drawing my attention to where he was rolling his eyes at me. Like he was in on something I had missed.

Curious, my gaze slid across the bar again, looking for what I might have missed.

The woman had her gaze trained on the door.

And the man - oh.

I half turned back to Cam, seeing his smirk, feeling one of my own pulling at my lips.

Because the man I thought was *her* man was flirting with a man to his side, stroking his hand down his tie suggestively.

And, on closer inspection, they had the same eyes.

Brother, not boyfriend.

I drained my drink, getting to my feet, making my way across the bar.

"Oh, well, boo, no one has to kno..." the man's voice trailed off, clearly picking up on a bi vibe from the man who outwardly seemed straight as his gaze fell on me. "Well, look at this fine ass mother fucker," he exclaimed, leaning back against the bar, a hand going to his heart. "Don't worry, Denzel," he added, shaking his head. "I know you aren't here for me. Bitch, stop looking at the door. This fine piece of man meat wants to chat your pretty ass up. Thaddeus," he told me, reaching out his free hand. The other was still holding the tie of the curious man to his side.

"Virgin."

His brow raised at that. "A nickname, I hope. Not a declaration. Because, no offense, but my little sis deserves a man who knows how to slide her on into home, not some fumbling first timer."

"Road name," I clarified, making his eyes move over to the leather cut over my black tee.

"Oh, shit. He rides a bike. Are you listening to me?" he demanded, snapping at his sister who turned back, brows furrowed, apparently lost in her own head.

"Not at all actually."

"She's a work in progress," Thaddeus explained, excusing his sister for her lack of sociability. "Girl, this is Virgin," he explained, making the woman's gaze finally move to me for the first time.

Maybe she was good at distant and hard.

But there was no mistaking the way her lips parted, the way her eyes roamed over my face. The way she had to work at keeping them from roving lower.

"This is my sister, Freddie," Thaddeus went on when she said nothing. "Fred, this is where you say hi to the nice man."

Her gaze cut to him, eyes rolling a bit. But she was the sort who placated her big brother, so she looked back at me with a simple, "Hi."

"Not in the mood, huh?" I asked, shrugging a shoulder.

"Well..." she started to let me down.

"Um, hell the fuck yes, she's in the mood. Need I remind you of your rather impressive dry spell that..."

"Thad!" Freddie hissed, eyes going round. And, if I wasn't mistaken, her cheeks got a little bit red too. Blushing, now that I hadn't expected.

"Dry spell, huh?" I asked, watching as her gaze tentatively moved back to me, not quite making eye contact, making me wonder about my earlier assessment of her confidence. "I could help you with that."

"Really, I just came here to..."

"Stop being a cock-block to your big brother, see some new faces, get hit on by hot bikers..." Thad reminded her. "Listen, honey child, when a man with that Shamar Moore smile and that Channing Tatum body wants to buy your pretty ass a drink, you let them buy you a drink. And you let your brother talk to this gentlemen right here about whose place we are going to be hooking up at tonight," he said, giving the guy's tie a tug. "Go on with your cloistered self," he added when his sister didn't seem like she was going to budge, placing a hand between her shoulder blades and shoving her forward, making her stumble off heels it seemed like she wasn't accustomed to and into my chest.

My arm wrapped around her back, holding her to me as her hands planted on my chest, her head angling up. "Guess you know when you're not wanted, huh?" I asked with a smile as her brother *Mm-hmm'd* from behind her. "Come on. Let me get you a drink."

A bit caught off-guard, she let me right her on her heels, not shrugging away my arm from her hips as I guided her through the crowd.

It wasn't lost on me - though she seemed blithely unaware - that every set of male eyes watched her progress across the room. Eye-fucked her. Sent envious or angry looks in my direction.

Sorry, guys. You gotta nut-up if you want to get the girl. Pansy-ass, insecure bastards need not apply.

That was one lesson I was certainly glad I learned young thanks to the environment I was raised in. The women being as come-and-go as they were in the biker world, you didn't learn to base your self-esteem on whether you got laid or shot down one night. Because there was always the next girl, the next night. If you stepped up to the plate often enough, you were all but guaranteed a home run here and there.

"Freddie, this is Cam. Cam, Freddie," I remembered my manners - something literally pounded into me at some points of my childhood - as we stood in front of my booth.

"Nice to meet you," came from Freddie, as knee-jerk as my own call to social niceties. I'd bet good money on there being a hardass woman figure in her life just like there had been in mine from time to time.

Cam gave her a chin jerk. "Cam doesn't speak," I explained as I pulled out a chair for her to slip into.

I felt out of my depths with Cam, with his condition, not quite knowing if I was being offensive by explaining or providing a relief to the stress that new interactions no doubt brought along. I meant to ask Liv or even Astrid when she happened around, but never seemed to remember.

I figured it was better to explain than have someone ask why he wasn't speaking.

"Oh, okay. I, ah, there must be a sort of comfort in that at times," she said, giving him a wobbly sort of smile. Something telling. Uncertain. Like she was struggling. Like she wished she had an excuse not to talk to people.

Not to talk to me.

I glanced back at her brother, figuring if she wanted out, I would give her an out. I didn't fuck around with trying to convince a woman to want me. You did or you didn't. Either way, I was good. But her brother was making his way to the door, his arm holding the tie of the man over his shoulder, leading him out the door like a puppy.

Freddie's gaze followed mine.

"Seriously?" she asked, shaking her head. "He was my ride," she added when my brow quirked up.

"Cab. Uber. Back of my bike. Plenty of ways to make it home. What are you drinking?"

"Oh, um. Just a soda is fine."

"You clean?" I asked, thinking of Laz, of Beth, again wondering if I was being too blunt.

"Clean? Oh, ah, no. I just... I've never been much of a drinker."

"Fair enough," I said, going to the bar, ordering us both soda. Fucking soda. I hadn't had soda since I was a teenager. But, well, if I wanted her to take me up on the offer to drive her home - and, let's face it, I did - then I needed to lay off the drinks too. I walked back holding two cups topped with fucking umbrellas - the bartender had jokes, it seemed, seeing he knew I was usually one for harder shit.

"Thanks. I really am just going to finish this and head out. I have some, ah, *job* hunting to do tomorrow."

Something about the word *job* rang false to me. But what was there to lie about there? What other kind of hunting was there to do?

"What do you do?" I asked, sensing this was a swing and miss, but not wanting to be rude.

"I, um, cook." Again, a false note. And, again, why lie?

"I make a mean bowl of cereal," I offered, getting rewarded with a surprised, charmed smile.

"Everyone in my family knows how to cook," she told me, giving me a true note. "It was how we first learned to show love, I guess. Thad is better than I am."

"Is he a cook?"

"No. He teaches a cardio dance workout class at the gym."

"Which gym?"

"Ah, the one that used to be a nightclub."

I wasn't originally from the area, so that didn't help me. But I figured it wasn't Lo and Janie's place since they'd probably burn it down before they held a cardio dance workout class. Shane Mallick's place then.

I had a sudden, utterly uncharacteristic urge to take up a membership, see if I could weasel out some information from her much more outgoing brother.

That wasn't me.

I wasn't an investigator.

A Facebook stalker.

Hell, I didn't even have a fucking Facebook account.

I, in general, was a let the chips fall where they may kind of person. I didn't get riled. I didn't get wrapped up in some inconsistencies and try to figure them out, track down leads. No. That wasn't me. I just moved on to the next girl when something seemed off about one.

"What do you do?" she asked, looking between the two of us.

"We're Henchmen," I supplied.

"Oh," she said, those perfect lips forming a big O for a second as recognition hit.

"Gonna run screaming now?" I asked, sensing that she was clearly not like the typical bar chick who had fed on endless years of sexualized crime shows that left them with a thirst not just for *bad boys* but actually bad men. Criminals. Mob members. Gangsters. And, in my case, arms dealing bikers. Granted, it was just a fleeting thing. Just an itch that needed scratching. Just a fantasy that needed fulfilling. Not many women - the old ladies of the club aside, of course - signed up to lock it down with a man such as me. And, well the women that belonged to Henchmen men were, as a whole, a different breed of women, unique creatures entirely.

"Screaming, no. I'm not shocked - or scared - that easily," she told me, and even as she said it, the confidence that I had seen earlier came back, got stronger, made her harder, tougher.

Social conventions and flirting flustered her, shook her confidence. But crime bolstered her up?

Who the hell was this woman?

"But?" I prompted, sensing it floating in the air around us.

"But, like I said," she went on, taking a long sip of her soda before finishing, "I have places to be tomorrow. Thank you for the drink. And it was nice meeting you," she added, getting to her feet, making the two of us do the same. "I hope you find what you're looking for tonight," she added in parting, turning, and hustling her way through the crowd and out the door.

I turned back to Cam, finding his brows furrowed too, apparently as lost as I was feeling.

"That was fucking weird, right?" I asked, needing the confirmation. That she was off. That the interaction as weird. That I wasn't reading too much into it because she was a fantasy come to life. Camden's head was nodding, his shoulders shrugging. "She was lying about the job, about cooking..." Again, more nods from my silent brother. "Weird," I added again, dropping down, getting another round, knowing it was going to be a night I hoofed it since I planned to drink until the urge to chase her fine ass down evaporated.

I hope you find what you're looking for tonight.

The words haunted me.

Even after four more rounds.

Even after getting back to the compound, hanging with the guys, having some more drinks.

Even after a shower and climbing into bed.

Because, to be perfectly honest, I was pretty sure what I was looking for was her.

And that shit, yeah, that was fucked up.

Not like me.

But it was there, niggling at my brain even as sleep finally claimed me.

THREE

Freddie

"Woman," Thad said after coming in the door the following morning after spending the night with the tie guy, leaning back against the door, head tipped to the side, watching me make coffee. The third pot of the day. Since it had been so long since I made coffee that I had no idea how many scoops to put in. The first pot was hot, yellowish water. The second had been so dark and bitter that I had needed to spit my sip into the sink. Hopefully, the third time would be a charm.

"Yes?" I asked, turning to him.

"Where is he?"

"Where is who?"

"Where is who? That fine ass man who was drooling over you last night, that's who."

"Oh. I don't know. Home, I would imagine." Thad's eyes got small. Annoyed. Disappointed. A mix of the two perhaps. "I wasn't going to go home with a strange biker!"

"Lover girl, it has been a *decade* since you've had any action. A decade. You needed to go home with a strange biker. Especially one that fine."

"I don't do casual sex."

"Honey, you don't do *any* sex. And I gotta say, that just can't be healthy."

"It hasn't exactly been a choice."

"Well, yeah. But now it is."

"I didn't even know how to talk to him," I admitted, shaking my head. "I felt like a little girl confronted with an intimidating man."

"Oh, Fred," Thad said with a little sigh, moving over to me, wrapping an arm half around me, pressing a kiss to my temple. "You'll get there. There's time. Now let me just take a shower, then I will take you out to breakfast before work, okay?"

I nodded, turning to watch the coffee drip for a moment before there was a loud rapping on the door, something that made me insides jump - a knee-jerk reaction to hearing that sound startling me awake so many times in the past. For shakedowns or just morning wake ups.

Hearing Thad singing and the slap of water on the shower floor, I knew it was up to me to answer. And I felt oddly nervous about that.

"Thad open up. We gotta talk."

If I was nervous before, it was amplified by the sound of that voice. A familiar voice. One who called me weekly. Who visited me whenever possible.

Colson.

Thad's twin.

My eldest older brother.

By eight minutes and forty-two seconds.

A man I hadn't told I was free yet.

Even after Thad suggested we show up at his door before the bar the night before.

I, oddly, was worried about seeing Colson. Maybe because where Thaddeus was all light and love and easy humor, Colson was all seriousness and standoffishness. He'd taken much longer to come visit me after I was sent away, never really giving me a reason. It had hurt more than I would ever admit. He hadn't apologized. I hadn't brought it up. And, if I were being honest, there had been a bit of a wedge there ever since.

He wasn't going to be happy that I had been out for over two days and hadn't told him.

"Don't make me search for your key," his voice called through the door, sounding impatient.

Taking a breath, squaring my shoulders, I forced myself to move across the floor, oddly wishing that I had something on other than loose lilac silk pants and a black tee. Which was ridiculous seeing as all he had seen me in for a decade was a hideous prison uniform.

I slid the lock and pulled the door open.

A cursory glance would say that Colson and Thad were identical. They were both tall, broad, had strong jaws, the same eyes, nearly bald heads. But if you looked closer, Colson was almost two inches taller, longer around the trunk than the leg like Thad. He let his face go to stubble whereas Thaddeus was an almost compulsive shaver. Colson's cheekbones hollowed out a bit more than Thad's, giving him a somewhat angry look at times. His lashes - and Thad would slap me if he heard me ever say this - were much thicker than Thad's too.

His gaze found my face, his whole body shocking back at seeing me stand there. Like he was faced with a ghost instead of his own sister.

"Jesus Christ," he hissed, shaking his head.

"Bad words, Daddy."

Now *that* was a voice I had never heard before. I knew of the owner of it, of course. You didn't forget that you had a niece, even if you had never met her.

Jelena.

She was four and a half, short, sturdy on brushing thighs and with a slightly rounded belly. It was clearly a 'she dressed herself' kind of day since her shorts were black with neon stars and her top was a long sleeve rainbow print. Her hair was worked into an elegant wrap-around style braid that ended in a braided bun behind her ear, putting her cute slightly pointed ears with little diamond studs on perfect display.

I'd never met her mother. Neither had Jelena for that matter. But seeing as she didn't resemble Colson, I figured she must have taken after her mother with her sturdier frame, her large eyes that were golden with the faintest hint of green, her rounder face, her pouty mouth with a bigger upper lip.

"You're right, Jelly," Colson agreed, placing his giant hand on top of her small head. "Winnie," he said, voice an odd hiss. Deeper than usual. Thick with - dare I think it - emotion.

"Hey Colson," I said, giving him a wobbly smile. "I'm home," I added even though it went without saying.

"I see that. Jelly, this is Aunt Winnie," he told the little girl who looked up at me with those big eyes, something like recognition there.

And then her baby fat hand thrust out toward me. "I'm Jelena. Daddy calls me Jelly."

"And why is that?" Thad's voice asked from behind me, making Jelly's face light up as she dropped my hand.

"'Cuz I got jelly in muh belly!" she declared loudly enough for all the neighbors to hear, hauling her shirt up to show us all said belly.

"Yes you do, little boo. Come on in here. Uncle Thad will get you some strawberry milk," he called, making the girl barrel through the doorway and collide with him bodily, prompting him to wrap an arm around her middle, lifting and flipping her upside down. Her squeals carried out into the hall where I moved, closing the door behind me, sealing us away from the ears of an impressionable little girl.

"How long you been out?" Colson asked, hands slipping into his front pockets. A defensive move.

"Just about two days," I told him.

"And you didn't tell me because..."

"I didn't tell Thad before either. He found out because he called and I was already on my way here."

"And you didn't tell me once you got here because..."

Colson was not someone who backed down, who let you have your reasons without explanations.

"Honestly, I don't know," I admitted. "I was nervous."

"About seeing me."

"I guess."

"Fuck," he hissed, running a hand down the scruff on his face, glancing down the hall before he looked at me again. "How did we get like this?" he wondered. "Winnie?" he asked when my gaze slipped to my feet for a moment. "Spill it."

"You didn't come see me for almost a year," I admitted, knowing that one way or another, he would get the truth from me. I might as well use the band-aid technique.

Colson's head hung, shaking in either shame or regret. Maybe a mix of the two. "I'm a shit," he declared, voice rough. "Never meant to hurt you. You gotta know that."

"I know that."

While Colson and I might not have been quite as close as Thad and I had always been thanks to shared interests, he had always been there for me, had always been my protector, my shoulder to lean on.

"We can rebuild this," he told me. With conviction. Which was how he always spoke, honestly. But this was with determination. Like he had set his mind to it. Like he was going to do everything in his power to make it so. "With Jelly, it was hard to get out that way as much as I would have liked. But you're here now. We'll work on this."

"We won't need to work on it," I declared, moving toward him, wrapping my arms around him, feeling that warm sensation move through me once again as his arms folded around me, familiar, comforting. "It will all fall into place."

Until...

I pushed that thought away, refusing to harp on it. That was a problem for another time.

"Come on. I gotta get in there before she cons his gullible ass into giving her cookies for breakfast."

We moved inside, having coffee, deciding to all go out to breakfast together.

It was odd to see Colson as a father. She brought out a softness that I hadn't ever really seen in him. Colson had been the man of our family, even when he was nothing but a little boy. The weight of that burden had made him older than his years, heavier when Thad and I got to be young and light.

When he had told me on the phone that he'd gotten a girl pregnant, I had always known he would take care of it. I knew he would work to provide for it, be a part of its life. Then when, three months after Jelena's birth, her mother decided she was not cut out to be a mother and gave Colson the choice to take over, or have his daughter put up for adoption, he had, of course, stepped up. As I knew he would. I hadn't been able, when I had heard the news, to picture it. I could see him doing the necessary tasks. Feeding, cleaning, washing clothes for her. But I couldn't see him rocking, snuggling, being sweet and silly with her. I hadn't thought he was capable.

But sitting at a diner with him as he cut up her food, had a bubble blowing in their milk contest with her, as he entertained her with silly drawings on the placemat, I realized I had been wrong all along about him. There had always been sweet and soft and fun inside him. It had just taken a little girl with an infectious laugh to bring it out of him.

"Did you get a card from Auntie May?" Thad asked, making the entire aura around the table shift.

Auntie May.

That was a sore spot.

No.

It was a gaping, festering wound.

For all three of us.

See, Colson, Thad, and I were as close as we were out of necessity, the need to close ranks, protect one another.

Colson and Thad were eleven and I was nine when Child Protective Services ripped us out of our beds in the middle of the night, pulling us through the only home we ever knew, bringing us to a room with a social worker who told us our mother could no longer take care of us anymore.

That was not exactly a surprise.

We hadn't seen our mother in three days.

It was not an uncommon occurrence. And we had learned to take care of ourselves. Get up for school. Eat cereal. Get to the bus stop together. Come home, sit at the table and do our homework, watch TV, eat freezer meals cooked in the microwave, go to bed. Shower, rinse, repeat.

She would come shuffling in with greasy hair, purple circles under her bloodshot eyes, looking somehow thinner than she had been when she left. She'd fall into bed, shaking, crying, throwing up. Then she would get up and be gone again.

And then in a room in the social services building, we met Auntie May. Our mother's older sister who had washed her hands of her well before we were born. There had been no appearances on holidays, no birthday cards on birthdays. In fact, we hadn't been aware our mother *had* any family until she came into that room, her low heels clicking on the worn linoleum floors.

Auntie May was what our mother might have looked like had she lived an easier life, had she not spent all her money on drugs instead of food. Where our mother was rail thin, all sharp angles poking out of skin, Auntie May was softly rounded in the chest, butt, and belly. She dressed in a way the principal in our school did - straight and pressed slacks, a silky shirt underneath a tailored blazer, with oversized jewelry.

She looked like our mom in the face, though hers was much rounder. And, sure, while our mother's eyes were often sad or bloodshot, there was a warmth there. Auntie May's eyes were cold. The kind of cold that made us all huddle closer together.

I didn't remember the exact conversation, but the social worker had asked her if she would be willing to take us on.

Her response?

I guess I don't have much of a choice, do I?

From that day, our fates were sealed.

Free of the responsibility to care for us, whatever self-control our mother had evaporated. From what we knew, she spent the next several years in a cycle of drug use - using, running out of money, tricking herself out to get the next hit, overdosing, swearing she was recovering, then not. By the time I was twelve, she got hauled in for her first prison sentence.

Disgraceful, Auntie May had hissed after the call had come through. *Embarrassment to this family* was another of her favorite things to say about our mother. To our faces.

Auntie May did, on paper, all she was meant to do. She kept a nice roof over our heads. She made sure we ate, showered, did our homework, took us to doctor appointments, hired tutors if we were falling behind on work. Because Auntie May had the money for things like that - having spent her life working her way up the ladder in a big energy company, affording her a life full of luxuries but empty of a partner, her own children, friends.

What she didn't do was genuinely care. Maybe she loved us in her own way. But her love came with strict conditions. Like never embarrassing her by being unkempt, never talking back - especially in front of company-, never having her need to leave work to come pick us up from the principal's office, never doing anything that might in any way reflect poorly on her.

Not surprisingly, I never heard from or saw her again after I got locked up.

"Please," Colson said with a snort. "We all know how I have brought shame on this family," he said, putting his left hand - free of a wedding band - on his daughter's little shoulder. "She doesn't send cards anymore."

"Not *that* kind of card," Thad said with a smirk. Thad had handled Auntie May's rejection with the ease he handled everything. And maybe he had been more prepared for it, knowing that once he came out, she would want nothing to do with his *godless* ways. "It was technically from her attorney, I guess. About us getting cut out of the will."

"Who is she going to leave it all to then?" Colson asked, shaking his head, his gaze going to his daughter, knowing the opportunities he could afford her if he got even a small piece of her estate when she passed.

"Some scholarship for girls."

"Well, at least it is going somewhere decent," I figured. Since she hadn't been willing to help me get something more than a public defender for my case, I always figured I was out of her will years back.

"We don't need it," Colson added. "I am already working on a savings for Jelly."

A savings that would likely have a lot more in it had he not helped put money into my commissary.

Guilt flooded my system, stealing my appetite, making me push a plate of previously mouth-watering French toast away so I could rest my forearms on the table, hands cradling my lukewarm coffee cup.

I would make it up to him, to her, before I went back. I would get a job, sock it all away, put it into a trust for her. Or leave it with Thad with instructions to give it to Colson for Jelena when she needed it.

"And you know we will all be putting in," Thad agreed as he picked up the ketchup to trace over his golden hash browns.

"Of course," I agreed. "I owe you guys."

"Shush," Thad said, waving a hand that made four separate silver rings catch the light. "You're family," he said simply.

"So what's your plan, Winnie?" Colson asked, checking the time on his phone because Jelly had a dance class he had to take her to after we ate. I tried - and failed - to picture my big, somewhat scary older brother full of a room of leggings and tutus.

"Find a job," I told him. That was true enough. I couldn't rely on Thad's graciousness forever. And it seemed like it was going to take a bit to go through with my plan since a Facebook search hadn't gotten me any closer to finding *him*. "Which I am assuming will not be easy."

While I likely had a better shot than a man in my position, I knew no one saw 'ex-con' on the application and jumped for joy.

"This is Navesink Bank, boo," Thad said, waving a hand toward the window at his side. "Got different employers here."

"Right," Colson agreed with an eye roll. "But we don't want her to have to be in that life."

"I wasn't saying she should start selling..." he trailed off, gaze going to Jelena who was watching him with big eyes. "Tic Tacs," he decided. "But the Tic Tac *manufacturers* have many legitimate places for her to sidle up to a desk. That's all I'm saying."

"Like Mallick," Colson said, voice full of insinuation. Like it was Thad's place to try to get me a job at the gym.

"Exactly. Like any of those yummy Mallick boys, actually. Grassis. That gym that's owned by those... well... those hill people who all fill out their utility pants well."

"I'll figure it out," I assured them with more confidence than I actually felt.

I'd never even been on a job interview before. I had nothing to put on a resume. I didn't even have a valid driver's license anymore. Or a bank account.

"Baby steps," Colson said, seeming to read the growing panic on my face. "It's not gonna happen overnight. Jelly, you about done? We got to get going."

"Shit, me too. I mean shoot," Thad said, when Jelena giggled. "I have a 90s Hip Hop Dance class to teach."

"Who even goes to a class like that?" Colson asked as Thad stole the bill he was reaching for, leaving him to toss money on the table for a tip instead.

"Mostly the younger stay-at-home-mommies. You, dinner later?" he asked, offering me his cheek to kiss.

"Sure. I'll cook."

"Got your key?"

"Yep," I said, fishing it out of my pocket.

"You want a ride?" they both asked in unison.

"I think I will walk," I told them as we made our way up to the front where Thad dealt with the bill. "What? No," I objected when Thad slapped some cash into my hand.

"Shush," he said, slapping my butt hard before heading out the door. "Love you!" he called before disappearing.

I was still tucking the money into my back pocket when Jelena collided with my thigh, her arms wrapping around my leg as she left what I suspected was a syrup smudge on my jeans. "I stole some of your fat toast," she told me in a hush like it was a big secret.

"That's okay. I wasn't eating it anyway," I assured her, my hand pressing between the juts of her shoulder blades in a makeshift hug. "Go dance pretty, okay?"

"Okay!" she declared, turning to make her way to the door.

"I'll text you," Colson said, having gotten my new cell - a cell I wasn't one-hundred-percent sure how to use fully yet - number when we sat down. "We'll get together again."

"Soon."

"Yeah, soon," he agreed, giving me a one-arm hug before taking Jelena's hand and making his way out the door.

I waited for everyone to leave, watching their cars pull away, before making my way outside, the crisp air making me wish I had worn a jacket. And about five minutes into the walk, I wished even more that I hadn't worn the heels Thad had thrown at me. Another block later, I comforted myself that I would never have to wear them again seeing as I was darn near certain that the insides were now stained with my blood.

"Hey, baby," a voice called at my side, a shadow emerging from the overhang of a front stoop. "Where you headed?" he asked, coming down the stairs.

Prison had been a funny thing.

It exposed you to a violence you likely hadn't been around while free - violence from fellow women. But it also managed to shield you from the violence of men. Or, at least, that was the case in my prison where the male guards weren't - as far as I knew - predators. Just people who had a job to do.

A sliver of uncertainty slid down my spine, making my shoulders push back, my chin lift, wanting to give the aura of confidence and lack of fear even as my pulse quickened as I saw him step onto the sidewalk.

"What you too good for me?" he asked, his hand reaching out, closing around my wrist.

I'd been aware of the noise - a loud car on the street.

It wasn't until the noise got loud then cut off that I realized it wasn't a car at all.

"Fuck off," a deep, not unfamiliar voice called from my side. When the hand didn't immediately drop from my wrist, I watched as Virgin - what the hell kind of name was Virgin anyway - pushed down the kickstand with his boot, slowly lifting up off the seat, dragging a leg over it to stand towering over me. Every movement was in half speed, was pointed, almost... threatening. "I won't tell you again," he added in a deeper rumble.

The hand around my wrist disappeared, snatched back comically fast.

"Sorry, man. Didn't realize she was one of yours."

With that, he turned and jogged back up the stairs and into the apartment building.

"Thank you, but I could have handled it," I assured him. "And what did he mean by *One of yours*? You have several women?"

Why did I care?

"Not at the moment," he said with what I could only call a lazy grin. "You want a ride where you're going?"

"I--" I started, only to be cut off.

"You're walking like your feet are killin' you."

"They are," I admitted with a small smile, knowing it was pointless to deny it. In another block, I would probably be saying to hell with the disgustingness of the ground, kicking off my shoes, and making it home barefoot.

"So you got nothing to lose and everything to gain from taking a ride, yeah?"

It was hard to argue with that logic.

"Where were you headed? Is that a hard question?" he added, white teeth peeking out of his lips in an amused smile when I didn't answer.

"I am supposed to be looking for a job. But... I don't even know where to start."

"You new in town?" he asked, picking up on my feeling of complete loss.

"In a way. Sort of. I grew up here. But I left ten years ago. I just got back the day before we met."

"You need a job this fast?"

"Yes. I mean, Thaddeus is happy to spot me until I get on my feet again, but I don't want him to have to. But all the restaurants around here have changed."

"Well, let's see. There's the Mexican and Chinese places, but I doubt they're hiring. More family business kind of things. The pizza place is the same. There's Famiglia and Abby's though."

"Abby's?"

"It's a delivery-only place that does comfort food shit. Soup. Mac n' cheese. Open all night. Great if you got the flu or something. Abby is the chef, but the way that place is growing, I figure they could use some help. And Famiglia is an upscale Italian place. Run by the mob. Just so you know. Dunno if that is a deal breaker for you."

"No." Actually, it sounded like a place worth looking into.

"Interesting," he said with a smirk I didn't quite know how to interpret. Pleased, maybe. But why? Because I was okay with the mob? Or, more likely, because I wasn't scared of being affiliated with them. An illegal organization. Like the one *he* belonged to. I mean, not that he wanted to be involved with me. Of course. Everything about the man screamed *I'll give you the night of your life, but leave before the sweat dries*. Not that I knew much about such things, but any woman knew that vibe when she found it in a man.

"Where is Abby's?" I asked, looking both ways down the street.

"Closer to my end of town. By the compound," he clarified, moving to toss a leg over the seat of his bike, reaching behind him for the helmet. "Come on," he offered, holding the helmet out toward me.

"You don't wear a helmet?"

"Not in town."

"That's stupid," I told him, taking the helmet.

"Yeah, probably," he agreed, not at all offended. "You gonna put it on?" he asked when I didn't move to do so, thinking - for the first time in years - about my hair. But, in the end, the throbbing in my feet said there was no way I was getting to the other end of town without a ride. And this one was free. "That'a girl," he told me with a nod as I slammed it down on my head and secured the buckle. "Ever been on a bike?"

"No."

"Climb on. Close ranks. And hold on."

Close ranks. He wasn't joking. From the looks of things, I would be plastered to his body. And to prevent myself from flying off the back, I'd have to wrap my arms around that solid body of his - a thought that made my chest feel tight, made an odd, aching sensation move across my belly.

Pretending to ignore that, I attempted to throw a leg over, forgetting my teetering heels and my, well, shortness, that made me wobble and almost miss, my hand slamming down on his shoulder for stability.

"So, I'm assuming dance wasn't your childhood extracurricular activity, huh?" he asked, a low rumble of amusement in his voice.

"No one would ever call me graceful," I admitted, shaking my head at myself as I finally got my leg over and settled in, the seat forcing me to slide forward until my thighs gripped the outer sides of his, the juncture between pressed intimately against his body.

"Gotta hold on," he reminded me, but before I could do so, his hands reached back, grabbing my wrists, pulling them around his sides, securing them across his stomach. A rock freaking hard stomach, I might add.

When I drew in my next breath, it was shaky for reasons I couldn't even pretend I didn't understand. But then the next second, the engine roared to life, the bike peeled away from the streets, and my stomach just seemed to drop straight out of my body. And then dragged along the street for the short five-minute drive to the other end of town.

"You can relax now," Virgin told me, voice amused, making me realize how tightly I was still clinging to him even though we were stopped by the curb.

"Mhm. After my stomach climbs back up into my abdominal cavity, that is exactly what I am going to do." But even as I was saying the words, my arms were untangling themselves from where they had curled around his midsection, holding on for dear life, the grip so tight it must have made taking a proper breath difficult work at best.

"Not a fan, huh?" He asked, waiting for me to climb off before doing so himself. "I practically grew up on one. Forgot that not everyone has the stomach for it."

"It's not that. It's like a rollercoaster. Freaky when it is happening. And you swear you will never put yourself through it again. Until your feet are back on solid ground. Your belly settles. Then you are running back to get on line again."

"Spent a lot of time in amusement parks?" he asked, seeming a mix of amused, curious, and almost... sad? But sad seemed wrong. For such a big, scary biker guy.

"My brothers and I learned that the best way to survive summers was to avoid our aunt. So we got passes to Six Flags when we were teens and drove down in the morning, came back before she got home from work." It was the most adventurous thing I had ever done. No one would believe that since I had a record that said quite differently. But sneaking out and lying to my aunt was as daring as I had ever been.

"Not a great family, huh?" he asked, tone seeming to hold familiarity, intimacy. Like he knew that feeling all too well.

"Well, my brothers are everything," I admitted, feeling like that was too much, over the top. But it was true nonetheless. They were everything. "And my niece is a sweetheart too. But growing up, we had some rough times."

"I grew up in a heroin-dealing MC. I know about rough times too."

"Your mother was okay with you being around that?" I asked, figuring if he was willing to talk about it without prompting, that it wasn't being nosy to do so.

"My mother dropped me off there and never came back for me," he admitted.

"How old were you?"

"Four?" he half told, half asked.

"And you grew up with bikers? Just bikers?"

"It was an interesting childhood," he admitted, reaching up to rub a hand across the scruff on his face, holding back a smile.

From what I heard about MCs, I imagine he grew up with next to no rules and a revolving door of half - or fully - naked women around.

Yeah, I bet that would have been interesting for a growing boy.

"So, you gonna nut-up and go in there?" he asked, jerking his chin behind me, making me aware of what we were doing. Not getting to know each other. Not exposing shared wounds or little childhood rebellions. No. He was driving me to apply for a job.

Half-turning, I saw a small storefront wedged between two much larger ones - a laundromat to the left, a pet store to the right.

Abby's.

It was in the spot that a small Chinese place had been when I had left. The all-glass front had been frosted, the only thing to see through the white being the bold lettering at eye-level saying the name of the establishment.

My brow furrowed, wondering why - with a place that small - you would choose to close yourself in, block out the world.

I guess, if I maybe, possibly, got the job, I could ask.

"Go on," Virgin encouraged, not really doing anything to help the nerves.

"Are you just going to stand there and watch me?" I asked, pulling the helmet off my hair, reaching up to hopefully fluff it into place.

"Yep."

"Don't you have anything else to do?"

"Nope."

"I can take a cab home after."

"Nah."

"I wasn't going to invite you up anyway," I added a little pointedly in case that was what he had in mind.

"Okay."

Frustrated, a low grumble escaped me. "Well, can you at least look over there?" I asked, waving an arm out toward the end of the street.

"Like this view better."

Alright. I was only human. I had to admit that those words sent a little swirling through my belly.

"Go on now," he told me, jerking his chin toward the restaurant. "I might hire you for the eye candy alone, but I think Abby might want to talk to you."

Shaking my head at him, forcing my measly breakfast to settle in my belly, I turned on my heel, cursing them in new and inventive ways in my head as I made my way to the door. Pulling, I found nothing but resistance. But I knew if I didn't do this now - with an audience - that I wouldn't be able to force myself to come back. My hand lifted, knocking a few times, hopefully loud enough to be heard over the clangs of pots and pans and the loud TV from within.

There was some more slamming, followed by the muting of the TV. Then a female voice.

"If you are not the cops, a coffee delivery, or a free ride to the nuthouse, I don't have time for this!" she declared just a second before yanking open the door, shocking me enough to take a step back.

Abby was younger than I would have expected for a restauranteur. She couldn't have been much older than me with a tall, willowy - just shy of lanky, all limbs - build, an impish, delicate face with oversized, black-lined see-through blue eyes made even bluer thanks to the vivid shade of turquoise of her pixie cut hair. Her thin arms were bare, displaying a range of black and gray tattoos. A full-body apron - that at one time must have been white but was currently a mismatch of reds, yellows, browns, and greens - was folded down at her waist, mostly covering her simple straight-leg jeans.

"Sorry," I told her. "I don't have a warrant. Or coffee. Or an electroshock therapy machine. I was just looking for a job."

"You cook?" she asked, rubbing the back of her wrist across a brow beaded a bit with sweat.

"Yes."

"Tomorrow, ten a.m. Come prove it." With that, she slammed and locked the door, making me almost unsure that I had heard her correctly.

"Well, that was a success. How are you going to repay me?" Virgin asked from behind me, making me turn to find him watching me with a smirk toying with his lips.

"I will offer you a cup of coffee. But that is it."

"That'll do," he agreed with a cocky smile as he got back on his bike, making me wonder as I took the helmet he handed me to slip on my head again if he thought a cup of coffee was the 'in' he needed.

Well, I decided as I climbed on again, he would just have to live with disappointment.

Mumbling off the address, I folded my arms around him again, feeling my stomach fly out, but bungee right back in, anchored by the sense of satisfaction building inside.

I had a job interview.

Granted, she didn't know about my record. She didn't even know my name. But with her level of frazzle, I figured that so long as I lived up to her cooking expectations, she might be able to overlook all that in favor of being able to get a little time away from her restaurant.

I would knock her socks off with some recipes I learned growing up. Then I would carefully mention my criminal record once she had dreams of sleeping in on her mind.

And I would wear *flats*.

"You gonna make it up the stairs, or you need a boost?" Virgin asked, that bemused smile toying with his lips as my hand went white-knuckled on the banister for the steps - ten in all - up to the front door.

"I don't have a ton of pride, but what I do have would not allow me - a grown ass woman - to be *boosted* up the stairs," I informed him, taking a deep breath which I told myself - even though I knew it was a bold-faced lie - that the breathing would cut the pain.

I could have sworn I heard snickering as I cursed my way up the last three stairs, reaching for my key as I did so.

"The fuck you wear them for if they hurt your feet?"

"That's such a guy thing to say," I told him, shaking my head. "They're new. I didn't know they would hurt my feet until I wore them for a day."

"They're icepicks attached to your heel and you didn't think they might not feel so great?" he shot back, brow raised.

I bit back a comment about how it had been a decade since I wore heels, so I had no idea how my feet would feel anymore. But that invited questions, ones I didn't really want to have to answer.

"Some heels don't bother your feet, believe that or not," I informed him with some authority I didn't feel as we took the elevator up to Thad's floor.

He towered over me as I opened the locks and moved inside, reaching down to free my feet of the torture devices, having to flex my feet up off the floor for a second before they un-stiffened enough to be able to walk on them.

"You're bleedin'," he informed me, making my gaze shoot down to find a bloody gash across the back of my heel.

"Seems about right," I agreed, making my way over to the coffee pot. "So this is Thad's place," I told him, waving a hand around.

"You got another sister?" he asked, hand touching the two kimonos on the back of the couch.

"Oh, ah, no. Thad has a kimono. And then a guest kimono. And I am, apparently, an idiot for not knowing one needs such a thing as a guest kimono."

To that, Virgin snorted. "I don't even have a guest blanket."

"I don't imagine you have many overnight guests."

"Can't tell if that is an insult or ego stroke," he murmured as the smell of coffee filled the air. Three scoops was the right amount, I had found.

"Maybe a bit of both," I admitted, reaching for the mugs, having to go up on my tiptoes to do so since I was vertically challenged and Thad was half giant.

"Need some help?" A voice asked. Close. Really close. So close that I felt the body sidle in behind me, strong thighs brushing against my ass, arms going around my sides, trapping me in as he reached for the almost-out-of-reach mugs.

And what was I thinking, you might ask?

Something absolutely ridiculous.

And cheesy.

We can't forget cheesy.

Because it was some freaking old school romance novel level of smarmy.

I might not mind imprisonment if it was between his arms.

See?

I was embarrassed by my own internal monologue.

In its defense, it had been a long, long time since there was even a clear and present danger about the imprisonment between a man's arms. And there had never been anything like the 'set the alarms to Def Con One' kind of threat that this stupidly good looking, obnoxiously sexy, unnaturally calm man with his front pressed against my back caused.

Sure that if I spent even a second more thinking of my current predicament - and how him bending me over the counter would not be a wholly unwelcome progression of events - my mouth blurted out the first thing it could drag out of the fog of my mind.

"Why do they call you Virgin?"

His arms - and the mugs nestled like little doll vessels in his giant hands - paused in mid-air for a moment, caught off-guard, before descending to the countertop with a quiet click, his hands abandoning them - *and how much they must have missed his touch* - and grabbing the counter instead. *Lucky counter.*

Jesus.

What the hell was wrong with me?

Did I fall *off* the back of the bike back there, slam my head, and find myself experiencing that lovely end-of-life reel of fantasies flashing before my eyes, as my brain fired off and died?

That was possibly the only explanation for my thoughts right about then.

"They call me Virgin because I don't give a fuck," he told me, voice - and therefore *mouth* - down near my ear.

Mouth.

Mouth and lips.

Lips and kissing.

Right at that little spot behind said ear, that spot that shocked off a thousand fireworks when touched just right. And something in me said he would know how to do it just right.

Okay.

Space.

I needed some space.

Ducking low - well, lower - I clumsily shoved myself into the small space under his arm, spinning outward, going toward the fridge as though it was imperative that at that very second, I get the half & half out for us.

A low, rolling chuckle let me know that he found my behavior - at worst - ridiculous, or - at best - kinda cute and amusing.

If I were a betting person, I would always put my money on the safest bet. Meaning the most negative thing when it came to me and my luck.

"That's funny. I mean... I doubt it was funny how you came to get that name. But it must be fun to explain that to people when they ask about it. Does everyone in your club have fun road names?"

"Some," he told me. "They call my best friend Sugar."

Oh, a third party.

That was safer territory, wasn't it?

"How'd he get that name?"

"You should ask him yourself. He likes telling it." My head jerked up, finding him watch me as I added too much sugar to my own coffee since I was distracted by trying to resist the urge to just tell him to take me, end the dry spell like he promised back at the bar. "Come to the clubhouse tomorrow night. Celebrate your newfound employment with some booze and interesting conversation. Don't," he cut me off when he knew I was about to object, "say anything now. Think on it. Decide later. Tomorrow night. After eight. Thanks for the coffee," he told me, taking a giant swig of mine that was now loaded down with so much cream it was barely warm anymore. "Go wash out those cuts," he added, making it to the door in about two strides, and letting himself out into the hall.

FOUR

Freddie

Root vegetable au gratin.

The perfect minestrone soup.

And baked macaroni and cheese with that crispy top layer and melt-in-your-mouth gooeyness hidden within.

That was what it took.

To go from a complete wreck to having to stifle a chuckle as Abby leaned back in her chair making vaguely pornographic noises as she ate.

"I forgot how good food tastes when you don't have to make it yourself."

By the time I had shown up at her door, Abby's apron already looked like it had gone to war. As did the kitchen area where she had six separate to-go orders in the works all by herself, making me wonder why she hadn't reached out for help instead of waiting for it to show up at her door.

By the looks of things, she might have simply not had the time.

Her only employees were two delivery people - one a single dad who worked the shift while his daughter was at school, an efficient, but unfriendly man who barely spared me a glance, and a part-time college student with striking good looks and an outgoing, friendly personality, all white teeth and shining green eyes, singing some song I had never heard as he collected the bags for delivery.

"So, what is your schedule like?"

Aside from the light stalking I did when Thad wasn't around to see it... "Open."

"I generally like working the night shift. It probably would creep anyone else out anyway - being here all alone. But it's the busiest time of day. I thrive on the chaos. But my shrink says I need to thrive a little less on the chaos. Meaning giving up eighteen-hour days and learning to delegate and trust people and yada fucking yada. So here I am. Offering you day shift. After a training period, of course. You can't jump into this without learning the curve. Um. I will look into benefits for you, but that might take a bit. And... what the hell else are bosses supposed to ask here?"

"References?" I suggested.

"I don't need anyone else telling me you can cook. I have taste buds."

Even if she doesn't ask, you gotta tell her, boo. Thad's words came back to me, making my palms wet, having to wipe them on a rag before starting to move my dishes to the sink.

"There is one thing I should probably tell you," I started hesitantly, back to her, hoping that would help me get the balls to say it.

"Should is a bullshit word. *Should* is what this guy told me about taking a chance on his pierced dick, saying it would rock my world when, in actuality, it, in fact, felt like my pussy turned into a tackle box. But go ahead."

"I just got out of prison." There. It was out. My heart felt like it was being squeezed by Andre the Giant, but it was out.

"Did you kill someone? With a cleaver? Melt them in a vat of acid? Oh, no, maybe shot the prick who was beating on you and threw him into a river with cement shoes? Maybe..." I turned as she spoke, lips curving up as her excitement - and the ludicrousness of her imaginary crimes - grew. "Sorry," she said, waving her fork toward the flatscreen hanging down from the wall. "I am a sucker for *Forensic Files, Cold Case Files*, pretty much all the files. And *A Killer in My Family, A Killer Next Door*... well... all the killers too."

"Maybe that is why you find it creepy in here at night," I suggested, wiping a few splatters of cheese off the counter.

"Maybe. But anyway... statistically speaking, there are enough laws on the books in this country now that the average citizen commits three felonies a day without realizing it. And you could get locked up on bullshit charges for inhumanely long stretches for any one of those when you catch a judge on a day when he has heartburn and his wife refused to fuck him for the tenth year in a row, and then get sent away because the prison-industrial complex makes bank off of the heads in the beds and because society is brainwashed into thinking prisons work when all the data collected since the eighties proves exactly the opposite... and, yeah, this is my way of saying fuck the system. You're still hired. But don't steal from me because I will meat cleaver the shit out of you and melt you in a vat of acid."

There was no stopping the giant grin that stretched across my face. Because she was insane. Because I was hired. Because I never imagined I could find someone who didn't look at me like I was dog crap on their shoe because of what had happened to me a decade ago.

"I accept the terms," I told her as she got onto her Doc Martin clad feet and came over to go under the counter to reveal a small fridge loaded up with various drinks - including two hard ciders she pulled out, handing one to me.

"Yes, I sometimes drink on the job," she told me, twisting off her top. "I would be a hypocrite to tell you not to. But don't get sloppy. Or I might have to kill you and-"

"Throw me in a river with cement shoes," I finished for her, twisting off the top of mine for a drink.

"Precisely," she agreed, finishing her food before starting in on her orders again.

Not having anything to do, I hung back for my first lesson, leaving later that afternoon covered in about two dozen different substances, my feet aching a bit, my hair sticking to the back of my neck with sweat.

But warm.

Happy.

Excited.

Things I was becoming perhaps a bit too accustomed to. Which was dangerous. Because I might not be able to give them up. And then the past ten years of concocting plans, of cradling my rage to my chest like a baby, might have been for nothing.

But those were thoughts for another day.

"I see you got the job," Thad said as I stepped inside, not even bothering to pretend like he wasn't having an elaborate selfie-taking session, just hamming it up for his camera as he spoke to me, his shutter going off every few seconds.

"I gotta meet her," he decided when I had told him the whole story before going to wash all of the aforementioned substances off of myself. "We should celebrate," he told me as I went through the strict routine he - or more accurately, his friend Benny - had taught me to get that perfect wavy curl look. "What?" he asked when a flash of something crossed my face. I was terrible at keeping secrets. Thad knew this. And he would absolutely use it against me to get what he wanted.

"Nothing. We *should* celebrate," I tried to cover, plastering on a smile.

"Bitch, that smile is as fake as the tits on that lady in my dance class today. Up to here, they were," he told me, cupping his hands into circles up near his clavicles. "Honey could put her chin down and rest it on the girls."

"Don't be mean," I told him, tossing my towel at his head.

"Not mean. Just honest. Ain't no woman got natural titties for a necklace save for top-heavy gals in inverted positions in yoga class. Could fucking suffocate themselves, I swear. But you don't have to worry about that," he told me, flicking the side of my tank top-clad boob, making me send a scathing look his way even though I had long since gotten over my adolescent insecurity about my small chest. What I lacked in boobs, I made up for in ass. It was fair. "Anyway. Back to my point. Did you have something specific in mind for celebrating?"

I could *feel* the *I've got a secret!* look as it crossed my face.

"Spill," he demanded, snatching the light pink lipstick I was reaching for, slapping the bright red in my palm instead.

"Why?"

"It's your signature look, that's why. Now, go on and tell me. You know I'm gonna get it out of you eventually."

"I sort of got invited to a celebratory thing tonight," I told him as I smeared on the lipstick, watching as it slowly went matte, letting me know it would stay on even if I had a heavy make-out session. Which, of course, I had no intentions of having. Not even if I did go to celebrate the way I was invited to.

"By whom?" he asked, making me aware I had completely *forgotten* to tell him all about the ride, the invite, the counter-pressing thing.

"Virgin," I supplied, watching his reaction out of the corner of my eye.

"And we're the fuck still standing here because?" he demanded, hip-checking me out of the way to grab for a little mattifying powder, swishing it over his T-zone with a brush.

"Um, I don't know if I was allowed to bring anyone."

"Honey, baby... there is no way I am letting you go into that den of Prime USDA Manmeat without me," he told me, waving a hand dismissively as he spritzed on his cologne.

"They're bikers, Thad. I'm pretty sure they're all straight."

"Mhmm," he agreed, half-ignoring me. "So was that boy Adam last night. But he sure sucked my cock like he thought the fountain of youth was in the motherfucker," he told me as he walked through the bathroom then down into my room, grabbing an outfit, tossing it at me.

"Thad..."

"Alright, listen," he said, leaning back against my bedroom doorway. "I want you to take a ride or fifty on that fine piece of masculinity. You earned it. You deserve to blaspheme the name of God while you get your lady business worked over for the first time in a decade. But that being said, you are my baby sister. He is a dangerous biker with a bunch of dangerous biker friends, so there is no way I am letting you take your fine ass into there without your big, scary brother to keep an eye on you. Now squeeze that round ass into those jeans, tie on that shirt, spritz on some perfume, and meet me at the door."

With that, he left me alone to do, well, just that. The top was white and flowy, but tied in the center of my stomach, showing off a bit more than a sliver of belly. I spritzed on the perfume, grabbed a pair of flats, and pretended like I was trying to talk myself out of it.

But, well, I wasn't.

I didn't want to.

If I was alone, I never would have worked up my courage to go.

But with Thaddeus there as backup? I wanted to go. I wanted to satisfy my curiosity. Maybe - just maybe - get to know Virgin just a little bit better. Even if the more rational side of me knew it was stupid. A non-starter. Doomed to fail.

It could go down in flames.

Brilliant, orgasm-filled flames.

It was funny how, when I was inside long enough, the urges went away. When there was no possibility for relief - no men to take it away, no privacy to take care of it yourself - your body kind of just shut it all down. But now that I was back out, it was back with a vengeance. And despite having used - when no one was home - the vibrator Thad had included in my basic necessities package until the thing damn near burned out on me, nothing seemed to ease the clawing, aching need, nothing would take away the oppressive weight on my lower belly, begging for an end to the torment.

I didn't just need an orgasm.

I needed touch after so long without.

I needed hands gliding over places that hadn't been grazed in far too long - shoulders, spine, lower back, hips, thighs.

I needed the feel of lips down the side of my neck, my belly, lower.

I needed the weight of a man on top of me, the feel of his hard lines on my softer ones, the scent of his skin on me, his words in my ear.

I needed a man who could give me an orgasm.

And if you were going to let yourself have a fling, wasn't it the smartest bet to go with someone who had what seemed like an immense amount of experience? Someone who was clearly a noncommittal sort so things never got confusing or grew roots.

I had enough roots that I would need to rip out if I went through with my plans for revenge.

"Fred, I'm not getting any younger over here," Thad called, snapping me out of my wandering thoughts. Grabbing my purse, I made my way out into the living room, finding Thad standing half out the door already.

"Oh my God," I snorted when we moved outside and - I could not be more serious (nor mortified) - when Thaddeus threw open a parasol. A gauzy, baby blue freaking *parasol*. Despite the fact that it was dark outside. "What are you shielding yourself from? The moon?" I asked as he twirled it on his shoulder.

"Look like a poster child for a passive gay man, right?" he asked, suddenly grabbing the base of the handle with both hands - one staying put, the other yanking outward. And I'd be damned if a long, lethal-looking knife didn't come out in his fist. "Looks can be deceiving," he added, popping it back in. "Here," he added, reaching in his pocket to produce a small pocket knife. "Stick this in your pocket. Or in your bra. You should have room," he added with a smirk.

"Watch what you say to a woman holding a sharp object," I warned, turning it at him. "You could be missing a part of you that you really hold near and dear."

"Listen to you, Shawshank. Threatening to make a Eunuch outta me. Weren't you the girl who almost fainted when Colson broke his leg?"

"His bone was sticking out of his skin!" I shot back as we started walking. Even just the memory made a shiver course through me. I could never unsee that.

"Oh, damn. Don't even gotta go inside to get a taste of the mancandy," Thad declared as we walked up to the gates of The Henchmen compound where a duo of men in what almost looked like military gear with semi-automatic guns strapped around their backs stood.

Not bikers something inside me said. But why would not-bikers be doing security at a biker compound?

"Look at you all baby faced and shit," Thad said to the guard on the left who, admittedly, did look like he could pass for a high schooler despite the muscle tone that suggested much older. "And you. I bet those lashes are real."

"Are you expected?" Lashes asked, sizing both of us up, eyes landing on the parasol for long enough that I wondered if he knew there was a knife inside it. Like there was some underground knowledge about frilly things that were masking dangerous weapons. Hell, maybe there was.

A snap - clear and unexpected - made all our eyes move to behind the guards where a man who obviously *was* a biker was standing. The one who had been with Virgin at the bar that night. Cam, I think his name was.

"He doesn't speak," I whispered to Thad, but one of the guards looked back, eyeing me a little harder even as Cam waved us in, making the guards move apart and unlock the gates.

"That's okay, honey. I speak enough for the both of us," Thad told Cam, taking down his parasol, sticking it under his arm as he walked with Cam toward the door, leaving me to trail behind.

The closer we got, the louder the music and voices were. A party was obviously going on.

Party.

I hadn't been to a party since I was seventeen-years-old.

I had a feeling grown-up parties were a lot different from teenaged ones.

Especially grown-up *biker* ones.

The door pulled open and we moved into a wide space with a full bar to the right, a pool table to the left, and a sitting area toward the back and a doorway that I suspected led to the kitchen since someone in a Henchmen cut was moving out of it with a heaping pile of finger foods on his plate.

For a biker party, it wasn't exactly what I had been expecting. Which meant, I guess, there were more women around - fully clothed women - than I had anticipated. One was jabbing a pool cue into the chest of one of the bikers, her cheeks red with what I could only assume was anger. Another hopped herself backward onto the bar then jumped off on the other side, reaching up on the back bar to pour a round of straight tequila. Another still was sitting on the lap of a huge, bearded man.

There were more men than women - most in Henchmen cuts, obviously. Men who belonged here in this space. Men who walked around with the comfort and confidence of familiarity. A couple others, though, clearly didn't belong. Judging by the butt-kissing they were doing, I imagined they were trying to fit in, belong, be a part of the organization.

"Oh, be still my heart," Thad said, putting a hand to his chest as his eyes worked over all the men present. Not an ugly one in the bunch. I shouldn't have been surprised. There was never any shortage of gorgeous, dangerous men in Navesink Bank. But this was a whole other level.

"So, you're pretty," a voice said from my side, making my body jolt, finding a tall, somewhat thin blonde guy with bright brown eyes and a great beard. Not a Henchmen due to his lack of a cut. But not as unsure of himself as the other outsiders seemed to be.

"Oh, um... thank you," I said, shaking my head a little.

A sigh at my side told me I was failing at the socializing thing. "This is Freddie. I'm Thad. And you are?" Thaddeus asked, giving me a *This is not hard* look.

"I'm West," he told me, reaching out a hand with bright red and black tattoos over his fingers, the back, and snaking up his arm. Covered. He was covered in them. The V in his tee showed more on his chest, up his neck. And one would imagine, all down his back and stomach as well.

"This is where you shake the hand instead of inspecting it, Fred," Thad told me, elbowing me in the side.

"Sorry," I said, putting my hand in his, having to fight back a blush when he didn't shake it like I had been expecting, but slowly rose it up to his mouth, kissing the tops of my knuckles.

"Yo, fuck off," a voice cracked liked a whip in the space. A newly familiar voice. One that I had maybe thought about while alone in an apartment with a battery operated device just hours before.

My head whipped over, watching as Virgin cut through the crowd, seeming to suck up all the air as he got closer.

"Was that too vague for you?" he asked pointedly to West who was still holding my hand, but was now swinging it between us like children at a playground.

"Not at all," he said, tone, body language, everything about him wholly unconcerned with the threat in the biker's voice as he started pulling me. "Let me just take my new girl with me. She's pretty, right?" he asked, seeming completely unaware - or simply not caring - about the look of death Virgin was shooting him.

"Yeah, she's pretty. She also isn't yours," Virgin clipped with a pointed brow raise.

Maybe West looked contrite.

Maybe he looked worried.

I wouldn't know.

Because my silly brain could only focus on the fact that he had called me pretty.

"Well, that's just not fair," West declared, giving my hand a squeeze before dropping it. "He gets to have that concrete jaw *and* the pretty girl? And me, I have to grow a beard and go home alone? Nice meeting you, pretty girl," he added, giving me a wink before turning away, easily going over to a group of three women, integrating himself in their conversation with the ease that made me wonder if he had sisters. Or was just that sure of himself.

"Yeah, that's about the look all the women have been giving him tonight," Virgin said with a nod as he looked at me. "Like he's a cute new puppy dog. But that puppy dog could rip a grown man's throat out," he added.

"Oh, well, now you're just making him even more appealing," Thad decided. "Who doesn't like a bad boy?"

"Hey Thad," Virgin greeted him as though they were old friends. "If you guys are here, I'm assuming you got the job."

"I did," I told him, not even trying to hide the smile. "Thanks to you in a way." At Thad's eyebrow raise, I shrugged. "He told me she might be hiring and gave me a ride."

"Oh he did, now, did he?" Thad asked in a tone that let me know I was going to hear it later. "Well, good. I am going to go get myself a drink. You two... have fun," he said with an utterly ridiculous eyebrow wiggle.

"Brought backup, huh?"

"He wouldn't have let me come into a biker compound alone. He has a knife in his umbrella."

Virgin's lips quirked up, teasing at those white teeth before his hand rubbed across his face, wiping the smile away. "Sounds like a good brother."

"The best," I agreed.

"Can I get you a drink? Food?"

"Food," I agreed, realizing I hadn't had a chance to eat much all day save for the samples of dishes Abby insisted on just so I got to know the menu by taste as well as ingredient and prep.

Virgin led me through the door I had - correctly - guessed was the kitchen. It was a medium-sized space full of masculine energy, nothing frilly on the windows, no cutesy hand towels hanging off the stove front. Everything was stark and economical. Which made sense, I guess.

Food was spread out across the counters.

Very familiar food.

"Did you order all this from Abby's?" I asked, suddenly feeling bad for her. It had to have taken forever to get it all done. There was enough here to feed an army. Mac n' cheese. Chicken wings. Mozzarella sticks. Sliders. Loaded potato skins. It was endless.

"She's used to us by now. If it's not pizza, it's Abby's. This is Freddie," Virgin said to a duo of women - one a pretty blonde, the other a delicate-faced brunette. "That's Penny and Bethany. They belong to Duke and Lazarus."

"Belong," I mused, testing the word out, finding it odd, foreign, too possessive to feel comfortable.

"Old ladies, not fuck buddies," he clarified. "Guys around here seem to shack up fast."

"Because the women in this town are top-notch," the woman who had been sitting on the big bearded man's lap said, coming up behind Virgin. She peeked around his arm, giving me a once-over. I'd hate to play this woman in poker, because whether she found me wanting or not was a complete mystery. "Has Lo met her yet?"

"Don't start shit, Janie," Virgin demanded, but there was a softness in his voice, an affection for the woman.

"Me? Start shit? No way," she said, devious smile in place as she moved over to join Penny and Bethany who had decided to keep their distance. Shy, I decided, in Penny's case. And maybe a bit standoffish in Bethany's.

"Go on. Load up," Virgin invited, passing me a plate, leaving me out of the loop. It was ridiculous to feel like the last kid chosen in Red Rover, but that was how I felt as I started picking out food, feeling Virgin at my side as he loaded up his plate as well.

I spent the next hour meeting enough people to ensure I would forget all of them save for the first few I was introduced to in the kitchen. Thaddeus was always somewhere in my periphery as Virgin asked some basic questions, seemed to accept my veiled answers.

Or so I thought.

"You gonna stop bullshittin' me, or tell me the truth?" he asked when we were alone - well, as alone as you could be while a party raged around you.

"I'm sorry?" I asked, my head whipping back in his direction, knowing I looked as guilty as I felt. I needed to find that Janie woman and ask her for lessons in poker faces.

Virgin's lips twitched. "You're a shit liar," he told me.

"I know," I agreed, shaking my head at myself, suddenly wishing I had something to drink that wasn't water from the tap in the kitchen. Why was no one serving up shots now?

"Why would you lie to me? You know I am an arms-dealing biker. You knew I grew up around heroin and clubwhores. Not exactly in a place to judge."

The words were out of me before I could think better of them.

"Have you ever been to prison?"

"Jail, yes. Prison? No. You?"

FIVE

Virgin

I didn't think she would show. Not really. Maybe I hoped. Because, apparently, all these relationships around me were making me soft or some shit. But something about her said she wasn't the type to show up at a biker compound even if she was invited by a member. I'd been around a lot of women in a lot of clubs. There was a vibe about them, an energy. Freddie didn't have that.

In fact, if I wasn't completely mistaken, she almost seemed to have a sort of goody-goody vibe to her. Which was not my type. Not by any stretch of the imagination. I wasn't one of those guys who got off on the ideas of corrupting good girls, dragging them down to wade in the muck of things.

I liked my life.

I liked the uncertainty, the familiarity of the crassness, the brotherhood that was the closest to a family I had known in far too long to even remember.

But it wasn't meant for everyone.

And it felt cheap to try to coax someone into it.

I probably shouldn't have even invited her in the first place.

Especially knowing it was a bit of an open house, not just the guys and their girls, knowing that whenever you brought in new, unpredictable men, you opened up the potential for unsavory things to happen.

Reign had about five guys who had been brought to him - or in West's case, just swaggered his cocky ass in through the gates - that he wanted us to all get a chance to vet.

It was almost distracting enough to forget to check the door for her.

Almost.

"What's the consensus?" Reign asked, tipping back a beer, watching the guys move around.

"The one with the gauged ears is out," Renny decided, always the first to nix a potential member.

"Gonna need reasons, Renny," Reign reminded him.

"The way he talks about women like objects, I get the feeling he roughs up his girls in his free time."

"So he's out," Reign agreed. Drugs and hurting women, those were the old man's triggers. It took some getting used to, coming from the MCs I had been in where drugs was where the money came from, where women were often treated like trash. "What about that fucker walking around charming all the women?"

"West," Repo supplied. "Dunno. Reminds me a bit of Shooter before he settled down."

"What's his story?" Reign demanded.

"He's a floater," Sugar supplied, shrugging. "Worked all across the states doing whatever paid."

"Such as?"

"Anything that involved fucking someone up," I pitched in.

"A lot of suppressed rage," Renny agreed.

"In a way we got to worry about, or like Wolf?" Cash asked from behind me.

"Best guess? Like Wolf. He's hard to read. But I would pick him over the others to prospect at least."

"We'll see how he does the rest of the night," Reign allowed. "Christ, what is that, the eighth woman he's hit on tonight?" he asked with a snort, pushing away from the bar.

My gaze followed the line his had, finding Wes standing there. Kissing Freddie's hand while her brother loomed behind her holding an umbrella under his arm despite the fact that it was dry and dark out.

"She yours?" Renny asked, those unsettling eyes on me. Eyes that were that way because of how much they saw, how many inferences they made from all they saw.

"I invited her," I clarified. "But she isn't mine."

But despite that being the absolute truth, there was no denying the possessiveness that swarmed my system - swirling and uncomfortable - at seeing her smile at West, seeing his hands touching her.

Mine something in me called. It was some prehistoric, caveman impulse to take, claim, own. Some biological drive that I had never felt before.

But there was no denying it as the night went on, as the men and women eyed her, sized her up, silently - or not so silently - placed their bets on our status, on her potential of fitting in.

Mine the voice called again, selfishly steering her away from them while staying in the party, in the line of sight of her protective brother.

No one would accuse me of being chatty, but I tried, threw out conversation starters, attempted to get to know her. She was open with stories about her brothers and her when they were young. But when I tried to get information about her over the past few years, she got ramrod straight, her eyes evaded contact, her words went from effortless to careful, calculated, awkward.

And then the words blurted out of her, an explosion of repression and uncertainty, and maybe even a twinge of fear.

Have you ever been to prison?

I didn't have to ask to know.

Not with her skittering gaze, her anxious tugging at her shirt, her hair, the hoops at her ears.

Freddie, the woman who I had thought of as a goody-goody not too long before, had been to prison. Not jail. Not some county stint while she waited for a court date where she would get out on time served.

No.

She went away.

Away away.

And, from the evasiveness of her answers, I imagined for a long while.

Her teeth sank into her lower lip, uncomfortable, waiting for my answer.

"Jail, yes. Prison? No. You?"

"Prison, yes," she answered in a choked voice, not even a hint of air in it.

"Am I supposed to look at you differently now?" I asked, watching as her eyes snuck a look from under their lashes. "You did time. So what? I once cracked a tire iron across a man's face. Done anything like that?"

"No."

"Then why would I think differently about you?"

"Yo, boo, you good?" Thad's voice called from behind me, making her head shoot up. "Tugging at her earrings. That's her stress thing," he added, moving toward my side, looking down at me with what could only be called accusing eyes.

"I'm fine," Freddie insisted, giving him a wobbly smile.

Thad's eyes narrowed, reading her like only a sibling could do. "Right. But you have to get some beauty rest so your fine ass can start bringing home the bacon tomorrow. So we best be going, yeah?" he asked, extending his hand down toward her.

She paused.

Her eyes lifted, looking at me, trying to read me.

Her hand eventually rested in her brother's.

But she paused.

Like she didn't want to go.

Like she would rather stay here. With me. Talk. Maybe do something more.

"Thanks for having us," she said as she was pulled onto her feet, giving me a smile. "It was nice to get out and celebrate a little."

"I'll be seeing you around, Freddie," I told her, getting to my feet too.

"I don't really get out too--"

"I'll be seeing you around, baby girl," I cut her off, watching as her lips parted, her eyes went hooded.

Oh, yeah.

I wasn't the only one who was having some feelings.

And hers could be ignited with a solid pet name. I was storing that information away for later.

"Oh, yes you sure will," Thad murmured under his breath.

"Let me walk you out," I offered, leading them through the crowd, out into the cooler night air. "Nice seeing you, Freddie. Thad."

"Not like you not to close," Sugar's voice called from behind me, jeering, amused at the idea of me being stuck with just my hand when I clearly wanted her.

He was right.

It wasn't like me not to close.

Not when we were both clearly interested.

"You running a long game?" he asked as I turned back, finding him leaning against the clubhouse, looking off at the town.

"I don't even know what the fuck a long game is," I admitted. If there was one person who knew me perhaps as well as I knew myself, it was Sugar. There was no shame in admitting that I was clearly on uneven footing with Freddie - a woman I just met. A woman who I had barely spent enough time with to get to know even a little bit. Everything should have been about the attraction, about getting her into bed, satisfying the desire we both felt toward one another.

I hadn't even tried.

It wasn't like me.

"You like her."

"I don't know her well enough to like her."

"Met her for two minutes and *I* like her," West declared from the doorway, shamelessly eavesdropping. And, for some reason, neither of us told him to get lost.

"Liked Peyton by the end of our drive in her hearse back to town. Not saying you're in love with the woman. I'm saying she's piqued your interest. In more than a 'I want to get up in that' way. So what? Get to know her."

"Not like I can bounce into her. She works at Abby's now. And then likely just goes home after."

"Well, if it helps. Her brother and her are having a spa day at Kennedy's next Saturday when he doesn't have a class to teach," West supplied.

Sugar and I shared a look.

We'd gotten good at the unspoken conversations over the years.

He had our vote for a prospect too.

"Eavesdropping is a favorite pastime of yours, huh?" Sugar asked, raising a brow at him.

"Never know what information might be useful," West said, shrugging, reaching to put a cigarette between his lips, cupping the tip to light it.

"So long as the information stays in the club," I added, tone barely masking a threat.

"I like this town. Wouldn't fuck up my chances of hanging around. I don't wanna be a loanshark. Or a fixer, whatever the fuck that involves. And I have a moral objection to selling Easy Lay."

"Easy Lay?" Sugar and I both asked at the same time, straightening up off the wall, turning to face him fully.

"Who is selling Easy Lay?" I asked.

This was the first we were hearing of it. And we all kept an ear to the ground about the organizations in this town. There was cocaine being dealt by a much more careful Abruzzo. And Third Street was doing the heroin. Maybe some meth. There was a trio of twenty-somethings selling pot. We overlooked all that. Adults made adult decisions. It wasn't our place to police the streets.

But date-rape drugs?

Had a feeling Reign would not sit back and let that fly.

In fact, none of the organizations would. Not now that they were all breeding like rabbits, had a bunch of girls aging up. In a town where GHB was easily acquired.

"You want to prove your loyalty, you tell us this," Sugar warned. "Otherwise, fuck off."

"I was planning on telling you," he said, shrugging, completely unconcerned with the ice in Sugar's voice. If I was right, Sugar was thinking about Peyton and her group of girlfriends going out on the town. To bars where maybe someone looks away from a drink for a minute. Long enough to have something slipped in. "Those bangers down on Third Street. Before I came here, I heard they were a pathetic facsimile of the organization they used to be. But it seems like they must have some new management because they are hopping to. Lots of little dudes on the street handing out GHB and Roofies. Lot of working girls on the street. With some bruises that makeup don't cover."

"We're going to go inside and tell the prez about this," Sugar declared, knocking the cigarette out of West's hand, grabbing the back of his neck, and turning him toward the door.

No one could claim Third Street were great to the women they pimped. But we'd never seen evidence of them being heavy handed with them. Or overlooking Johns who were.

Red flags.

These were all red flags.

Reign would want to check into it, put feelers out in town. Talk to Lo and her people at Hailstorm. Maybe even Paine who he knew kept tabs on the gang he used to run back when it was stable and - for all intents and purposes - a more respectable organization.

No beating on their women.

No selling date-rape drugs.

"Looks like we got a problem in town," Sugar announced, making Reign's beer slowly lower from his face.

I couldn't imagine what this man had seen over the years.

Sug and I had only been around for a short chunk of it, after most of the dust had settled.

His chest expanded and contracted with a small sigh.

"What else is new?" he asked himself. "Alright. What do we have now?"

SIX

Freddie

I understood why Abby was a workaholic.

And this wasn't even my business. My name wasn't attached to it. My life savings wasn't dropped into it. I didn't have the risks she had.

But I finally truly understood the pride of a job well done resulting in hard-earned cash.

My check felt heavy in my hand as I looked down at it, waiting for Thad to change after his shift so he could show me how to put it into my bank account through the phone app.

It had been a busy week even if you didn't include work.

I had needed to get a new driver's license, a bank account, work attire, and get myself a bike since Thad's and my schedule overlapped some days and I refused to let him throw down several thousands of dollars on a used clunker to get me from point A to point B.

Besides, I liked the bike. The wind. The sense of utter freedom - something so foreign to me. And the ability to get anywhere I needed to without having to worry about bus schedules and sketchy dudes. I even had Colson attach a basket to the front for if I needed to go shopping.

A basket on my bike.

The girl I was before I went away would be red-faced in shame at the very idea of something as, well, old-lady-ish as a basket on her robin's egg blue beach cruiser.

Funny how time changed even the little things.

I couldn't claim to love all things girly, but I had to admit that I was looking forward to a little spa day after being on my feet, losing five pounds in pure sweat all week.

And, apparently, my hairstyle was 'very high maintenance' and required 'a trim every week and a half.'

Besides, I liked Benny.

And we would be picking up Jelena to bring with us for some pampering too, allowing Colson an afternoon to himself for a change. For as long as I was around, that was a habit I wanted to keep up. For Colson who deserved an occasional day to do whatever he wanted after taking on the whole responsibility of being a single parent. But also for Jelena, who I was really enjoying getting to know.

I never gave much thought to children. I had been too young when I went away to have considered it. And when I was inside, well, it was useless. Not that I wasn't surrounded by it. When you're locked up with a bunch of women, a lot of what they talked about was their children. How they were going to clean up for them, do better, get them out of the system, be a more significant part of their lives. There were endless photographs taped to the walls or lining the desks.

But when my plan was to get back out long enough just to get my revenge, well, it was pointless to torture myself with things I could never have.

Being around Jelena, though, it was making me really get to see something I would be giving up. The chance to be a mother, shape a life with stability like my mother had never been able to give us, with love that my aunt had never provided.

I shook my head, finishing ripping the top off of a frozen push-up yogurt, handing it over the center console to Jelena, secured in her car seat, legs and arms flailing out as she sang along to a song Thaddeus had blasting that I was pretty sure Colson wouldn't approve of.

"Do you and Uncle Thad go to the salon a lot?" I asked when the song winded down and she finally permitted us to get out of the car.

My hands wrestled with the straps of her car seat for a second, forgetting how tight the pieces clicked together, before lifting her small body out, her glittery Doc Martens catching the light as I set her on the sidewalk, taking the hand she immediately thrust up at me.

"Mmhm," she informed me. "They give me a lolly," she told me. "A big one."

"Think they will give me one?" I asked, making my voice low and hopeful.

"I'll *make* 'em," she promised me with a little hand squeeze I swear I felt in my heart as well.

As one would expect of ten in the morning on a weekend, the salon was packed. Mostly women sat in the chairs getting cuts and colors or at the tables in the back having their nails done. As we were led to our saved seats, a woman was led out of a room in the back. Waxing, I figured.

"You need to get your lady business handled? I can make her fit you in," Benny told me in a voice that wasn't hushed at all, making me glance around to my sides to see if anyone was listening.

"Oh, no. I don't need..."

"Oh, fuc--" Thad started, then eyed Jelly. "Fudge yes, she does. The way that beautiful biker man was slobbering all over her last weekend, I give it another couple of days before he comes banging on her door. And she will need to be all tamed down there."

"I am... plenty *tamed* enough," I told him in a low hiss. "Not that it is any of your business if I am tamed at all or not," I added with a pointed eyebrow raise. "I don't ask you about your tameness."

"Girl, you wanna see? Smooth as bowling balls at all times," he told me with a smile. "No one likes a mouthful of little hairs when they are all up in your business. Am I right?" he asked, looking over at Benny.

"He's right. I mean for us and the strickly-dickly sorts," he said then cast a guilty look at Jelly who was not paying attention now that a girl who was clearly her regular hairdresser was pulling her hair out of her braids, talking animatedly to her about her next style choice from a book Jelena had in her lap. "I don't know if the same rules apply for the lady cave. But given that most men these days have a stroke if a woman has some leg or underarm stubble, I imagine you need your hardwood floors waxed."

"Okay we are so not discussing this," I informed him even as my lips turned up.

An hour later, my hair was trimmed - just barely - my fingernails were lacquered in a matte black that I knew wouldn't last more than the weekend since I couldn't wear polish and cook, my butt and back were getting a workout thanks to the massaging - and vibrating - pedicure chair, my feet slipped in warm water, waiting for the nail tech to come back. The music in the back was loud and soothing, quieting the noise in the front of the building, allowing you to lean back, close your eyes, relax.

Which was precisely what I was doing.

The air shifted, making me aware of someone taking the empty seat to my side. When no vibrating turned on, my eyes peeked open.

Did I find my brother? A woman from the salon?

Oh, no.

I found the star of my late night vivid, sweaty, torturous dreams.

Virgin.

"Big fan of pedicures?" I asked, hoping it would cover any possible longing that might be clear in my eyes.

Longing.

That was the only way to describe the deep, clawing ache inside.

A primal thing, surely. But also possibly more than that.

Ever since I found something I hadn't expected from anyone except my family. Acceptance. Maybe it shouldn't have surprised me after Abby had no issues with my past. But, I guess, I had been brainwashed into thinking no one would want to be my friend or want to date me because of where I had been. There was this niggling little voice in the back of my head that whispered *What do you have to offer someone*?

It was ridiculous, of course. Especially when thinking about an outlaw biker. It was silly to think that a man who made his living selling drugs - and then guns - would look down on me for my past.

But it had been a bone-deep fear until he had given me what I had been so desperately craving.

Acceptance.

Approval.

"'Bout to find out," he admitted, kicking out of his shoes and socks as the nail tech came back, filling his foot spa with water and salts for him to slip into.

My gaze slid down his long, solid legs to his bare feet, finding their appearance oddly intimate. You didn't usually see a man's bare feet unless you were close with them in a physical way. Or at the beach, I guess.

"If you didn't come here for a pedicure, why are you here?" I asked as the tech moved away again, an odd smile on her lips.

"'Cause West said you and your brother would be coming here today," he admitted.

"So... you're stalking me?" I asked, lips curling up. Maybe I should have been creeped out. But I found myself flattered by the attention from a man who could clearly have just about anyone he wanted.

"Lightly," he admitted with a smirk. "You could tell me to fuck off. I will. But something tells me you aren't gonna," he told me, leaning closer, dropping his voice a little, making the entire salon suddenly fall away.

Mouth suddenly dry, I had to swallow hard before I could get any words out. "Well, it would be a shame to miss out on your first pedicure," I told him.

"Eavesdroppin'?" he asked with a raised brow, making me follow his gaze to the woman I had thought of as the nail tech - blonde and super pretty with a determined sort of gait.

Her smile was at once amused and guilty. "Get over yourself, Virgin," she shot back, rolling her eyes at me like we were sharing in some secret. But I was completely out of the loop.

"I better not be getting ribbed about this because you pillow talk this shit to Pagan," he added, pretending to sound threatening when it was clear he had a soft spot for the woman.

A woman who pillow talked to a man named Pagan.

Which, well, had to be a road name, right?

Who else had a name like that?

So the nail tech was one of his brothers' women.

"Hey, how am I to blame if you're in here getting your spa day on?" she asked. "I think the Tickled Pink polish would go *great* with your skin tone, by the way," she added with shining eyes as she moved away. "Or, at least, that is what I am going to tell Pagan you picked."

"That's Kennedy," Virgin supplied when we were alone again.

"As in Kennedy's?" I asked, meaning the name of the salon we were sitting in.

"Yep."

"You're going to get a lot of crap for this, aren't you?" I asked, lips curving up.

His gaze slipped there for a long second before moving up to my eyes. "It'll be worth it," he declared, reaching for the remote on the arm of his chair. "So how does this work?" he asked, holding it up to me like this was the most natural thing in the world - sharing pedicures. Like we were the oldest of friends. Or the most intimate of lovers.

Fifteen minutes later, I was laughing as Virgin jerked and hissed his way through his foot massage.

"You like this shit?" he asked, hands a death grip on the arms of his chair to - I imagined - avoid slapping the poor nail tech who was clearly tickling him as she worked.

"I *love* this shit," I corrected as my tech slipped the pad of her thumb along my aching arches, making my head slam back on the chair, my back arching, a low, somewhat sexual noise escaping me. A sound that made Virgin momentarily forget about his own feet, his eyes moving over me, the lids seeming to go a little hooded.

"Keep that in mind," he murmured, filling my mind with fantasies of being sprawled out on his bed, my legs over his lap, his hands massaging the aches out of my sore feet.

"Aunt Freddie!" Jelena yelled, launching herself at me from my other side, landing on my lap with a giant smile. "Like my hair?" she asked, touching one of the little knots that were positioned on each side of her head, a part down the center, little cornrows leading up to them, the other half of her hair left in a curly mass almost down to her shoulders.

"I love your hair," I informed her.

"Daddy is gonna grumble," she told me with an eye roll that she had to have learned from Thaddeus.

"Why?"

"It's gonna get knotty," she told me, pulling at the free strands.

"Well, you're gonna have to let him comb it so it doesn't get knotty."

She made a noncommittal grunting noise as she swirled herself on my lap, her little back to my chest, her head resting against my breast like a pillow.

And my heart did a little flip-flop as she snuggled in like she had always been there.

For some reason, my head swiveled, finding Virgin's gaze on us, something strange, unreadable behind his eyes that made my heart do another flip.

"Alright, boo, let your auntie get her toes done," Thad declared, moving up at my side, reaching his arms out to Jelena who reached back, happily settling on his hip when he hoisted her there. "Why don't we go and get you some ice cream?" he suggested. "I can trust you to get her home, right?" he asked, directing his attention to Virgin.

"She's safe with me," Virgin agreed, tone almost determined.

"I'm counting on it," Thad told him, giving me a wink. "See you later. This is all paid for," he added, even though he knew I had wanted to pitch in now that I was working.

"She come to visit you while you were... gone?" Virgin asked, choosing the word carefully, knowing *'away'* either meant jail or rehab, and aware that we were not alone.

"No," I told him, a little sad about the lost time even though I had made it clear that I didn't think it would be appropriate for Colson to bring Jelly when he came to visit, not wanting her to meet me after getting patted down like a criminal herself.

"So you just met her?"

"Yeah."

"She has taken to you fast."

"I think that she was kind of looking for a female presence in her life," I admitted. "I mean Thad takes her to do all the girly stuff. And Colson goes with her to all her dance classes and such. But I still think she was craving a woman in her life."

"Her mom bailed?"

"Yeah. When she was just a couple months."

"That's fucked."

"Yeah," I agreed. "But Colson is doing a good job with her."

"What's he do?"

"What he can," I said, shrugging. "It's not easy to work around her schedule. School is off a lot of days. And he has to be around for her classes and such. He works night jobs. A custodian and a security guard at some dive bar a couple towns over. It gives him his days free for Jelly. Then an older lady in his building watches her at night."

"Can't be making much," he mused.

He didn't intend for it to, of course, but the words made guilt stab into my belly. For all the years I allowed him to fill my commissary when he should have been saving the money for Jelena.

"I guess not," I agreed.

"Just sayin'," he started, shrugging. "If he doesn't have some moral objection to a different lifestyle, Reign is looking for good men. And the hours are flexible. And the money is good."

"I will... mention that," I told him, even though I wasn't sure there would ever be an appropriate opening for something like that. *Hey, Colson. This apartment is really nice. But if you ever want to worry less about paying your rent, you can become a gun-running biker.*

"Figure single dads need to keep their options open," Virgin added, shrugging it off. "So, you gonna let me take you home after this, or be a pain in my ass and insist on walking?"

"She could smudge her nail polish," the nail tech told him with a knowing smile.

"Hear that? You could smudge your polish. After all this work. Can't be having that, can you?" he asked, then suddenly yanked his feet away from his tech. "I'm gonna go ahead and skip the polish," he said with quirked lips and a head shake.

"It's clear."

"And shiny," he shot back, reaching for his socks and shoes, then his wallet, handing a twenty to his tech as he got to his feet. "You go dry up. I'm gonna square up and grab coffee. You actually take it as sweet as you made it at your place, or were you... distracted?" By him. He knew I had been practically drooling over him.

"Three sugars," I told him, sidestepping the last part of his question with the same precision as I sidestepped the leg of a chair so I didn't smudge my polish on the way to the dryer.

I had barely slipped my butt into my seat and my feet into the dryer when I felt his body move behind my chair, curling forward to tower over me, his hands moving down to grab the armrests, lowering his mouth to my ear.

"Be right back, baby."

He had likely made it outside before the shivers inside died down.

Easy.

I was so damn easy.

And I couldn't even get mad at myself about it.

"Here you go," Kennedy said, dropping a glass of water that had come from a giant dispenser with cucumbers and lemons floating in it. "I remember that beginning phase. If I had a block of ice for you to sit on, I'd bring it over," she added with a smile before she moved away to talk to Benny.

My shoes in my hand, new reusable pink flip-flops with Kennedy's on the bottom on my feet, I made my way toward the door where Virgin was waiting with two cups of coffee, his head ducked to the side slightly, lips tipped up just the tiniest bit.

And it didn't escape me either that just about every woman's eyes were on him, eye-banging him, thinking about how nice it would be to have that smile of his aimed at them.

That's right, ladies, that smile is for little ol' me.

It was an oddly possessive thought for me to have, but there was no denying how good it felt to step up to him, have him hand me that coffee he got just for me, then look down at my feet to compliment the color. I'd swear I heard *sighs* around me at that.

His arm rose over my head, holding the door open, then as we stepped onto the street, his hand went to my lower back, staying planted there. A comforting - and incredibly distracting - presence.

"My bike is at the compound," he explained when he saw me looking at the street for it. "Hence the coffee. Figured we could finish as we walked the block or so. How is it?"

"Perfect," I admitted. "Have you recovered from your tickle torture?" I asked, watching as his smile went almost bashful.

"I can take a back rub any day of the week. But I don't know how you tolerate that shit. You ticklish anywhere?"

"My ribs," I told him. "Don't use that against me," I demanded, locking my elbows down at my sides. I'd endured endless torture sessions at the hands of brothers who wanted something from me. The idea of it happening as an adult filled me with dread.

"If I got my hands on your skin, baby, I wouldn't be tickling you."

"Oh."

Yeah, that was eloquent.

And totally the right response to something that, well, swoon-worthy.

The hand on my back suddenly slipped to the side, sinking into my hip, using it to turn me, press me back against a building.

There was a swoop and crunch as Virgin's arm tossed his coffee cup in a nearby bin, freeing his hands.

So that they could slither their way up my sides, barely grazing the ribs that didn't feel the least bit ticklish at all, sliding up the sides of my breasts, up over my chest, the sides of my neck, stopping only as they framed my face, tilting it up.

And they met absolutely no resistance.

In fact, I was pretty sure my body was incapable of resistance.

Everything went weak, fluid.

It was a miracle I was still able to keep upright as his body shifted inward, his hard lines pressing into my chest, belly, hips, pinning me gently to the wall as his eyes held my gaze for a second before his head started to lower.

My heartbeat tripped into overdrive, and a silly, insecure, niggling little voice wondered if he could feel the pulse pounding in my throat from where his hands were.

But then his lips pressed to mine and all thoughts about anything fell away.

The contact set off a jolt through my body, my muscles all involuntarily tightening and loosening in the span of a blink, and I was vaguely aware of the fact that my hands had spasmed as well because there was the hot splatter of my coffee on my bare feet as the cup dropped, the clink of my shoes falling at my other side.

But my mind couldn't seem to think to be bothered about that, just pleased that my hands were free to rise, slide up Virgin's strong arms, curl around the back of his neck, an action that nearly lifted me off my feet, forcing my body to plaster to his as his lips pressed harder, demanded more.

A low, throaty whimper escaped me as my lips slipped open, inviting his tongue to move inside and claim mine.

The hands left my jaw, disappearing for a long second before sinking into my ass, dragging me up and off my feet as his teeth nipped my lower lip hard enough to drag a moan from deep inside.

It was a car horn and cheering that broke the spell, making my body jolt in a much less intoxicating way than the last time. My hands planted on his shoulders and pushed until he settled me back down on my own feet, but pressed me back against the wall. As if he knew my legs were feeling just a tad wobbly.

I pulled in a deep breath that made my chest shake as Virgin suddenly started to lower down, his head level with my crotch.

"What are you doing?" I hissed, wanting to sound horrified, but there was definite heat in my tone.

At the sound, his head tilted up, lips curved, eyes bright with what I could only call masculine pride. I couldn't even fault him for it. He'd earned it.

"Might be a one-percenter, baby, but I don't litter," he told me, lifting his hand to show me the takeaway coffee cup that had fallen from my hand, the lid bent in, coffee saturating the thick paper outside.

Then he slowly - and there is a definite emphasis on the *slowly* - moved back to his feet, his gaze staying level with my crotch, my belly, my breasts, then my face for what felt like minutes each before he finally moved away to toss my cup where he had discarded his, giving me a second to shake some sense back into myself, trying to calm the chaos of desire coursing through my body.

I pushed off the wall, ready to try to act like I had it together even as the pressure on my belly all but assured me that I would go through an entire pack of batteries later without any real relief.

Virgin turned back, stooped again, this time coming back with my shoes which he clicked together and held at the heels in one hand, his other going to my lower back again. Possessive. Maybe even a little protective.

Or was that my wishful thinking?

Wouldn't it be strange - and wonderful - to actually find a man who wanted to protect me instead of, well, the exact opposite.

I shook my head, not wanting those thoughts. Not now. Not when they could easily sour a sweet moment.

"So, you gonna let me see you again?" he asked as we walked into the yard of the compound, moving over toward the long line of glistening bikes settled at the side.

Glistening because they'd just been washed.

By, it seemed, the guy who had kissed my hand at the party.

West.

"Hey, pretty lady," he called, wiping some sweat off his brow with the back of his heavily tattooed arm, giving me one of those smiles that women would be hard-pressed to find a better way to describe other than *panty melting*.

I, however, seemed suddenly immune.

"Hey West," I greeted him with a small smile. And it wasn't until my shoulder brushed his chest that I realized I had moved closer to Virgin as I spoke to his brother. "How are you?"

"Oh, slaving away for these schmucks," he said, waving a hand toward the bikes.

"Hey, at least you don't have to clean the bathroom with your toothbrush," I told him, knowing the horror of that from my adolescence. My aunt was many things, and one of those was a complete and utter neat freak. When she took us in, there was no longer a need to pay for her twice-weekly housekeeper. Why, when she had three sets of hands that could provide free labor?

"You have clearly not been inside to see the bathrooms. Yes, plural. Because Reign is an evil bastard, each of those bedrooms in there has its own bathroom. And since I am the only probie, I am stuck cleaning them all. The horror I have seen," he said, shaking his head solemnly.

"Sugar still here?" Virgin asked, his hand leaving the center of my lower back and out to my hip, fingers curling in.

"Yep."

"Tell him I will be back later to take over your schedule."

"How much later?" West asked, eyes dancing, lips curled up. There was no mistaking the innuendo there.

"None of your business, prospect. Isn't there a SUV you should be washing too?" Virgin asked pointedly, leading me over toward his bike, handing me the helmet with his free hand, seeming like he refused to let his hold of me go until West walked away.

"Yes, sir," West agreed, saluting him, then walking toward the side of the building where the garage must have been located. "Hey," he called, popping back out. "Is it true there used to be a tank in here?" he asked, making my brows raise up.

"Gonna have to explain where you heard that to Reign later. But yeah. It's been moved since the SUV is more practical now."

"Hm. Cool," West said, but there was a light in his eyes like a little boy being told he could tour a fire truck for the first time.

"He's gonna ask to see that tank," I told Virgin as I secured the clasp under my jaw.

"Looks like it," Virgin agreed, dropping his hand so he could climb on his bike. "You gonna answer me?" he asked a few minutes later after we pulled up to Thad's apartment building, cutting the engine, waiting for me to climb off.

"Answer you?" I asked, pulling the helmet off, putting it back on its spot at the back of the bike.

"About letting me see you again," he clarified.

"Oh." Yep. There was that eloquence again. "Sure." That was not much better.

"You working tomorrow?"

"Yeah."

"Monday?"

"Half day."

"I'll pick you up there."

"And do what?"

I cringed a bit at that, the words sounding almost suspicious. Like he was going to kidnap and murder me. Which was only on my mind because freaking Abby had her true crime TV shows on nonstop.

"We could eat," he suggested, almost awkwardly. Like he was no better at this than I was.

I found myself somewhat charmed by that, flattered that I was the only woman he had come across that he felt the need to go on dates with.

"I like eating," I said with a small smile. "Is there a dress code involved?"

"Pretty sure anyone would let you in anywhere even in a sack. Wear what you want. What time you get out?"

"Six. But I have to come home first to get changed. I will be covered in various substances by then."

"I'll drive you home."

"No, it's fine. I have my bike."

"Baby, I have a bike. You have a bicycle," he clarified with a smile.

"It has a basket," I told him, beaming a little. I really liked the basket.

"Christ. You're making it worse," he said, shaking his head at me. "Alright. I will meet you here at seven then."

"Sounds good. Aren't you going to... take off?" I asked when he just stayed there, watching me.

"Yep. Once you're inside," he agreed, jerking his chin toward the door.

Oh.

That was sweet, right?

The little skip in my heart certainly thought so as I gave him one last smile before making my way up the path, my shoes dangling from my fingers.

It wasn't until I was safely inside the apartment that I heard his bike rev and pull away.

And me?

I sank against the door, smiling like an idiot, and incredibly thankful that my brother was not around to see it. Then shower me with questions. Demand answers. Answers I didn't really have.

Like was this going somewhere?

What were his intentions?

What did I want?

Well, I could answer the last one.

I wanted Virgin.

In a deep, aching, undeniable way.

But I had never had much of a chance to simply want a man before. To experience something casual. I had no idea how - or even if - I would handle a situation like that.

"Ugh," I grumbled, taking myself across the apartment, dropping down in my bed, those worries overtaking all the light, girlish excitement I had felt for a few short moments.

It plagued me all night, making Thad claim I was a Debbie Downer and he was going out to find some more fun.

It was still with me when I got to work the next day, Abby's eagle eyes watching me for a long moment.

"What's his name?"

Surprised, not thinking better of it, I blurted it out without considering it. "Virgin."

"What? No fucking way! I know him. Well, I don't know him know him. But I've talked to him a few times. He's yummy. Does he fuck like he seems like he fucks?"

"What way is that?" I asked, feeling my spine stiffen in a way that could be called protective, defensive.

"Like he can make you scream god in tongues."

"Oh," I said, choking out a laugh. "I wouldn't know. We have just run into each other a few times."

"Well, when you *bump into each other* in the more fun way, let me know how it is. Promise? I won't stiff you. The guy meeting me here can make me come hard enough to forget my own name. He's dumb as a stick, but no one said I have to sit around and listen to him after. Oh, speak of the stick," she said when there was a knock at the door, prompting her to drag her giant hobo bag out from under the counter, hauling it up on her shoulder as she made her way to unlock the door.

"Hey Abby," he said, giving her a long once-over as he stepped into the doorway.

"Robby," Abby replied, eyeing him up as well. "We're going to my place this time."

"Where do you live?"

"About two inches above your face, sweet cheeks," she said, making me have to cover a laugh by slamming a pot down. "See? Right over his head," she said, shaking her head at his blank look. "Lock this door. And make sure the delivery guys lock the back when they come in and out too. Come on, Wallbanger. You have some work to do."

With that, they were gone.

And thanks to an onslaught of orders, I was able to drift out of my thoughts for the afternoon, half aware of the creepy show on the TV Abby never did tell me where the remote to was, working me up to a fit of nerves until the phone rang and I nearly jumped out of my skin.

"Hey, your plans with Mr. You'llSpeakInTongues aren't tonight, right?"

"No, tomorrow."

"Would you mind swinging a double? I will pay you overtime. Wallbanger must have been chugging energy drinks and wild yak essence because he is still hard as steel. And this girl needs as much stress relief as possible or I am going to have to take that script my shrink keeps trying to throw at me."

"No problem," I agreed, shooting the recreated kidnapping on the TV a wary look. The restaurant didn't close until two in the morning. By then, I should be jumping at my own shadow with this crap. "Can I..."

"Thanks so much. You're the best. Oh, well, yes, you may have a little snack..." Abby said, voice dipping low enough that I decided to go ahead and hang up before her end got decidedly X-rated.

The orders died down around half after one in the morning, giving me time to load the dishwasher, wipe down all the surfaces, and leave Abby a note about what we were running low on for when she got in early the next morning like she always did to check on stock.

With that, I took a deep breath, slipping the pocketknife Thad had given to me into my palm as I made my way through the restaurant to check the back door before going out the front where I would find my bike locked into the bike rack installed between Abby's and the store next door.

My head peeked out before I moved outward, turning to lock the door then pull down the metal cage, locking that into the ground, making my way to my bike to work *that* lock free, my heart wedged pretty firmly up in my throat.

"Baby, the fuck you doing here this late?"

Yeah, so, I screamed.

And not one of those kinda quiet inward breath screams.

No.

I screamed.

Like a girl in a horror movie who has been haunted by ghosts for months and then someone suddenly grabs her shoulder out of nowhere.

That kind of scream.

"Christ," Virgin's voice hissed, his hand going over my mouth. "It's me," he added when my whole body jolted. "You good?" he asked before he let his hand drop from my mouth, making me spin to find him standing there, the streetlight casting him half in shadow.

"Sorry. I'm jumpy. Abby has the stupid TV set to all those true crime shows. It's making me paranoid."

"Paranoid in this town isn't a bad thing. But, Freddie, babe, the knife works better if you open it *before* a threat shows itself," he told me, reaching down for my hand, pulling out the knife, flicking it open. "Jab," he told me, closing my hand around it, then pulling my arm out to jab toward his chest. "Or slice, but this way," he told me, turning the knife so that the blade was parallel with my forearm when it lifted. "Your arm is stronger this way," he explained.

Finding myself oddly breathless - and not from the scare - I swallowed hard twice before I could find words. "Were you waiting here for me?"

"Honest answer? When I noticed your bike here when I drove home an hour ago, I figured I would chance a walk around at closing time to make sure you aren't driving that damn bike home at this hour."

"Actually, my..." The flash of headlights stopping behind Virgin made my words fall away.

"Brother?" he asked, half turning as the door to Colson's SUV flew open, his body hopping out, muscles tensed, ready to beat the hell out of the strange man with me alone at night... when my knife was out.

"Wait," I said, holding up a hand, palm out. "It's alright, Colson. I know him," I told him as he got to Virgin's side in about two angry, protective strides. "He was actually making sure I was safe," I added as Colson sized him up. Virgin, it seemed, was doing the same.

"Since when do you socialize with Henchmen?" Colson asked, and I would have sworn there was a hint of suspicion there, making my heart and belly sink to my feet.

My head started to fall before I forced it back up, my jaw getting tight.

"Oh, since I started selling illegal guns for them. This whole cooking thing is just a cover for my criminal activities. Once a criminal, always one, right?" I asked, bitterness dripping from my words, not even caring that we had an audience.

Virgin's brows lowered, looking confused, maybe a little angry as his gaze went to my brother.

"Christ, Winnie, that's not what I meant. You know that's not what I meant."

"It sounded like what you meant," I shot back.

"Alright," Virgin cut in. "I know this isn't my place, but maybe this isn't a discussion to be having right now. You're worked up," he added, looking at me.

"Yeah, come on, Win. Let me get you home. You're dead on your feet. And you have to be back here tomorrow."

"I'm taking my bike," I objected, jaw set to stubborn.

"No you're not," Colson said.

"Like hell," Virgin objected at the same time.

"I am a grown ass woman. If I want to ride my bike home at two a.m. *naked*, then I can do that. And you can't do anything about it."

"Come on," Virgin said, reaching for my bike's handlebars.

"What are you doing?" Colson asked, stiffening.

"I'll walk her back to the compound. Grab the SUV. Then drive her home."

"You're not getting to know where she lives."

"He already knows where I live," I shot back. Typically, I would be warmed by my brother's protectiveness. But I felt nothing but hurt and anger.

"Jesus, Winnie..."

"It's fine. Thanks for coming out anyway. But Virgin is taking me home. I will talk to you some other time."

"Winnie..."

"I'll make sure she gets home safe," Virgin assured him, making Colson's gaze move his way, sizing him up. Maybe I would have found myself feeling guilty for the way his shoulders slumped, his head ducked, but I was too annoyed right then to care as he turned, got back in his car, and drove home to his daughter. "You alright?" Virgin asked, voice quiet.

"He cut off contact with me," I admitted, eyes avoiding contact. "For a while. After I was locked up."

"Your brother loves you."

"Yeah, but I don't think he sees me the way he used to either," I told him, my breath sighing out of me, defeated.

"Sometimes our choices, our actions, do that to people around us. Or society. I don't expect everyone to look at me without suspicion when I am walking around with a one-percent badge on my chest."

"The difference being that you actually did... you know... never mind," I said, shaking my head, ripping the lock off my bike, tossing it into my bag. "You don't know my story," I told him with a rare surge of honesty. "So you can't explain my situation to me."

At his silence, I felt the regret course through me. Never having been someone who could be outwardly snippy or confrontational, the reality of being able to do so with him, this outlaw biker I barely knew from Adam, made uncertainty flood my system. My eyes slipped upward, finding him watching me with a gaze I could only call curious. Not offended. Not pissed. Just... interested.

"Maybe you'll tell me your story someday and I can understand," he suggested, reaching to grab my bike, turning to walk, leaving me to jog up a few steps so I wasn't following behind him like a puppy.

"Sorry I was snip..."

"Don't gotta apologize to me," he cut me off, shaking his head. "We all have our moments."

And he wasn't just saying that. He wasn't feeding me platitudes while passive-aggressively storing this away to use against me at some point down the road. *Remember that time you were a complete bitch when I didn't even deserve it?* No. He was just... okay with it.

They call me Virgin because I don't give a fuck.

That was what he said.

Meaning he was laid back. Easy going. A roll with the punches kind of person.

I couldn't imagine that kind of freedom.

I gave fucks. I gave all my fucks. About damn near everything. I couldn't claim it made me happier to be that way, but I wasn't sure it was possible not to be that way either.

Virgin led me back to the compound, loaded my bike into the back of the SUV, then opened my door for me. All in silence. Not seething, angry, or uncomfortable silence. Just silence.

He was not a silence filler.

I was used to Thad who was convinced every silence would be better filled with his voice. But I still found it enjoyable as he climbed into his seat, flicking on the butt warmer in my seat like he somehow knew after endless hours in a hot kitchen, the combination of dried sweat and tiredness was giving me a chill.

Soft, oldies R&B hummed from the speakers.

And, apparently, the combination of the music, the heat, the gentle glide of the car down the streets was downright hypnotic.

Because it wasn't until I felt a giant hand close around the area just above my knee and give it a gentle squeeze that I realized I had fallen asleep.

"Home," he murmured when my eyes fluttered open, finding warm eyes and a matching smile only about a foot from my face.

"I never fall asleep that fast," I admitted honestly. I was a toss and turner since going away, since I learned that sleep meant vulnerability and that some people like to use that vulnerability against you.

"I'd claim it was because you're comfortable with me, but the seats are like butter and the butt warmers are like Ambien," he told me with a smirk. "I'll go grab your bike," he told me, leaving the car on so I could bask in the cozy comfort for another few minutes before I saw him standing outside the passenger side door, reaching to pull it open. Suppressing a grumble, I climbed out of the warm car, fishing in my bag for my bike lock for the front rack because I simply wasn't in the mood to try to wrestle it into the elevator and hang it up in the apartment. Thad claimed the building was safe enough to leave it outside without a lock. I was just going to trust him. And my padlock. "Still on for tomorrow night?" Virgin asked after I secured my bike and stood back up to face him.

"Yeah. I promise I won't be so snippy."

"I promise I can take it even if you are," he told me with a lip twitch.

"Thanks for driving me home," I told him on the top step, turning to unlock the door.

My hand barely got a chance to raise before the wrist got snagged, yanked higher as his body pressed me against the brick wall, pinning my arm above my head as his lips crashed down on mine.

The brick scraped at the skin of my forearm. His stubble scratched the sensitive skin on my face. His body heat moved through his shirt and into mine, making a shiver move through me as my lips parted, demanded more. My free arm rose, grabbing the back of his neck, holding him as though he showed any intention of pulling away.

His free hand slid down my thigh, sinking in behind my knee, yanking it upward, curling it around his waist as his hips pressed in. His hardness pressed against the aching need, making a moan escape me, only mildly muffled by his lips on mine.

The sound of someone clearing their throat made my face rip away, my leg dropping to the ground heavily even as Virgin's grip slowly loosened on my wrist, his head dipping down to place a kiss at my throat.

"Sorry to break up the necking session, you two, but it was getting a bit steamy for the apartment entryway," Thad informed us, and I didn't have to look to see the amused smile he had on his face. "Your brother called to let me know some dangerous criminal was driving you home," he added as Virgin let out an airy chuckle against my neck before straightening, slowly pulling away and turning.

"Hey Thad."

"Hey you handsome thing, you."

My gaze went to my brother, finding him standing there in his kimono in his furry *No, Officer, I didn't kill my rich husband* slippers, a sleep mask sitting on his forehead, gold strips under his eyes that he claimed worked wonders on dark circles.

"You knew who it was. You didn't have to come down here to walk me in."

"Walk you in, no. Spy on you? Yes, I sure did. You two kids have fun?"

"Oh, God. Stop," I grumbled, moving away from Virgin, almost sure that when his hand brushed mine that it was on purpose. "Thanks for driving me home. I'll see you tomorrow."

"Goodnight, baby."

"Oh, goodnight to you too, baby," Thad called, giving him a wiggly finger wave as he turned to walk away.

"Could you be more embarrassing?"

"We both know I could," he told me, curling an arm around my hips. "Your lady bits need some ice?"

"There's not enough ice left on this ever-heating planet," I grumbled, closing my eyes, taking a deep breath.

"Well then, we're lucky you have a date tomorrow so you can finally seal the deal. Don't think I didn't see the empty battery package in the trash, you horny bitch."

"It's a first date. We aren't sealing the deal."

"Oh, psh. You'll be lucky if you make it to the restaurant from what I just witnessed. Don't be close-minded for the sake of some antiquated idea about when it is appropriate to fuck. The only *appropriate* time to fuck is when you want to. Now let's get us back upstairs. Colson interrupted my REM cycle, and we both know I am bitchy when I am sleepy."

A long shower washed the cooking off of me, but did nothing to ease the aching inside.

As I fell asleep, I wondered if Thad was right.

If I could jump into bed with Virgin, a man whose real name I didn't even know.

But maybe if I asked him his real name at dinner...

--

"Girl, go," Abby demanded, slapping my ass with a wooden spoon hard enough for me to wonder if she was going to leave a bruise. *That Virgin might be seeing later.*

"It's early," I objected, looking up at the monitor above our heads where the orders scrolled as they came in.

"Yeah, but, Fred, doll, you just put sugar in the macaroni and cheese," she told me, making my eyes shoot down to what I had been doing. And, sure enough, the gooey golden cheese was speckled with granulated brown sugar I had meant to throw in the bacon brown sugar chicken pan. "You are clearly already in date-mode. And, judging by your stint at a woman's facility for the past decade, I figure this will be your first male-female rendezvous in ten years."

"It will be my first rendezvous at all in ten years."

"Really? I mean, I'm not into the lady cave that much either, but in a pinch..."

"I haven't been in that tight of a pinch," I said with a smile.

"Christ. You must be wound like a clock, huh?" she asked, dumping the macaroni and cheese in the trash, then filling up a new pot with water to start over.

"I guess."

"Well, go. Get yourself all cleaned up, dolled up, the usual. Do you need condoms?"

"My brother already threw a box at me this morning."

At my face, in particular.

From what I saw last night, he's a Magnum man, he had told me with a finger wave before heading off to work.

As I went home and showered, shaved, did the hair process again since I had just wrapped one of Thad's colorful scarves over my hair to go to work, then worked on my makeup, picked out my clothes, his words came back to me again.

From what I saw last night, he's a Magnum man.

And this time, they sank in. Magnum. I had been so wrapped up in the sensations the night before that I hadn't given size much thought. But now, alone in the apartment, I was unnervingly aware of the fact that I hadn't had sex in ten years, that I barely even had a chance to engage in it before I went away.

The women at prison used to joke about being re-virginized.

They used to claim that after a spell, it was nearly like the first time all over again when they went home. Or, at least, the child-free ones said that. The ones with kids made crude jokes about how with the way their babies battered their way out of their bodies that nothing would ever *pinch* let alone hurt like the first time again.

My butt sank down on my bed, still only clad in black lacy panties and a matching bra.

And that was exactly where Thaddeus found me about an hour later.

"Alright, what is it?" he asked from my doorway. "And don't be trying to tell me it is nothing because no one pulls a The Thinker pose in their panties over nothing."

"Do you think it's going to hurt when we have sex?"

"Aw damn," Thad said, pushing off the doorway to drop down on the bed beside me, nudging his shoulder into mine. "Look, I can't claim to know all about what you have going on down there," he told me, waving a hand to my crotch. "But the way I see it, if you want it enough, and you're primed enough, your body will do what it is meant to do even if it maybe pinches a bit at first. What I *do* know is that if you get all up in your head about it, you'll psych yourself out of it for no good reason. Now, let's get some clothes on you for that handsome man to peel off later."

With that, Thad got me into a white sundress with red flowers I never would have picked for myself even if I had to admit it was flattering.

"Flats," I told him when he held out a pair of wedge sandals.

"It's a date. You don't wear flats on a date."

"You are not the one who will get blisters," I shot back. "Go let him in," I told him as the buzzer went off, shoving him toward the door before going into my closet myself, finding a pair of sandals similar to the wedge ones, slipping my feet into them, then spritzing on some perfume.

"Look at you," Thad said in his flirtatious voice as the door closed. "Freddie, your gentleman caller is here!" Taking a deep breath, I checked my reflection one last time before moving out into the central area of the house.

Walking out, I found Virgin out of his jeans, boots, and leather cut for the first time. In their place, he had black slacks and a matte black dress shirt. No tie. Slip-on loafers.

He'd shaved too.

And he looked good.

Good enough that I almost didn't want to go to dinner.

"And this, dear children, is where you stop eye-fucking one another," Thad told us. "And you," he said, pushing Virgin, "tell her that she looks beautiful. And you," he went on, pointing at me, "tell him he looks good all dressed up."

Virgin's lips curved up as he moved closer toward me, ducking his head down. "You look beautiful."

"Thank you. You look good too." He smelled better.

"So where are you taking her?" Thad asked, never one to miss an opportunity to butt in.

"Famiglia."

"Oh, fancy. Well, you two have fun. I am heading out to date Danny. You know, Danny-On-The-Down-Low. He got a room. I will see you in the morning." He was being ridiculously obvious. "Here, boo," he added, holding out my purse. "You have some Mags in the tampon zipper and your nightstand. You are all set," he told me in a blessedly quiet whisper. "You two have fun!"

"Thanks, Thad."

"Mmhmm."

"Take care of my girl," Thad told Virgin as he moved past, voice losing the light, amused tone, getting uncharacteristically serious.

"Got nothing to worry about with me," Virgin assured him before stepping out into the hall with me. "What's the matter?"

"I'm gonna have helmet head at a fancy restaurant," I declared, reaching up to touch the curls that came out perfectly, like they were excited for the date as well.

"Took the SUV tonight," he told me, hand going to my lower back as we waited for the elevator, stepping us both to the side to let off the lady down the hall who always stole Thad's magazines before giving them back to him claiming they were in her mail by mistake. We moved inside, the doors closing with a quiet click that somehow still made me jump. "You're nervous." It wasn't a question, but I answered anyway.

"Yeah. I... haven't been on a date in a long time," I admitted.

"Baby girl, I've never been on a date," he told me with one of those smiles that made his eyes go all warm. "So we can just trip along this whole thing together," he told me, hand slipping to my hip to give it a squeeze.

Trip along.

I liked that.

"Are you nervous?" I asked, watching as the button froze on the main level.

"I don't really get nervous, but I second-guessed these shoes for fifteen minutes. So that counts."

The drive to Famiglia was short.

I had never been inside the restaurant myself, but had walked the docks beside it, watching all the men in their suits walk in with their ladies in dresses, everyone looking altogether very fancy and wealthy since I knew the food was expensive because it was where my aunt made her dates take her when she managed to find someone who wasn't put off by her gruff personality.

It looked like I remembered it, but somehow nicer and brighter at the same time. The lights from the outside deck shined down on the choppy water below the stilts holding up the building. Inside, everything was dimmed to the perfect intimate lighting level, the colors black and gold and just a hint of red here and there.

"So did you and your brother work it out?" Virgin asked after we ordered our drinks, as we looked over the menu while we sat in our fancy rounded booth in the back of the restaurant that was saved just for us in a way that implied it was a big deal, like maybe had an *in* with the owners or something.

"We haven't spoken yet," I admitted, feeling guilty. Now that the anger had died away, I knew I had overreacted, that I read too much into his tone.

"Got some wounds there that need stitchin' up," Virgin told me, glancing up at me over his menu. "And I don't mean about last night."

"I know," I agreed. "It's a sore spot. I was pretending it wasn't because I was just happy to have him around again. And I didn't want to rock the boat or make things awkward. But we are going to have to have that uncomfortable talk, I guess."

"Your family loves you. That is worth working on. Even if it isn't comfortable."

"Are you close with..." I lost my sentence when the waiter came over with a bottle of complimentary wine *From Mr. Grassi*. "Do you know the owner?" I blurted out when he walked away again.

"I've met him and his sons. I wouldn't say we know each other. But there has always been an understanding with The Henchmen and the Grassi family."

Grassi family.

Family.

"Do you mean family as in *family*?" I asked, half leaning over the table to whisper it.

"Yeah. That kind of family. The established organizations in Navesink Bank have respect for one another even if we don't do much business together."

"Who else is in an established organization in town?" I asked, having been too young and too into my own little life when I was last in town to know anything about them except for The Henchmen who always openly flaunted their illegal activities by wearing their cuts and one-percent badges.

"Mallicks. Hailstorm on the hill. And then there is Abruzzo. Though he stays clear of us now."

I wanted to ask, but also figured that asking questions was not what an outsider did in this kind of situation. "That's it? It sounded like so much more."

"There are a lot of, ah, independent contractors. Then there is Third Street."

"The gang?" I asked.

"Yeah, them," Virgin agreed with a grimace.

"I'm confused," I admitted.

"About?"

"Why you are grimacing about Third Street when you aren't about all the other organizations. What makes them worse?"

"Reign doesn't like 'em because they deal all sorts of shit. Heroin when they can find it, meth. I have nothing against drug dealers, obviously, from where I came from. What I have a problem with is the way they treat their working girls."

"Working girls. Like... prostitutes?"

"Are you surprised?" he asked, smiling.

"No, well, maybe a little." I shouldn't have been. There were more than a few women in prison with me who had worked the streets or in makeshift brothels. I knew all about the business. I knew more than I wanted to know, in fact. "Just that it is happening here and I never noticed, I guess. But, I'm guessing they are rough with them?"

"Rough is an understatement. I don't think I ever see one of those women without bruises or dried blood. And if they are doing that to their own women, you can only imagine what they let the Johns do. That shit doesn't fly with me. And now we are hearing that they are selling Easy Lay."

"What is Easy Lay?" I asked, feeling like I used to in high school when people would talk about weird sex acts then make fun of me for not knowing what they were.

"Date rape drugs," he told me with a dark look in his eye.

"Oh." The sound came out of me, weighted, heavy, knowing what that meant for the women in the area. All women in the area. Anyone who went on a date with a new man. Anyone who went to a bar where the bartender was paid off to slip something into the drink. Any girl who went to a high school party and woke up to find herself sore and bruised.

Yeah, no, there was no respecting an organization who sold those kinds of drugs. For me, while I had never used - and would never use - drugs, I understood the sale. Supply and demand. It was no different in my mind than selling illegal guns or whatever the Grassi and Mallick families did. But there was a line to be drawn in the sand. On one side, you could sell as much product as you wanted to someone who was okay with messing their own lives up. On the other, you catered to the lowest of the low and became slime yourself when you sold things that enabled someone to screw someone else's life up.

"This probably wasn't appropriate first date talk, huh?" Virgin asked, picking up on my dark thoughts.

"Well, we did agree there would be some tripping involved," I told him, shrugging it off as the waiter came back to take our order. "Besides, neither of us really know what appropriate first date talk is anyway."

"I think it is all about getting to know each other."

"That sounds about right." And also somewhat terrifying, to be perfectly honest.

"So, Freddie. Why don't you tell me your story?"

We both knew what he meant. He already knew what I did for a living, where I lived, what my family situation was like.

He was asking for the other stuff.

The stuff I didn't like talking about.

The stuff that lead to me losing ten years of my life.

And I wasn't sure I was ready for that yet.

Would he even believe me if I did tell him?

No one else did, save for Thad and Colson.

Reaching for my wine, I took a tentative sip, trying to find the courage to launch into it.

But what came out of my lips wasn't my story.

"You first," I demanded, watching as his shoulders went a little tight, as he struggled with the possible ramifications of telling me his story.

But, in the end, he leaned back, kept almost unnerving eye-contact, and went into it.

SEVEN

Virgin

My earliest memories were of a brown carpet in a mostly empty room where the walls had concave spots from angry fists. Whether they were from people who lived here before us or my mom and her endless string of boyfriends, I had no idea. I just remembered staring at those spiderweb-like holes, my heart skittering around in my chest, sure something was going to pop out of them if I looked away.

I slept on that brown carpet in that small room with the closet door that hung off the top hinges, so it didn't really open. But it opened enough for a skinny four-year-old me to climb inside when I heard raised voices in my house.

The carpet wasn't comfortable. It wasn't the kind like they had in the house of the lady next door who watched me when my mom went... wherever she went - all plush like you sank into it. It was hard, and the strings all stuck out wild and itchy. When an extra blanket was clean, I spread it out over the carpet to sleep. When one wasn't, I pulled my arms into the armholes of my shirt and slept with them pressed against my body, so they didn't get scratchy.

It hadn't occurred to me at the time why I didn't have a bed like my mom did. Or why I couldn't sleep on the couch in the living room. All I knew was that when I was home, I had to stay in my shoebox of a room and *Out of my mom's hair* like she told me all the time.

And since all she did was scream at me or slap at me when I did come out of it, I was happy to stay in until she and her friend were in her room making noises. Only then, I would sneak out, go to the bathroom, snatch some quiet food from the kitchen. Quiet food meant anything that didn't come in a crinkly, noisy wrapper. No cereal or chips or crackers. Usually, I stole stuff off the plate my mom left in the kitchen cold and a cup of water, rushing back to my room before the bed stopped knocking around, eating, curling up on the floor, trying to sleep, comforting myself with ideas of the house next door.

Squishy carpets.

A TV that was always set to cartoons.

A lumpy couch to sit on with a heavy knitted blanket the lady with the glasses who insisted I call her Mama Rita told me she made herself, though I didn't understand how you could make a blanket.

She gave me big glasses of watery milk she said would feed my bones, make me grow big and strong.

There was always butter and cinnamon toast for a late morning snack. Then lunch would usually be canned tuna fish mixed with mayonnaise and a bit of hot sauce. Some days, she would chop up pickles and mix it in. Those were my favorite days.

My mom never cooked.

Sometimes, she didn't even shop, so there was nothing around to eat unless I was at Mama Rita's.

The biggest blow in my young, sad little life was when I came out in the morning to have my mom walk me to Mama

Rita's before she did... whatever she did during the day and she told me to go back to my room.

"Rita croaked," she told me with a shrug. "As if I needed this shit in my life right now. The fuck am I supposed to do with you now?" she asked, but I knew she didn't want an answer. She liked to talk at me, not to me. "Know what, never mind. I will drop you off with my mother," she declared, grabbing my arm, dragging me along with her, still in my clothes from the day before.

"I raised my kids. I'm not raisin' yours." Those were the first words I heard out of my grandmother.

She looked nothing like my mom who was tall and skinny - all arms and legs like I was at the time as well. My grandmother was short and round all over with perfectly curled hair, small, angry eyes, and a dress that was too tight around the chest, making the buttons pull apart, create little holes between them that you could stick fingers through, making her dark brown bra visible from certain angles.

"Raised me," my mom scoffed. "That's a joke. Watch him. You have nothing else to do. I'll pick him up later."

Except she didn't.

My mom always came home right when the sun was going down.

But the sun went down.

The streetlights outside went on.

And she didn't come back for me.

My grandmother's house wasn't bare like my mom's house, but not comfortable and cozy like Mama Rita's either. The furniture in the living room had slippery, uncomfortable plastic on it. The TV was there, but my grandmother sat on the slippery couch drinking something out of a big bottle as she watched her shows on it - all angry grown-ups or grown-ups kissing. Sometimes both. Yelling and kissing. Kissing and yelling.

There was no cinnamon toast.

Or tuna on rye bread with mayonnaise and hot sauce and maybe, if I was super lucky, pickles.

There was no food at all.

Or milk.

But there were orders.

To not speak unless I was spoken to.

To always say 'ma'am' when I answered her.

To move the heavy, wet clothes from the washer into the dryer.

To sweep the floors.

To empty the trash bin in the kitchen. Then, when I had trouble getting the overfilled bag out and spilled some of the slimy garbage all over, she'd slapped me hard across the face, then made me clean it up. Then scrub the floor on my hands and knees.

Later, hungry and exhausted, I fell asleep on the linoleum floor under the table that night, more scared than I remembered ever being at the idea of having to live here, wishing my mom would come and pick me up, promising myself that if she did, I would be good. I wouldn't annoy her or get in her hair. I would do whatever she wanted me to do.

If she would just come and get me.

Take me home.

"What the fuck is this?" My mom's voice demanded, shocking me awake, my body trying to shoot up, but my shoulder hurt from laying on the hard floor ,and my leg was asleep, all tingling and overrun with pinpricks.

"Don't be coming in my house at seven in the morning hollering," my grandmother demanded, slapping a hand on the counter.

"You made him sleep on the floor."

"I didn't make him do anything."

"So he *chose* to sleep on the kitchen floor like a dog?"

"How should I know? He disappeared when my shows were on."

"Get up," my mom demanded, reaching under the table, dragging me up until I found my knees, pushing myself up, trying to ignore the churning, grumbling feeling in my empty belly. "You're a real piece of work, you know that? Piece of fucking work, Mom. The fuck am I supposed to do with you?" she asked herself out loud as she dragged me out of the house. "You know what? I can't do it anymore. I'm done. Done done done. Come on. Get your ass in the car," she demanded, ripping open the door, barely letting me climb in before slamming it shut.

We drove for a long time.

I sat silently in the back, listening to her talk to herself about things that made no sense.

One-night-stands.

Low hormone birth control not working like the original one.

Deadbeat dads.

Child support.

How she was supposed to get a man with a baby hanging on her all the time.

I didn't know what baby she was talking about.

I wasn't a baby anymore.

I had fallen asleep by the time we made it to wherever we were going.

"Get up," she demanded before climbing out, slamming her door, coming around the car to yank open mine, grabbing my arm, half dragging me down the walkway to a long, squat building with blacked out windows.

Music and voices were coming from inside, loud, loud enough that the sounds vibrated through my little body even as my mom wrenched the door open and stormed inside.

Like she'd been there before.

Maybe a lot of times.

Some heads turned.

Then some men whistled, yelled things at my mom that I didn't understand, but made me move closer to her, wanting to be further from them and their ugly sounding words.

"There you are!" my mom yelled suddenly, dragging me toward a group of men.

"Sherry? The fuck you doing here?" the man she had been looking at demanded.

I didn't know much about giants, but I was pretty sure at the time that he was a giant. To me, my mom was larger than life, always towering over me, refusing to get down on my level, making me look up at her until my neck ached. But this man made my mom crane *her* neck up. I wondered as we stood there if her neck hurt too.

"What am I doing here? This is what I am doing here," she declared, yanking me up off my feet under one arm, settling me on her hip. "He look familiar?"

"He looks all gangly. Like you," the giant added to a chorus of chuckles from his friends, making me think that whatever *gangly* was, it wasn't nice.

"He's yours, Dwayne," she told him with a flick of her neck.

"Not for nothing, Sher, but I once saw you take three dicks at once. So excuse me if I'm not sold on the paternity thing based only on your word."

"Well, you can go ahead and get him tested on your time then, because I am done. He's all yours," she declared, dropping me down onto my feet hard, making me fall back on my butt, having to blink away a couple tears that started in my eyes.

My mom didn't say sorry.

Or try to help me up.

She was too busy yelling at the giant, slapping his chest and arms.

I didn't ask for her help, getting back onto my feet by myself because I didn't want her slapping me like she was slapping him.

It was then that I felt a hand press down on my shoulder.

But not the hand of a grown-up.

A hand of someone who was about my size.

He pulled me slowly away from my yelling mom.

"You're a man now," he told me, pulling me along with him. "So we can't cry," he added, nodding his head reassuringly. "But don't worry. I have toys."

I didn't have a lot of toys.

I had an action figure man who was missing a leg, a T-rex, and a yo-yo that Mama Rita gave me for Christmas. And I didn't have any of those things now. At this strange place full of so many men.

That was what hit me first. I'd been around a lot of women in my life. My mom. Mama Rita, her friends that stopped over, my grandmother.

The only men I knew of were the revolving door of them my mother had over.

This place was mostly men.

There were three women around.

One, my mom.

Another, a lady in a short skirt that had slipped up to show her whole butt, sitting on the lap of a man in a corner, rocking up and down.

And a third was coming out of a room with two men, wiping her runny makeup out of her mouth and eyes.

But there were dozens of men. All of them were watching me and this boy who was leading me away from all of them and into a back room where there was a bed and a box piled with toys in a corner.

All I knew for the next few hours was this boy, Sean, his toys, and the sounds outside the room that got louder, scarier as the night went on.

I never saw my mom again.

It wasn't until both Sean and me had both fallen asleep on the floor by his toys that we finally had company.

Two men came into the room. One was the giant. The other was another giant.

"That's my dad," Sean told me proudly, straightening up, getting to his feet.

"So, you're with me, kid," the first giant told me, extending a hand toward me.

"It's okay," Sean told me, reaching down in his toy pile to find the Army man I had been playing with. "Here, you can take this with you," he told me. And, not having much of a choice, I followed the giant down a hallway, clutching the toy to my chest like he could protect me from whatever might come my way.

"Alright. So. Your mama left you here with me. I would give you my sympathy, but that woman was a fucking lunatic. Think you might be better off here in all honesty. Look at you," he added, waving a hand. "When's the last time you had a shower? And your clothes don't even fit right. Maybe if she wasn't so busy whoring around and blowing her money on who-knows-what, she could have gotten you some shit that doesn't look like it's cutting off circulation. Anyway, I'm Dwayne. Your mama says I'm your father, so I guess we are going with that. You do kinda have my eyes," he added, softening a little.

I didn't know what to say.

The concept of a father was as foreign to me as having a pile of toys like Sean. But maybe his father got him those. Maybe my father would get me some of my own.

And some food.

My belly was grumbling so loud.

"Gotta be honest with you, don't know a fucking thing about raising a kid. Barely got a chance to be one myself. So you're gonna have to grow up fast, little homie. Can't promise you all that soft shit women can give you. But at least you can have clothes that fit and some food. You're all fucking bones. And we can show you how to be a man. That's what I can give you. Sound good?"

Honestly, I didn't know.

All I knew was he would give me food.

And I needed food.

"Sounds good," I agreed.

That night, he got me a shower, borrowed clothes from Sean for me. Clean clothes that fit. And then he got me two giant pieces of cold pizza and a bottle of soda.

Then he dragged in a squeaky cot from a closet, unfolded it, put a pillow and extra blankets on it, turned on the TV to some old black and white TV show, then left me to, I figured, go talk to his friends.

Alone in a strange place, I had a full belly, new clothes, a comfortable bed, a toy on the mattress next to me, a TV, and, it seemed, a new friend.

And a father.

Things, I figured, could be a lot worse.

I wouldn't claim it was easy at first. All the men around me were loud, violent with one another, teasing toward me. But I had Dwayne. And Sean. And Sean's dad Phil.

Eventually, I got a whole drawer full of clothes that fit. I got a box of my own full of toys that were mine, though I shared them with Sean.

Within a few months, the fear of the men lessened, finding instead that while they did so with a lot of yelling and cursing, they were kind of amused by the presence of two small boys in the club, making us fetch them things, do basic cleaning tasks, sometimes tossing balls with us outside the way they all wished their own fathers had done with them when they were young.

By the time we were in school, we realized how unique our world was. Maybe we didn't have moms around, didn't have soft and sweet things. No home cooked meals. No nighttime kisses. No one to wipe our brows with cold compresses when we were sick.

But we had freedom all our classmates envied.

We had no rules except to stay out of the club member's way when they were trying to work. We could run free all day, shirk our homework without getting in trouble, bring home solid Cs every semester without anyone getting on our case about our wasted potential, get into fights in or out of school without getting lectures.

We were inseparable.

Brothers in every way we possibly could be.

And then one day, Sean's dad went to jail, and his mom showed back up again.

And ripped him away from me.

The days after that were long and lonely, feeling oddly left behind, left out, knowing that Sean was getting things I never would. All the softer things in life.

It didn't last long, though.

Three months later, Phil was out, and he brought Sean back with him. Back to me.

Unfortunately for me, every once in a while when Dwayne got locked up or was gone for any stretch of time, I was - for some unknown reason - shipped back to my grandmother. I didn't even know how they knew about her, where they found her, why they couldn't just let me stay there with Sean and Phil. But it wasn't my place to question. What the president wanted, he got. And that meant my banishment when my father was gone.

As an adult, I figured maybe it was a law thing. Maybe the president didn't want child services sniffing around when they got word that my dad was locked up, that it was safer for them to ship me off to my next of kin since they couldn't have the law in their clubhouse around all the guns and drugs and fugitives.

All I knew at the time though was the feeling of being unwanted, the rejection, the aloneness as I found myself at a doorstep I had seen years before in a house with plastic covers on the furniture and a table I once slept under.

And that the woman who owned it was no longer just a chain-smoking, soap-opera-addicted, mean woman.

No.

She was a fucking lunatic.

Made that way by too much booze and maybe some kind of dementia, making her meaner than a rabid cat, coming at me with rolled up magazines, frying pans, a belt that once belonged to her late husband. Not for any real reason. Just because I was there. Or because I wasn't there - as in at school - when she wanted me to do some menial task. Then, as time went on, for no actual reason at all except the warped voices in her head claimed I was guilty of something I had no part of.

Just when I was sure I couldn't take another beating, another screaming match, another incident of full-blown insanity, Dwayne would get out, and I would be brought back to my club, back to my people.

When we changed clubs a few times over the next few years due to massive incarcerations or lousy leadership, Dwayne, Phil, and Sean were the only constants in my life.

In the next clubs, we weren't seen as the club's kids, everyone imparting their fucked up little life wisdom on us, treating us like the kids they all actually hoped they didn't have, not wanting the actual responsibility of having one of us show up at their doors, just liking the idea from a hands-off distance.

The new club didn't want us around, didn't try to make it seem like they did. We endured. We did the dirty work. Took their taunts without argument.

It was there that I got my road name, a couple years after Sugar got his with that whole raid incident.

After some asshole taunted me about my 'slut mother,' my 'whack job grandmother,' my 'gay' friendship with Sugar relentlessly, trying to get a rise out of me.

But I had long since learned to lock all that shit down.

It all started that first night when my mom dropped me off at the club, and Sean told me we were men now. Then every single visit back to my grandmother's where any reaction on my part brought about worse treatment on hers.

And, hell, once you learned to lock those emotions down for long enough, they stopped really coming up at all. That calm you used to fake became your new normal.

"He doesn't give a single fuck," the brother declared, smirking. "Maybe we can call him Virgin."

It wasn't until a couple years later that I realized the name could be seen in a negative way, that I would have to keep explaining it for the rest of my criminal career. But it was mine. I kept it.

"How did you and Sugar end up in Navesink Bank?" Freddie asked, ripping me out of my memories for a moment, realizing for the first time that it had been a long time since I thought of those things. My mom, the room I lived in, the neighbor who had been my only sliver of warm and soft, my crazy grandmother, meeting my dad for the first time, finding my best friend in the world.

Heroin gang to cocaine gang to enforcing.

It was the third club when we finally grew up, got bigger, stronger, meaner looking. We got licenses that allowed us to run more errands, to become useful to the older members of the MC.

The inevitable happened around then too. Phil got locked up on a two-year stretch, leaving Sean fatherless. My father was in and out of jail more than he was around, taking the fall for the men who were actually at fault for the things he went down for. But that was what you did. Whatever the president wanted you to do. Even if it meant giving up some of your freedom.

It was then that it all changed for us.

We were allowed to do something we had never been able to do when our fathers were around. We got to prospect, work our way into being actual club members, not just annoyances hanging around.

By the time our fathers were back, we each had cuts, had patches.

We weren't technically adults yet, but according to the club, we were.

There was no more of our fathers protecting us from things, shielding us from some aspects of the club.

We were given drinks, access to the clubwhores, did jobs.

In fact, we were given more jobs than our own fathers were. Not because of their age, but because of our own. Because we were underage. Because if we got caught, we would merely go to juvie for a short spell, not a couple years upstate. It was a smart move to risk us instead of the more established members of the club.

And, inadvertently, it also pushed Sugar and I closer than ever. We were part of a brotherhood, sure, but he and I, we were our own sort of brotherhood. All we had was each other when we were out on jobs, taking on enforcing all by ourselves. Often outnumbered. Expected to do the damage, get the money, keep the club afloat.

Sugar was the one there to pour alcohol on my bleeding, aching knuckles. I was the one in a seedy motel room in a town we didn't know using tweezers and a cheap sewing kit from a convenience store to pluck a bullet out of his flesh then stitch him up. He pulled my unconscious body out of a bad situation by the back of my shirt. I hauled his battered body over my shoulder like a soldier in a war to escape a hailstorm of bullets.

That was our life for years.

Then Phil had a heart attack when we were in our mid-twenties.

A year later, while Sug and I were out of town doing one job, my father caught a bullet on another, taking his life before I could get a chance to say goodbye, to thank him for taking me in when he didn't have to, for giving me a life free of hunger, for giving me skills as a kid that would help me as a man.

"I'm sorry," Freddie said, voice a little thick, reaching across the table to put her delicate-looking hand over my big, scarred one.

"It was a long time ago," I hedged, not liking the feeling that came up at those words. I'd never heard them. Not even right after his death. Sug had clamped a hand on my shoulder, and we had both bowed our heads in silence when we got the news.

If someone had apologized, it would have implied something bad happened. Dying for the brotherhood, that was seen as something to be proud of.

By the time we got back to the club, the body had been buried, the booze had been poured. It was business as usual.

"Still. That couldn't have been easy," Freddie insisted, only pulling away because the waiter came back to the table with our entrees.

"Life usually isn't," I agreed.

"So what happened then?"

It was life as usual. We stayed in the club that was home for all intents and purposes, that was the only family we had left.

Or so we thought.

Until the betrayal.

Sug and I had been left at the clubhouse while most of the other members went to a biker rally that they were doing security at. I remembered feeling relieved, glad to be able to hang back for a change. We'd been on so many jobs for the months leading up. The idea of doing more traveling filled me with dread. So when we got to stay behind to hold down the fort, we were glad for some downtime.

We didn't even know some shit went down until we got a call from the hospital.

Most of our men were dead or in prison.

With no central leadership, the club fell apart.

We did what we had to do. We took what we could and left, traveled around, trying to find a new club.

That was when we got word about The Henchmen having an open house, looking for new members after their own numbers got decimated.

You weren't in the one-percent lifestyle without knowing about them. They were one of the most prominent arms-dealing MCs in the country period. And they were - since Reign took over after his father - notoriously particular about their members.

We went to the open house with low expectations.

Because there was one other thing known about Reign.

He fucking hated drugs.

His men weren't allowed to use.

It went without saying that they also didn't sell.

And we figured that once he heard about our first two MCs - about the heroin and the cocaine - he would get rid of us quick.

But we'd managed to get a positive vote from his men at the time - Pagan and Renny and Duke and the list went on and on. It got us a meeting. Where we were given the chance to explain.

Reign, as it turned out, was the kind of man who let you tell your story, gave it thought, and didn't hold things out of your control - like the decisions of your fathers - against you. I guess coming from the shithead father he and Cash had growing up, he knew a thing or two about the sins of the fathers.

After a promise that our old connections held no loyalty anymore and that we never touched drugs ourselves, we were allowed to prospect.

"Is it as bad as TV makes it sound?" Freddie asked as she twirled spaghetti on her fork.

"Prospecting? Depends on the MC."

Compared to our previous MC, prospecting for The Henchmen had been a breeze. The guys simply weren't the bastards we were used to. Sure, we got all the dirty work. We cleaned the clubhouse, did the shopping, washed the bikes, did the oil changes, took the worst of the guard shifts. But we weren't deliberately made miserable. We were treated like brothers almost immediately. Which was likely due to the small number of men left in the group.

It was a shorter prospecting period too, not the years we had needed to endure when we were young.

"Are you happy here?" she asked, surprising me.

That wasn't something you got asked much. As a man in general. As a criminal in particular. A lot of society didn't exactly think you deserved to be happy if you operated on the wrong side of the law.

Hell, I never thought much on happiness myself.

I had brothers who didn't generally get off by beating each other. I made good money. I got the security of knowing we had good leadership. The women were a different aspect I had never known in my life. They created a family feeling I had never really experienced.

The lifestyle was a little more tame.

But as I got older, I found myself content with that.

"Yeah, I think I am happy enough here," I decided.

"Your story is kind of crazy," she told me when I was done.

I hadn't given it much thought. My story seemed almost average in this lifestyle. When you were surrounded with men who had stories similar to yours, you forgot how out there they seemed to people who didn't live a life like yours.

"Maybe a little," I agreed. "So, I told you mine," I told her, watching as she stiffened a little, knowing what I was about to say. "Now it's time to tell me yours. How did you end up in prison?" I asked, point blank, knowing it was a sore subject for her, figuring it would be better to launch into it, not try to eke it out of her.

Her head dipped, gaze on the tabletop for a long time, long enough that I was sure she wasn't going to tell me, feeling a stab of disappointment, not just because I shared my story expecting her to do the same, but because I genuinely wanted to know more about her, something new to me.

Her breath sighed out of her, and her head lifted, chin going up, shoulders going back.

And then she gave it to me.

EIGHT

Freddie

I wish I could say I wasn't your typical teenage girl.

There were girls like that in my school, unique for their own reasons. The compulsive overachievers, the ones who were in every single club in school to increase their chances of getting into the best colleges. Then there were the girls who, even at seventeen or eighteen, had decided to dedicate their lives to causes, who always had flyers or pamphlets they were handing out, spent their weekends at marches or rallies. Hell, there were even just the punk or goth girls with their dark makeup and 'fuck society' mindsets that set them apart.

I was not one of those girls.

In hindsight, I wished I had fallen into one of those crowds. Even if I very much doubted I would look good with thick black eye makeup or spiky, colored hair, and I didn't think I had strong enough arms to carry picket signs all the time.

But being a typical girl certainly didn't work out so well for me.

I didn't know at the time, though, that being average would lead me where it did.

All I knew was Thad and Colson had worked almost nonstop after they graduated the year before, got themselves a clunker of a car, then moved out of our aunt's house.

Left behind was a bit of a silly way to feel, I guess, since of course they needed to grow up and start their lives. But it was how I felt. My aunt's focus, usually cast in three directions, was suddenly squarely on me. All the chores that used to be split three ways were now my responsibility.

And I had no one. No brothers to sit with in those precious hours between when school let out and when our aunt came home to sit and commiserate, to make plans for the future.

I was, for the first time in my life, lonely.

Loneliness and a teenaged girl usually meant one thing.

Boys.

I wasn't allowed to date. It hadn't been a double standard in the household. Thad and Colson weren't allowed to date either. We'd heard the lecture a thousand times over the years.

There will be plenty of time to date after college and after you get your careers started.

We'd once even - maybe cruelly, I would think in hindsight - wondered if she had ever had sex. We'd never seen her spend the night out or have a man over.

It wasn't even that her advice was bad, to try to teach us to prioritize education and a secure future over dating.

The problem was, it was simply unrealistic. I mean, even our schools told us that abstinence-only approaches to dating and sex generally didn't work. Hormones were strong, primal drives. People as a whole wanted connections. Especially those with the opposite sex.

Maybe if my aunt had been more lax about it, had allowed me to date around, maybe I would have gotten a taste of it and decided it wasn't what I wanted, not really. I just wanted companionship, someone to talk to, share my time with, share my stories with.

What I got instead of some casual dates with a few different guys was Tanner.

"Tanner," Virgin cut in, brows raised, looking amused.

"Yeah," I admitted, wishing I was able to smile about it.

"Alright," he said, letting it slide even though there was a smile in his voice.

Tanner was everything I hadn't been at the time. Popular, outgoing, a little edgy. And older. Only by two years, but older was older, and when he used to come to pick me up after class, all the girls would tell me how envious they were.

Everywhere we went, he seemed to know everyone, seemed important. And as a girl who had felt altogether invisible and wholly *un*important, I thrived on being attached to that attention, on the attention it got me just for being at his side.

And Tanner was everything a lonely, needy girl could ask for. He made time for me. He called me pretty. He told me I was smart and interesting and that he couldn't wait until I finished school so I could move out with him.

To this day, I still wasn't sure how honest any of that was. If he, at the time, meant those words or not.

"Why was he so popular?" Virgin asked, dragging me back to the present.

"Hm?"

"He wasn't in school. Why was he so popular? Most people grow past that shit once they leave high school."

That was true.

But at the time, I hadn't given the idea much thought.

I never thought to ask. I was just charmed by it, by him, by our potential as a couple. Because, despite my aunt's best efforts to try to turn me into some girl hellbent on being a career woman, I had no idea what I wanted to do with my life, if I was going to college. So hearing from Tanner that he would take care of me, help me get on my feet, let me take time to figure out my future gave me a sense of security.

The woman I would become, the woman sitting across from a really attractive man, telling him about her young naivety, was immeasurably embarrassed that I had ever believed such grandiose, unrealistic promises from my first boyfriend, someone only slightly older than I was.

"He didn't even really have a career of his own," I admitted, shaking my head at myself.

"What did he do then?"

"Sold mixtapes."

"He was a rapper?" Virgin asked, eyes dancing. "Grand ideas of being the next Eminem, huh?"

I snorted at that. "Eminem," I scoffed. "Please, he made Paul Wall seem like a lyrical genius."

"Paul Wall, huh?" Virgin asked, big smile on his face. "Baby girl, we gotta update your musical references."

"If what the guy across the hall from Thad plays is what today's music has to offer, I will happily stay stuck a decade in the past."

"Fair enough," Virgin agreed. "Go on. Didn't mean to interrupt you."

I was shocked at how popular his CDs sold when I had heard his songs, had needed to hold my true opinions to myself about them. But sold them he did. Enough that I started to help him here and there, gleefully accepting the small salary he threw my way for it. With that and my babysitting money, I was sure I would be able to afford my own car in no time. Move on like Colson and Thaddeus did.

"Babe..." Virgin said, tone full of understanding, knowing where this was going.

But I had to say it, get it out, tell someone who would believe me.

One week after my high school graduation, I was standing outside Tanner's apartment building with a stack of CDs, handing them out to the people who came up to me.

It never occurred to me that it was not normal for people to know to come to me to pick up random mixtapes.

I was down to my last five when the police approached.

And I offered to sell them a CD.

"Fuck," Virgin hissed.

That about covered it.

Because they weren't just CDs.

Sure, the CDs were there. Because Tanner was a narcissist. He wanted people to listen to his Godawful raps, believed someday he would be rich and famous. But nestled behind the CDs bought at Staples and burned off his home computer, there were little baggies.

I had been selling heroin for weeks without knowing it.

And while Tanner had been all of fifteen feet away from me when the cops slammed me against the hood of their car and wrapped handcuffs around my wrists, he never tried to take the blame, never even seemed to feel regret over the fact that I took the fall for his crime.

That was what I remembered most, his face as I stared at him, silently pleading for him to save me.

There was nothing there.

He was utterly blank.

Like it was nothing.

Like *I* was nothing.

If I thought I had felt lonely before, it was nothing compared to how I felt when I was placed in the back of a squad car, too shocked to cry, too scared to find words to say.

The drive to the station was the longest of my life. The short interrogation showed me that no one was going to believe that I was an innocent in the situation, that I didn't know there were drugs in the CD cases. And since Tanner's face wasn't on the CDs, his prints weren't on the CDs, his real *name* wasn't on the CDs, there was nothing pointing to him, nothing I could use to accuse him.

They put me back in the car, drove me to county.

I got through intake, got my mug shot taken, got my phone call after they threw me into a holding cell with other women.

And with no one else to call who could help, I called my aunt.

Don't ever call me again, she'd told me after the words were out of my mouth. *You brought shame on this family again. I should have known you'd turn out just like your mother.*

It was painfully obvious that this was it.

I was going to go away.

You had forty-eight hours to post bond.

No one was coming for me.

I sat on the cold, hard concrete bench, staring at the wall, waiting for the inevitable.

Then it happened.

The worst day of my life.

I was led to a back room.

The 'dress in' room it said on the front of it.

I was made to strip.

And I learned there was nothing more humiliating in life than getting naked in front of a stranger who was slipping on gloves, and having to endure a search, feel the most basic right you had - the one over your own body - taken away as you felt hands on you, as you were made to bend over to be inspected for drugs or weapons or whatever else people shoved up their body cavities.

And I didn't cry.

I wanted to, but I didn't.

I didn't know much about jail, had led a relatively sheltered life since my aunt took us in, but I had a feeling that the standard phrases were true.

Like they can smell weakness.

And nothing said weakness like showing up to your first day of jail with swollen eyelids and tear-stained cheeks.

So I buried the tears.

I did what I had to do.

I got tough.

My palms were sweaty as I was led out of intake.

I was handed a pillow with a blanket rolled on top, a pillowcase, a change of clothes - one - slip-on shoes, a small bag of travel size shampoo, toothpaste, a toothbrush, and a bar of soap, then a roll of toilet paper.

By the time I actually was led down the hall toward the housing tier, I was actually too exhausted to feel fear.

The unit itself was two floors of long lines of green painted doors, gray walls, gray floors, gray tables in the lower level common area. Everything cold in a figurative and literal way.

I was led to the second floor and all the way to the corner, ignoring some of the questions yelled out at me.

Where are you from?

Who are you with?

What are you in for?

Even if I had chosen to respond, no one would have liked my answers.

The nice side of Navesink Bank.

No one. Absolutely no one.

And possession. Distribution.

My first cellmate was a woman about ten years my senior, in county for the fourth time in five years, awaiting her trial for a drug offense. Luckily enough for me, she didn't want to make connections, had her eyes set on her freedom that she was sure was just a couple months away, that she would get out on time served.

You're going away, baby doll, she had told me, not one to sugar coat things. *They like making examples these days. Getting tough on the ones selling drugs. It's not so bad though. Prison will be easier.*

I couldn't fathom such a thing.

A cage was a cage was a cage.

But it was something I heard day in and out while waiting for my court date, while trying not to get discouraged about my incompetent public defender since I knew I had no one else, that my aunt would never pay for a decent attorney, that my brothers couldn't afford one, not even if they got together.

"How long were you in jail?"

"Three months. Then I had my trial. Which went exactly as my cellmate told me it would."

It was a first offense for an honor roll student who had just turned eighteen.

But they threw the book at me.

Ten years.

They wanted ten years of my life for a mistake of misplaced trust.

It was a whirlwind that day.

The sentence was handed down. The next thing I knew, I was on my way out of Jersey and into Pennsylvania to the minimum security women's prison.

It was not what I had been promised from the women in county jail.

Did we have the right to get jobs, to load up on commissary, to have better visits, more access to things like the small library, better outdoor spaces for exercise, and some classes? Yes.

But we also didn't even get the relative privacy of a cell with a single roommate.

Nope.

We lived in one large room full of low beds where you got to store your things underneath and in a footlocker.

Forty women.

In one big room.

That was why I could never sleep. That was why their crying or nightmares or talking kept me awake night after night. It was hard enough to adjust to sharing a room with one woman, but to share it with thirty-nine others was a whole different beast.

During the day, the noise was loud enough to drive you half mad most of the time. People talking, yelling, laughing, singing.

I was the only new woman in our unit, so everyone else already had their cliques, their alliances, their friends. And while I wouldn't say they were opposed to the idea of new women trying to join in, I guess I just never put in the effort.

I never felt like I fit in.

I wasn't a criminal.

I hadn't done the crime everyone thought I did.

And while everyone liked to boast their innocence when guards were around, when we were all essentially left to our own devices, they would admit the truth to their friends.

They all knew they belonged there, that they had to do their time, even if they maybe didn't agree with the length of their sentence, or the laws themselves.

I didn't.

I didn't belong in the first place, and found it hard to try to act as if I did.

So I did what a few of the older women around did.

I behaved. I read when books were available. I took any classes that would get me out of our common area for a while. I took my time outside to walk the yard, get some exercise. When I had been there long enough to do so, I got a job in the kitchens.

I was behind bars when Thaddeus finally got the courage to come out. Though I had known for years, it was the first time he had openly admitted it. It was big. And I should have been there for him when he did it. When my aunt disowned him for it, when he had to face that rejection all by himself. And I knew how that felt. I knew how lonely that felt.

I wasn't there when he got his physical therapy certification. Or his fitness certification when he decided that helping people rehab from injuries wasn't what he wanted to do with his life, that he wanted the fun and freedom of helping people get in shape, in making his own hours.

He was, at first, all I had. He was the one filling my commissary. He was the one writing letters and calling, visiting when he had the time and money to travel.

He had believed me.

When the courts hadn't, when my aunt hadn't, when - it seemed - Colson hadn't.

And he had been the one trying to keep me grounded, trying to remind me that I would still be young when I got out, that there was no reason to feel like I lost my whole life because of this. He wanted me to think of the future, of what we would do when I got out, what I wanted to do with the rest of my life.

I suspected it had been Thad that finally got through to Colson as well. I had never asked. But one day, there had been a letter. A week later, a call. And as I found out, I hadn't hardened up enough that I didn't need my big brother, didn't crave that calm, steadfast energy he had always had, something that had only grown in time as he got older, matured, got his life worked out.

Their calls and visits had been bittersweet for me.

Sweet because they were all I had, all I had ever had really.

But bitter because their lives moved on without me while mine stayed stagnant. Thad got so busy that his visits became less frequent. Colson found out the stick turned blue, and his life needed to be about something much more important than me.

I convinced myself it was for the best.

Because the longer I was there, the more time I had to think about Tanner, about how his life got to just go on while mine got ripped away from me.

I had been a good girl.

I didn't cut class.

I didn't drink.

I didn't do drugs.

I had only had sex two and a half times.

"Wait wait wait," Virgin cut me off, lips twitching. "How do you have sex two and a *half* times?" he asked. I sent him a lifted brow look that made him shake his head. "Got it," he agreed, clearly amused by Tanner's lack of prowess. "Go on. You were thinking about that shithead."

I did a lot of thinking about that shithead.

And the pain that had once been there, the aching, crippling betrayal, was suddenly gone.

All I had left was rage.

Oddly, the rage helped. It kept a fire burning in my belly, helped me get through the endless days and the longer nights.

"You didn't make any bonds inside? In all that time?" There was a silent question there *How the fuck did you cope without connections*?

It wasn't like I didn't talk to anyone. I did, obviously. You couldn't spend a decade in prison without speaking to anyone. Well, one woman could. None of us could tell if she was deaf, or maybe out of her mind, or simply had no interest in interacting with any of us. She'd been there before I got there, was still there when I left. But I wasn't like her. There were times when I craved normalcy, when I did reach out.

I let one of the girls who worked as an esthetician on the outside put homemade face masks on me out of commissary items - honey and Pepto or aloe and cold cream. I helped some of the girls make a 'spread' - a special food dish made out of items entirely purchased from the commissary - to celebrate birthdays or holidays.

Then there were the women in the kitchen.

We became our own little community twice a day - brunch and dinner always being served - three-hundred-sixty-five days a year. When we were there, we felt like we had a little more freedom. Sure, we had a schedule. And the knives had to be unlocked and then accounted for before we were allowed to leave after a meal, but we could move around without anyone scrutinizing us, do things we had been able to do in our old life.

Cooking for a prison was a challenge too.

There was, roughly, a sixteen-cent stipend per inmate per meal which meant we generally got the cheapest of everything to cook with. Rice. Boxed potato flakes. Beans. The crappiest, grisliest, fattiest cuts of meat. Canned or frozen vegetables. Limited spices. No salt. We had to be heart-healthy, after all, according to state guidelines.

So we had to somehow figure out how to make something even halfway edible out of those ingredients. We had lucked out with a kitchen manager who was open to suggestions, not stick to the 'toss everything in the pot and serve everyone a gruel-like substance' rule most prisons were known for.

Chili was a favorite - meat or veg and beans, depending on the day. Soups - vegetable, minestrone, potato. Black bean and lentil loaf.

I had always enjoyed cooking, but there in prison was when I had truly fallen in love with it, with its potential, with the fun that was trying to make bland foods tasty. I had entertained the idea for a while that when I got out, I might try to get into some sort of culinary school, find a cooking job somewhere.

But then as the years stretched on, as more time passed me by, things like plans and hopes and dreams slipped away.

Who would give me a loan for school?

And even if I had figured that out, who would want to hire me?

Tanner had fucked me.

Not just out of the ten years the law demanded of me.

But my life.

All of it.

Because I would have a record. I would be unemployable. I would be viewed as less than other people who wanted the same job. And if given the choice between two equally educated persons, one with a criminal record, and one without, well, who would you pick?

Exactly.

So there was no use trying to, as Thad had suggested, map out the rest of my life.

That was when the plan started to form.

That was when I decided I had to make Tanner pay for what he did to me.

And the determination I found in that decision was what had helped me get through the rest of my sentence.

"You know where he is now?" Virgin asked after the waiter had taken our plates, making me realize I had barely tasted what I had eaten. First, I had been too engrossed in Virgin's story, then too overcome with memories of my own to try to figure out what the cooks used in their sauce, if the ratio of garlic and parsley to butter in their garlic bread was perfect, or even think to try out Virgin's dish.

My first time at a fancy restaurant and I had zoned out while eating.

"Tanner? No," I admitted, reaching for my wine. Virgin had politely tasted his glass, but hadn't touched it since, apparently not a wine drinker.

If I were being honest, I hadn't even been looking very hard. The woman I had been behind bars would have chewed me out for wasting my time building bonds, getting my hair and nails done, screwing around with new dishes at home to maybe suggest to Abby someday. The woman who had been caged like an animal would have been pissed that I was even thinking of 'someday,' when all I should have been doing was searching for Tanner, making him pay.

It was interesting what a little space from that hellhole managed to do.

Restore things I had forgotten.

Love. Hope. Plans. Possibilities.

I wasn't sure there was enough of that old woman left in me to do anything even if I did happen across Tanner.

I didn't even know if I could find the strength to approach him, have my say, make it clear what he did to me since he clearly hadn't spared me a thought in all the time I took a fall for him.

Let alone do what the dark, ugly parts of me had dreamed of as I sat up in bed at night.

Thoughts that involved guns and bullets and shots fired and cuffs on my wrists and the rest of my life behind bars. This time for something I had actually *done*.

"You think he is still in town?" Virgin asked, tone almost a little cautious? But why would that be? Because he was worried I might find my lady-balls and do it after all?

"I haven't seen him here, but it is a big town. There are so many people. He could still be here. Or, for all I know, he is locked up."

Which was another thing I had never considered while I wasted all those years in hate and loathing.

What if his ways had already caught up with him? What if he was serving time for his crimes? Behind bars where I couldn't even get to him if I tried.

"What's he look like?" Virgin wanted to know, something that made my brows go down, wondering why he would want to know. To look out for him for me, maybe? Did I even want him to do that? Open up that possibility for me?

"Ah. This was a long time ago. He could look a lot different now. But he was tall, but not as tall as you. Maybe five-ten? On the thin side. He had this really badly done spiderweb tattoo on the left side of his neck. Brown eyes. Kinda on the small side. Dark hair."

"And white," Virgin specified.

"I thought that was implied when I told you his name," I said with a smile. I couldn't claim to know everything about every culture, but names like *Tanner* did tend to belong to the lighter complexioned folks. "My school didn't have much diversity back in the day. In fact, I think my brothers and I and the adopted girl from India were the only people in that whole place who had any color."

"Imagine growing up in MCs," Virgin commiserated with a smirk. "You can't really find a *less* diverse group of people. The Henchmen have been the only club I have been in where I wasn't the only person of color, aside from my dad. Got Roderick here," he explained.

Roderick. I rolled through my mental Rolodex of names I had thrown at me while at the party, vaguely remembering a tall, well-built, stupidly good-looking Hispanic guy.

"The Henchmen are an interesting group, though. Cam who doesn't speak. The guy who practically lives up in that glass room..."

"Roan."

"He looks like a lion." As soon as the words were out of my mouth, my lips pressed together, eyes going big, realizing how incredibly silly that sounded. A lion? Who said a person looked like a lion?

"Never thought about it, but he kinda does," Virgin admitted. "All that hair, the beard, that wild look in his eyes. Wanna hear a secret about Roan?"

"Yes," I decided immediately, leaning over the table a little.

"He used to be a spy."

"Like... an actual spy? Secret stealing and all that?"

"Yep."

"How do you go from a spy to a biker? I mean, that sounded judgy, but that seems like an odd career move."

"I think a lot of people who work secret government type jobs end up doing things afterward that aren't exactly legal. But in his case, he got burned. Someone claimed he was working for the other guys," he explained when I obviously had no idea what getting 'burned' meant. "The government freezes your assets, pretends they never met you. So, essentially, you start over with no money, a giant gap in your resume, and all these skills that really are only good for less than legal purposes."

"That's kind of cool. I mean, not for Roan. That must have sucked. But interesting. Does everyone in the club have crazy backstories?"

"Pretty much," Virgin admitted, suddenly sliding around the table, reaching out to grab my wrist, pulling me with him until our sides were pressed close, something that made my chest start to feel tight. "But I kinda don't want to talk about my brothers on our date," he told me, his hand sliding down my arm, resting over my hand. Not exactly holding it, not in the traditional definition of the word, but covering it, staying there.

"Oh, okay. Ah... what do you want to talk about then?" I asked, keeping my eyes forward, knowing if I looked at him, I wouldn't do so great with the whole stringing thoughts together thing.

"How about what you want to do once we leave here?" he suggested, his finger starting to trace over the back of my hand. It was a chaste, nothing little contact, but it was sending off shocks through my poor system.

"What do you mean?" I asked, knowing damn well what he meant.

"Lots of options that are clearly up to you. We could end things here. Drive you home. That's that. We could go for a drink. For dessert."

The idea of ending things here brought about an instant and unanimous objection from every single inch of my body.

"Dessert sounds good," I admitted. "But maybe I can make it," I suggested.

It was as close to an admission of wanting him to stay the night that I could make myself say.

Luckily, Virgin wasn't exactly dense.

Out of the corner of my eye, I saw his lips tease up at one side.

"Whatcha gonna make me?" he asked, reaching with his free hand for his wallet, deftly pulling out a card, throwing it onto the book the waiter had discreetly dropped off without a word.

"What do you like?"

"Watching a beautiful woman make me something sweet," he said casually. "Or so I would imagine," he added, reminding me how new he was to all of this too in a way.

And, somehow, the knowledge of that was enough to make me feel a lot more comfortable with the situation.

"So... it looks like brownies," I decided when we got home and realized that I really needed to hit the grocery store.

Brownies weren't exactly a wow-factor dessert, but if you did them right, they were kind of hard to beat in terms of deliciousness. I couldn't count the number of times Thad, Colson, and I would sit and eat a whole batch. Right out of the pan. Like a bunch of animals without even a hint of self-control.

"Sounds good," Virgin declared immediately, dropping his big body down on the couch, his gaze focused on me.

"Are you really going to sit there and watch me?"

"I'm really going to sit here and watch you," he declared shamelessly.

And so then he did.

Never had I been more acutely aware of every single one of my movements as I was while I moved around the kitchen, grabbing ingredients, bowls, a tray.

Flustered, I reached for the iPod Thad kept in a dock on the counter, picking his *Smooth Like Molasses* playlist at random, not realizing until it was too late that the playlist was straight up sex music. Of the classy sort, but sex music all the same. And I couldn't change it because that would seem like it bothered me. Yet leaving it on might be seen as forward, right?

Never before had I so thoroughly overthought a playlist as I did while I broke eggs into flour, cocoa and baking powder, sugar, salt, and butter.

"Relax," Virgin's voice demanded.

But not from where it should have come from.

Not from the couch, a safe distance away.

Oh, no.

His voice was directly behind me.

Even as I realized this, I could feel his body move in close.

Big hands came down on my shoulders that were, admittedly, tense.

"You mix," he suggested, thumbs pressing into the knots in my shoulders. "I'll work on the relaxing part," he suggested, his hands working magic across my shoulders, neck, upper back.

Then, as I poured the batter into the pan, the center of my back, lower, over my hips where I didn't think it was possible to hold tension, but hold it there I did, the muscles loose, lax by the time his hands slid forward.

I sucked in a shaky breath, not realizing I was leaning backward until I felt my shoulders press into his solid chest.

His hands paused at my hipbones, seeming to give me a moment, to pull away, to push him away.

Virgin didn't strike me as a passive man, a take things slow kind of man.

But it struck me that he was being careful, going at my pace. Because he knew it had been a decade. Because, as he found out over dinner, I had barely gotten a chance to engage in the physical sides of a relationship with a man even before I went away.

Realizing how unexpectedly sweet that was, my heart skittered around in my chest, chasing away the nerves that had situated there sometime early in the morning in anticipation of this reality.

Seeming to feel me relax into him, his hands moved again, flattening over the tops of my thighs, sliding down. The thin skirt material was a pathetic border. I could even feel the heat of his hand searing through as his hands kept sliding downward. At my knee, his hands started scrunching up the material, making it glide deliciously over freshly shaven skin until it was all in his palms.

His thumb held the material up as his hand flattened again, this time on the bare skin above my knee, the sensation soothing and exciting somehow at the same time.

Virgin's palms were rough from years of working with his hands, oddly smooth in other spots - scars from his enforcing days.

My head turned, resting just inward of his clavicle, as his hands slid up higher, teasing near the smooth skin of my inner thigh.

"Wait." I hadn't even known I was going to say anything until the word was out of my mouth. It didn't even sound like me, quiet, airy.

His hands froze but didn't move away.

Waiting.

Like I asked.

"Yeah?" he asked, his head shifting, his lips pressing a sweet kiss to my temple.

"What's your name? Your real name," I clarified.

Virgin paused, seemingly hesitant. I wanted to say never mind, that it wasn't a big deal. But, in the moment, it felt like a big deal. I felt like it was impossible to go this step with a man whose name I didn't know.

But before I could feel worry that we might be at an impasse, he spoke, voice low and rumbling, a sexy sound that shivered across my skin.

"Ty," he told me, sounding like he was telling me a secret. "Tycen, but... Ty."

"Ty," I rolled the name around, finding I liked it more than his road name, that I liked the honesty of it, the privateness of being privy to it.

A low, rumbling, almost... growling sound moved through Ty's chest at me saying his name.

"We un-paused now?" he asked, voice rough, a little impatient, needy.

Even as I thought that, I could feel his hardness pressing against me, as desperate as the throbbing, aching need between my thighs.

"Yes."

The word wasn't even fully out of my mouth before his hand shot upward, pressing hard over the panties between my thighs. My one arm flailed, looking for something to hold onto. Finding nothing, it moved upward, winding around the back of his neck.

"Soaked for me already," he rumbled, his one finger sliding upward, pressing into my clit, sending a shock of unexpected pleasure through my system.

Suddenly impatient, his hand slid up slightly, snagging my panties, dragging them downward hard enough that I heard a tear before they were free of my ass, and slid harmlessly down my thighs, legs. I stepped out of them on instinct just a second before I felt Ty's hand on my bare skin, tracing up my cleft, pressing into my clit without the barrier, something that seemed to steal all the strength out of my leg muscles.

Ty's other arm went across my belly, anchoring me to him as he worked my clit in achingly, torturously slow circles, driving my body up toward something it had only experienced from my own hands that, it seemed, were not as adequate because they never brought the havoc on my body like Ty's did.

My chest, already tight, got tighter. My breasts felt heavy. My nipples hardened enough that the brush of my bra sent off sizzles of need. The pressure on my lower stomach was impossible to ignore, demanding more, everything.

My hips rocked, trying to get there faster, trying to make him give me immediate relief from the clawing need growing stronger with each passing second.

"Ty, please," I begged, my nails digging crescents into the side of his neck, ones that would likely bruise, leave marks, something that seemed to excite me all the more. Marking him. Letting everyone know I had been there, that we had shared something.

At the sound of my pleading, Ty's hands moved suddenly, sinking into my hips, turning me, lifting me up off my feet, planting me up on the counter as he lowered down, burying his face between my thighs before my mind could even wrap itself around what his intentions were.

His hands planted on my thighs, holding them wide for him as his tongue slid up my cleft, finding my clit, circling it again but faster, harder, more demanding, driving me up harder, faster.

One arm rose above me, grabbing the cupboard, sure I was about to fall off the counter. The other slapped down on the back of Ty's neck, holding him to me though he showed no signs of planning to pull away.

I could feel my muscles tightening, my breath catching, my body pushed to the edge before his lips closed around my clit, sucking hard, pushing me that one last bit, sending me flying, falling, crashing through the orgasm.

Teeth nipped my inner thigh.

That was what seemed to bring me back into my body, looking down with half opened eyes to watch as Ty kissed down my thigh slowly before getting back onto his feet, moving his whole body into the space between my spread legs, both hands going up, framing the sides of my head as his lips pressed down on mine.

Not hard and demanding.

Soft, sweet, coaxing, seeming to sense my need to slowly ease back after an orgasm that had felt like it had torn me apart for a long moment.

My arms rose, wrapped around his back, held him to me as my lips demanded more.

I wasn't sure how long we stayed like that, only that my lips tingled when he finally pulled away, his hands sliding down my back, over my thighs, grabbing me under the thighs, wrapping my legs around his lower back.

My legs tightened, holding on as he moved a few steps backward, his hands moving back up my thighs to cup my ass, holding me against him as he turned, walking out of the kitchen, making his way down the hall I had emerged from hours earlier.

Only hours.

It felt like a lifetime.

That was, after all, what we had shared with each other since then. Every soaring high and crushing low. Every scar and wound. Every hope, every crushed dream. Every secret and public shame.

I felt I knew Ty better than I had ever known Tanner, better than I knew my own brothers in a way. You protected your family from things, from your unattractive parts, not wanting them to see those parts of you, to think of you differently because of them, wanting their love always to be pure, pretty. And, well, no person was pure and pretty. We all had dirt, all had ugly.

I had Ty's dirt and his ugly.

He had mine.

He suddenly didn't feel like a guy I had just met a week or so before.

A low, surprised laugh escaped him, making me pull back, look down at him.

"This is a fuckuva lot of pink, babe," he informed me, making me cast a look around at the space I had never given too much thought to before. I figured this, being his only guest room, was likely where Jelena spent a lot of her time before I showed up. And Thad had likely painted it bright pink to suit her. And bought her pink sheets. And a pink and purple comforter.

"I barely noticed," I admitted, squinting a bit at the garishness of it all.

"I'm bringing sheets next time," he declared, dropping his ass down on my bed with me still straddling him.

Next time.

That didn't exactly escape me.

It was my last real remaining worry.

The idea of a one-night-stand. In getting attached because he was the first man who had put hands on me in a decade, because he gave my body what it needed. And then having him want nothing to do with me once he got a taste.

"And maybe sunglasses," he added, hands squeezing my ass playfully.

Feeling oddly charmed by the lightness, the familiarity of the moment, I felt oddly emboldened, planting my hands on his chest for balance as I slid off his lap, dropping down onto my knees between his spread legs.

My gaze found his as my hands planted on his thighs, slowly moved upward, finding the button of his pants, then the zip, working them free, watching as his eyes went hooded with need.

Taking a steadying breath, hoping that enthusiasm made up for a lack of experience, my hands reached for the tight boxer briefs beneath, slipping them down, freeing his cock, finding it every bit as intimidating as I figured it might be, but feeling nothing but a thrill inside as my hand closed around him, stroking him to the hilt before leaning forward, tracing my tongue around his head before closing my lips around him, sucking him into my mouth.

A hiss burst from him as I worked him as deep as I could, his hand slamming down on the back of my neck, holding me, but letting me set the pace, letting me find our rhythm.

His hand got tighter and tighter, crushing in, likely leaving bruises that would be hard to explain except for with the truth.

But before I could drive him through an orgasm like he had given me, his hand slipped into my hair, tugging, pulling back until his cock left my mouth with a little pop, making my eyes shoot upward, finding his jaw tense, his breathing ragged.

Close.

He had been so close.

But he wasn't going to let me have the satisfaction of giving a selfless orgasm. At least not this time.

"Stand up," he demanded, voice somehow soft, yet brooking no argument at the same time, making my legs curl under me and move upward without me seeming to give them the demand to do so.

His hands snagged my hem again, slowly dragging it upward, having to lift off the bed slightly to pull it over my shoulders, up my arms, over my head, tossing it to the ground behind me.

I was suddenly very aware of my lack of panties, at only my bra hiding a part of me from view.

His hands went behind my back, sliding upward, grabbing the clasps of my bra.

Insecurity was a sudden, almost forgotten thing. My body had been nothing but a vehicle for so long that the idea of someone else seeing, touching, judging it was foreign, but strong, visceral, an uncomfortable fist closing around my belly.

The clasp tightened, then released, the bra straps slipping down my arms.

"Come here," he demanded, grabbing my wrist, pulling me forward. Sensing my hesitation, or simply wanting me closer, I wasn't sure. But he pulled me back onto his lap, his hand discarding my bra before, unexpectedly, his arms raised to his sides, inviting me to free him to my view.

Greediness overtook me, crushing down my insecurity with curiosity.

My hands slid down his sides, already feeling the muscles beneath, moving down to slip inward, find his bottom button, working my way slowly upward, eating up the view of each sliver of skin as it got exposed until there was a gap all the way up. I planted my hands at his shoulders, pushing the material wide to slide down his arms.

I knew, of course, that he was well-built.

But knowing it and seeing it were two very different things.

His skin pulled tight over muscles you could sink a finger between. He wasn't flawless. Pink and off-white scars marred his chest, his arms. There was one particularly long, deep one that seemed to go straight up his stomach. But somehow, I found the flaws all the more attractive, little testaments to the life he had lived, the experiences that had shaped him into the man he grew to be.

My finger moved to trace down the largest scar.

"Knife," he declared quietly as I watched in fascination as his muscles contracted under my touch.

"Ouch."

"Mmhm," he agreed, his hand moving up my side, sliding over my ribs carefully - so, it seemed, as not to tickle me, then moving inward, covering my admittedly less than a handful breast, his thumb moving out to stroke over the hardened peak in a way that made all thoughts of things such as insecurity scramble out of my brain.

"This one?" I asked, touching one that slipped across his left pectoral muscle.

"Piece of pavement ripped me up during a fight."

"And... oh," I whimpered as his thumb and forefinger grabbed my nipple, turning it in a delicious circle.

A cocky, sexy smile pulled at his lips as his head ducked, sucking the other peak into his mouth, sucking hard enough to arch my back, trying to get more of the sensation as the need rekindled in my system. He worked one, then the other, before suddenly taking his feet, turning, tossing me down onto the bed, making me bounce with a small laugh before I noticed him kicking out of his shoes, then his pants.

There was nothing to laugh about at seeing Ty standing there before me, naked, straining, looking down at me with hunger in his eyes.

My breath caught for a moment as he lowered down, his face level with my belly, his lips pressing down into the skin, making goosebumps prickle up over me, working slowly upward, between my breasts, over the side of my neck.

His arms slid up to rest at my sides, balancing some of his weight, then pressing the rest of it against me.

This.

This was what my body, mind, soul had been craving. Not just the orgasms, the touch, the scrape of skin, the sweat, the weight of a man pressing down on me.

My legs folded around his lower back. My hands slid over his broad shoulders, down the slope of his back, pulling him more firmly against me, begging for more of him even as his lips found mine, his teeth nipping, his tongue seeking mine.

Mindless with need, my hips thrust upward against him, demanding more, wanting an end to the hollowness deep inside, something only he could fill.

"Hold on, baby girl, hold on. I need to get..." he started to tell me, trying to pull away as I dragged him closer, as I whimpered my protest.

"Nightstand," I told him, my lips pressing into his neck as he turned to find the small pile Thad had left there for just this reason.

If he was amused by their presence, by the idea that I had wanted and prepared for this moment, he didn't let on as he snagged a foil, nipping the edge with his teeth, then making short work of protecting us before his weight pressed into me once again.

His lips came into mine as his hand went between us, stroking his cock up my cleft, rubbing against my clit for a moment before moving downward again, pressing.

Pressing.

My lips ripped from his, my eyes seeking his as the pressure became something a little uncomfortable, just a slight searing, a pinching as he pushed inside me. Just an inch or two, pausing, giving my body a minute to adjust to a foreign invasion, waiting, it seemed, until my need overtook my body's hesitation, until my hips shifted around impatiently.

Another inch or two.

The resistance, the pinching giving way to something else, something deep, aching in a more delicious way, wanting more, wanting everything.

My nails raked down his back as my hips moved upward, taking him fully, demanding motion. Which he happily gave, slow and deliberate at first - just shy of careful, then building, harder, faster.

"That's it," Ty growled, sinking in more roughly, deeply as my walls tightened around him. "Come for me, baby," he demanded.

As if my body had been seeking permission all along, the orgasm slammed suddenly through me, dragging me down wave after wave, crying out his name, clinging with arms and legs as he worked me through it, dragged it out, before settling deep, coming with my name on his lips.

I wasn't sure how long we stayed exactly like that. Long enough for the aftershocks to subside, for our breathing to settle, our heartbeats to return to normal.

"Gotta let me up, babe," Ty told me, pushing against the mattress, pulling against my hold.

With a grumble, my legs and arms fell away.

A shiver coursed through me as the cool air met my heated skin while Ty got to his feet, turned, giving me the glorious view of his ass for a moment as he walked away, found my ridiculous guest kimono, wrapping it around his waist like a towel as he moved out into the hall.

I heard the door close in the bathroom, scrambling up in the bed, sliding under the sheets, feeling suddenly insecure now that the heated part of the evening was over.

I wasn't entirely sure how this would go once he came back. If he would grab for his clothes, quickly dress, get out of here as fast as he could.

The idea made a hollow space open up in my belly.

But as I heard footsteps in the hall again, I schooled my features into something neutral - or so I hoped - before the door opened and he walked back in.

He came to the side of the bed, but didn't reach down, seek his clothes. Instead, he dropped the kimono with the rest of the discarded clothes, grabbed the edge of the sheets, pulled them up, and slipped underneath with me.

His arm moved around my back, curling me onto his chest, staying around me as an anchor as I allowed myself to sink into him.

"So," he said a long moment later. "I'm not sure how long is an appropriate amount of time to let pass before asking this... but... those brownies..."

Of all the ways I had maybe envisioned the events after sex for the first time in a decade, getting up to bake brownies in the nude, then climbing back into bed to eat them with Ty was not even in the realm of possibilities.

But it ended up being the truth.

And it was better than anything I could have chosen myself.

Way better.

NINE

Virgin

The list of things I *hadn't* done in life was maybe shorter than the one I had done.

But, somehow, in one night with Freddie, I had managed to do several of the few things I had never experienced before.

A real date.

Telling someone my life story. No filters, no omissions, nothing to ease the often ugly parts of it, the bits that - admittedly - made me feel something completely foreign to me.

Vulnerable.

Then sex that wasn't exactly just sex.

Sex had always been something base, something primal, something that required attention and skill, but nothing else. Certainly not feelings. But there was no denying that there were feelings involved when I was inside Freddie.

After that, another first.

I didn't immediately get dressed and leave.

After that, yet another.

I had a woman bake for me. Just for me.

Then, finally, the last thing.

After we ate almost a whole pan of brownies, I had scooted back down in bed, curled her back into my chest, and stayed.

I'd *stayed.*

The whole night.

The slamming front door was what woke me up.

Not Freddie, though. I figured that was a bit of the institution left in her, used to endless loud noises, cells opening and closing, guards yelling, other women talking, shouting. You had to find a way to sleep through it after some time.

She shifted in the bed, sliding off of me, the freedom making pins and needles ravage my arm for a long moment as I listened to Thad slam around the house.

While no one would likely accuse him of being a quiet sort, I had a feeling he was being deliberately loud this morning. So that we knew he was back. So no one came out of the bedroom naked or something.

I shifted off the side of the bed, reaching for my underwear, pants, fishing in the pocket for my phone, making sure nothing important had come in from the club, realizing I really shouldn't have had the SUV out all night without permission.

All I had, though, was a text from Sug.

So, you gonna try to tell me again that this isn't going anywhere?

I didn't respond. Because, quite frankly, I didn't know how to. My head turned over my shoulder, finding Freddie there, the girly pink sheets twisted around her, draped just high enough to cover her ass and nothing else, leaving her whole back on display. There were little marks on the back of her neck, put there by my fingers - no doubt - when she had been going down on me. One cheek rested against the pillow, her face softer in sleep, lips parted slightly.

There was a foreign sensation as I watched her, an odd tightness across my chest. I didn't even know what to call it, but I was pretty sure that whatever it was meant I wasn't going to just be able to walk away like I had done countless times before, just wash my hands of her like this was nothing. Because, quite frankly, I knew it wasn't.

It was something.

Otherwise, I wouldn't have given her my story. I wouldn't have wanted hers. I wouldn't have been *invested* in it as she gave it to me. I wouldn't have asked questions, demanded clarifications.

I wouldn't have pictured finding that dickhead ex of hers and pounding his face unrecognizable.

For what he did to her. What he stole from her.

And also, just be-fucking-cause.

Because a man had to own up to his actions. You didn't pawn your shit off on someone who loved you, trusted you. You didn't let someone you cared about take the rap for your fuck ups.

That wasn't how it worked.

Maybe I was a different kind of criminal. More of an old school one. Like the mob with their code of honor. Brotherhood meant loyalty up to and including self-sacrifice. It meant taking your charges. It meant doing your time. Hell, it even meant doing the time for someone else if it was asked of you.

It would never have crossed my mind to let someone take the fall for my shit.

But this bastard didn't just let some schmuck in his crew go down, lose some years that would be repaid at some later date.

No.

He let his woman go down for him.

A woman who wasn't even knowingly involved in it.

If there was a list of people I couldn't stand - snitches came first, cowards were a clear second.

I couldn't fuck with cowardice.

You didn't get into a criminal lifestyle and expect freedom. That wasn't how it worked. And when shit went down, you manned the fuck up and dealt with the consequences.

I understood her rage. Hell, I didn't even lose ten years of my life, and I felt something similar as she told me the story, as I had a night to chew on it, let it settle deep in my stomach.

That being said, if this was going somewhere with Freddie and me - and something in me said it was, regardless of what I might have insisted to Sugar and everyone else at the clubhouse - I was going to have to find a way to bring it up again, reason with her, make her see that losing more of her life wasn't worth making him pay.

On that thought, I stood, slipping into my clothes, moving toward the door, figuring that Thad would purposely hang around in the main space until we emerged and he could get some words in.

And I thought it might be better if I went out first, got it over with. I didn't think Freddie was quite ready for the teasing yet. At least not in front of me. I knew she would get it in private. But that was different.

This - sex in general - was somewhat new for her.

Hell, even if she hadn't told me, I would have known it. The woman was a fucking live wire, sparking at every touch, her body demanding more at every turn.

Luckily, I could definitely give her more.

"Well well well. I figured that was your SUV parked out front. A bulletproof SUV, too, wasn't it?" Thad asked, standing in front of a coffee pot that was steadily dripping.

"Yeah. Reign likes safety," I agreed as I lazily buttoned my shirt.

"Not gonna lie. That is a good thing to hear. You know, you don't really get to pick who your little sister shows interest in, but a gun runner wasn't super high on our list of potentials for her."

"I get that," I agreed. And I did. If one of the guys with kids had their daughter grow up and fall for some out of town biker, they would have a fucking stroke. "But I'm what you got anyway."

"Mmhm," Thad said, pursing his lips a little. "So, I'm gonna assume that means this wasn't a 'get it outta my system' sort of thing?"

A 'what are your intentions toward my sister' conversation.

Would the new shit never cease?

"She's not out of my system," I told him, not wanting to make some promise that I might not be able to keep, not knowing if she would get out of my system, if I would be out of hers.

The idea of that made an uneasy feeling slosh around in my stomach.

I'd never been in this position before.

Wanting more, but not knowing if the other person did.

"Good to know," Thad said, turning to reach to pull down two mugs, setting them down on the counter, pouring us each some. "You can stop looking at her door, handsome. She thinks she is a terrible sleeper, but since she got out, she sleeps like the dead. And until her alarm wakes her up. Plus, figure she might be a little more wiped out than usual," he added with a smirk. "Uh oh," he said when there was a knock at the door.

"Uh oh?" I asked, reaching for the mug he handed to me as he took his own toward the door.

"You thought you'd just have to deal with the fun, easy going brother this morning. But it is, apparently, a two-for-one kinda morning. Yo, Colson," he called even as he was pulling the door open.

"Is Winnie up? We need to talk about the other... what is he doing here?"

I couldn't even be bothered by his glare. Like Thad had said just a moment before, I wasn't what they wanted for their sister. And I got that. Apparently, Colson was not as easily swayed to the idea as Thad was though.

"He is your little sister's new gentleman friend," Thad explained, passing his coffee mug into his brother's hand, going back to get another for himself. "Took her out on a fancy dinner date and everything."

"Did he leave his guns at home?" Colson asked, closing the door behind him, staring daggers at me as he did so.

"Left 'em in the *car*," I told him, it being the truth. I didn't go anywhere without a way to defend myself. Not since I was a teenager. But I hadn't brought any into Freddie's apartment, not knowing her feelings on that kind of thing yet. She knew my job, of course, but that didn't mean she expected to be exposed to aspects of it. Like my illegal personal gun.

"You're seriously okay with this in your place?" Colson asked, directing his anger to a safer target, one he was more accustomed to shooting at.

"Okay with Freddie having whatever company she wants to have in *our* place? Yes. Since I ain't her father, I am okay with her making her own decisions like the grown ass woman she is. 'Sides, did you get a look at his fine ass?" he asked, sending twinkling eyes at me.

"Look, I get that you like being the nice brother, the one who doesn't say shit so he doesn't have to deal with the backlash of it, but I can't be the only fucking one worried about her future. And if we can..."

"Politely mind your own business and let me live my life for the first time in a decade," Freddie cut him off. Involved in each other, we had somehow missed her getting up, throwing on a simple tee and a pair of silky purple shorts, moving into the doorway. "That would be great," she added, lifting her chin as she stared down her brother.

"I know you think I am being overbearing and overprotective, Winnie, but I just... I want you fucking *here*, okay? Not catching another charge because you end up with another asshole who cares more about himself than you."

"Normally, I'd say this wasn't my business," I cut in, voice low, rough. Angry? Yeah, angry. It wasn't a sound you often heard from me, but there was no mistaking it when it was there. "But don't you fucking dare compare me to that asshole ex of hers. I might not be on the side of the law you'd prefer, but I would never let her go down for *my* shit.

"Aw damn," Thad said, smirking. "You done gone and pissed off an outlaw biker."

"And why the hell should we believe you?" Colson shot back, getting closer.

"Okay, enough," Freddie declared, voice raised, stepping between us, her back to my chest. "You need to leave."

Colson and I both seemed to realize what just happened at the same time, both of us stiffening, looking at Freddie, then each other.

She'd stepped between us, sure, and there was nothing strange about that. The testosterone was stinking up the joint. He was riled. I was ticked off. And neither one of us seemed the sort to back down from a fight. Of course she wanted to stop that from happening.

But she had told her brother to leave.

Not me.

Maybe to someone else, that seemed small.

But to me, and to Colson, it was clear it was significant.

And there was no mistaking the shock of pleasure in my system at realizing she was siding with me. But I squashed that shit down. It was petty. Selfish, even. You didn't make someone choose loyalty like that. It wasn't fair.

"Nah, it's okay, babe," I said, reaching up to squeeze her shoulders. "I will get going. You two have been overdue for a talk for a few days. I'm just in the way."

"You're not in..."

"It's alright," I cut her off as she spun on her heel, looking worried, like she thought I was heading out, never to be seen again. "You gotta repair this shit, or it is just going to keep being an issue," I told her, voice low even though I knew Colson could easily hear and that Thad was doing his best to as well. "Talk to your brothers. Suss this shit out. We will meet up when you're free again," I told her, reaching for my phone, handing it to her. "Put your number in."

I had to admit, her confused slow blink up at me was fucking cute as shit.

And *cute* was not a word I had ever - in my recollection - used to describe a woman before.

Yet another first.

She reached for my phone, adding in her number, pressing it back into my hands.

Aware of morning breath, I leaned down, pressing a kiss to her forehead, giving her wrist a squeeze.

"I'll call," I told her, moving out. "Thad, nice seeing you. Colson," I added, simply giving him a nod, then making my way out.

It was a short drive back to the clubhouse, not nearly enough time to figure out what the fuck was going on. With me. With Freddie.

And seeing Reign's bike parked out front that early in the morning had me parking and all but running inside to make sure nothing was going on.

I swear to fuck, the second I opened the door and stepped inside, the stereo system started blasting "*Another One Bites the Dust.*"

"You got jokes?" I asked, zeroing in on West who was pretending to innocently put the iPod down. "You think that's smart given my position and yours?" I asked, shaking my head, wondering what kind of disgusting, ass-breaking job I could throw at him.

"I picked the song," Sug announced, moving out from the kitchen with a coffee mug. "Can't be too pissed at him for being the only one with it on his iPod. So... this thing with that girl, you still trying to tell me it's casual?" he asked, taking a pointed look at my clothes from the night before.

"Why is Reign here so early?" I asked instead of answering, something that made Sugar's lips twitch.

"Roan scoped Third Street over on our side of town last night."

"Selling?" I asked, feeling myself stiffening, wondering if I was going to get chewed out for not being around.

"Looked like it from up in the box," Repo chimed in. "But you know Reign. He wants to be sure before he starts shit. Third Street has always minded its business, stayed on their turf, obeyed an unwritten rule around here."

"Too much turnover lately," Cash agreed, coming in out of the hall. "It was easier when it was Paine or Enzo, back when there was a definite leader for some span of time. They got a new boss every other week the past few years. Some not even from the area. Either don't know how shit works, or don't care."

"Well, whatever leader they got now, apparently, needs to be reminded how shit works in Navesink Bank," Reign pitched in, coming in from the basement which was the backward way of getting up to the glass box. "It went down too fast for Roan to snag a picture and Lo's guys just didn't have a good enough angle to see it, but he was sure he saw a deal. And that fuck has eagle eyes. I don't think he's mistaken. But I don't want to act until one of us sees it up close."

"You want us casually strolling the streets at night?" Repo asked.

"Everyone'll have to take turns. They'll get suspicious if they see the same people over and over. But, yeah, I want someone to see the deal go down."

"And then?" Sugar asked.

Reign's look was all the answer we needed.

It wasn't a pretty part of the lifestyle, but a necessary one nonetheless. You couldn't keep an organization going if other organizations thought they could walk all over you, could get away with whatever they wanted on your turf.

So whoever saw the deal go down would wait till the buyer was gone, check for cops, then drag the bastard in for a beatdown.

After that, I imagined we'd all get on bikes, drive on down to Third Street, and drop their man at their doorstep as a warning.

"And if that doesn't cut it?" I asked.

"Then Third Street will need to be looking for a new leader," Reign declared, shrugging.

I wondered, not for the first time, how much blood was on his hands. My old presidents had been delegators, rarely down in the real muck of it, letting everyone else do the dirty work in case shit went down, and the law got involved.

Reign wasn't a hands-off kind of leader. And his club had endured more than its fair share of ups and downs, interference from outside influences. Hell, there was the war alone he had raged after his men were gunned down in their own clubhouse. We'd only heard it secondhand from Edison, but he'd described the bloodbath, the beaten and prone bodies of men on the floor he'd needed to step over as they dragged him out of the place, the savage look on Reign's face, the blood and brain matter all over his body.

I'd been there to witness how hard he went at Abruzzo when his daughter went missing.

Reign was someone who kept his cool, collected information, ruled with a level head. But when he needed to have business handled, it was raw, brutal, unapologetic. It was easy, at times, to forget that. You saw him with his kids, with his wife, saw him being a family man, and you forget that he was a man who had beaten faces in, shot men dead, tortured answers out of tight-lipped people.

He was calm now, seemingly, but as soon as he had the kind of proof he wanted, he would take a hold of every neck in Third Street until they remembered that *he* was the big dog in town, and that he fought when you rattled his fucking cage.

"I know it might be hard to fit a patrol into your new relationship," Reign went on, eyes dancing, lips quirking up. "But you're gonna have to pen it in."

"Shit, you too?" I asked, laughing despite myself. It wasn't often Reign took it upon himself to rib any of us. It made a man forget he was capable.

"Dunno when you fucks are gonna learn not to say 'Not me' about relationships. As soon as you say it, you are the next to find yourself a woman. Wanna stay single, keep your mouth shut."

West mimed locking his lips.

"Eh," Reign said, shaking his head a bit apologetically. "Lo has decided you're her new project. So you're fucked whether you keep your mouth shut or not," he declared. "Anyway. Tonight is gonna be me, Sugar, and Virgin. Tomorrow, we will rotate it. But you all need to be available by cell in case shit goes down over this," he told us, making his way toward the door. "I'll be back when it gets dark."

"Whoop, yo," Pagan said, almost barreling into Reign on his way in. "Something up?"

"They'll fill you in," Reign declared, jerking his chin toward us as he made his way out.

Pagan's head swiveled around, a bright red scrape down the side of his face, testament to some scuffle he had gotten his crazy ass into. "The fuck is this? You got a modeling gig or some shit?" he asked, giving my outfit a distasteful once-over.

"Didn't you hear?" Cash asked, looking way too excited to pile on. "Virgin got himself a girl."

"I did hear actually," Pagan informed us, going behind the bar to grab a beer despite it not even being noon. "Don't give me that look. You'd be drinkin' too if you woke up to a busted pipe then a contractor who wanted to fuck you over. Fucking *me* over," he scoffed, cracking the top of his beer.

"That where you got the new accessory?" Cash asked, motioning to his face.

"Well, how the fuck is he gonna learn?" he shot back. "Anyway, Kennedy told me you dropped down in a pedicure chair and moon-eyed some new chick in town. Also said you got ticklish feet," he added, adding even more gasoline onto an already raging fire.

"You got ticklish feet?" Sugar asked, trying his damnedest to hold back a grin. "How do I not know this about you?"

"Shut the fuck up," I demanded, but without malice. "You know, I don't remember fucking with any of you this hard about spending some time with a woman."

"What can we say, we're short on hobbies lately," Cash said, pushing off the bar. "I gotta go up to Hailstorm. Chris is having a lesson with Edison and Lenny. Not sure how this is gonna go."

Chris had made progress as a whole. Had started training up at Hailstorm with Lo, Janie, Maze, Alex, Lenny... most of the girls club. But she lost her shit when she tried to spar off with any of the guys. Fucking understandably so, but we all knew she would never really have full training until she could shake off a man, until she didn't shut down or bug out. I guess they settled on Edison this time because he did his pressure point shit that didn't require full contact.

Lo had taken to motherhood the way everyone had expected her to. Effortlessly. She'd been, after all, a mother figure to everyone in her organization for years already. And because Lo was safe, Chris had taken to her as well, clinging to the calm, confident, capable woman who promised to show her how to be all those things as well. In time.

And Cash, well, he tried. He was there. Present. Persistent. Patient. Even though Chris hadn't been great about showing any kind of affection toward a man yet.

We figured if she were ever capable of feeling that for a man, it would be Cash. Who was, essentially, one of the easiest going, loving men I had ever been around, always good with the kids, quick with a joke, not easily pushed away or offended.

We were all silently hoping for him. For Chris. For all of them and their newfound family unit.

"Only been like a year," another voice joined our conversation. One of the roughest ones we had. Not Edison, Wolf.

And, well, he would be one to know about women and recovery from the horrible things done to them, being with Jstorm.

"How does someone as massive as you walk around like a cat?" West wondered aloud, making heads turn to him. West, it seemed, was born devoid of that hindrance called a filter. Everything he thought, he spewed right out. I had a feeling it would either be refreshing over time, or completely fucking intolerable. Time would tell.

Wolf's gaze slid over, brows pulled together slightly. "Shop floors are dirty," he declared, then made his way toward the bedrooms without another word.

"The shop floors?" West clarified.

"Repo's shop," Sugar clarified.

"What kind of shop?"

Pagan's lips tipped up. "Antique car shop. Good luck with those oil stains, man," he added, clamping a hand on his shoulder before moving off.

"He's serious? He wants me to clean shop floors?" West asked.

"Maybe you can call up Finn for some ideas on cleaners," Sugar suggested.

"Who is Finn?" West asked, lost.

"He's got a lot to learn," Sugar told me as I moved into step beside him.

"Mmhmm," I agreed, both of us enjoying this way more than we should have seeing as Sug and I were in West's shoes not that long ago, having to figure out all the intricate ins and outs of the complicated Navesink Bank criminal underbelly.

"So you gonna see her again?"

"Told her I would."

"Is that a yes?" he demanded to know, not letting me evade.

"It's a yes," I declared, going into my room before he could ask me anything else.

Once some of the guys cleared out, I was given some slack, everyone speculating more on what was going on with Third Street instead of about my fucking feet... or what was going on with me and Freddie.

I texted her, though.

Another first.

Just casually asking how things went with her brother.

She hadn't answered, and I figured it was because she was likely at work.

"Stop checking your fucking phone," Sugar growled at me as I came back in from a casual stroll, my third of the night. Sugar and Reign had been out at least as many times as well.

Nothing.

But then again, it wasn't like Roan saw it every night either. Just once. Maybe it had been a fluke, some newbie who didn't know the rules. Or maybe we just needed to wait it out a couple more nights.

"Do I give you shit about how much Peyton texts you?" I shot back.

"She finally answer? What? Think I didn't know?" he asked, smirking. "Had that sad puppy look all fucking day until, what, she got outta work and answered you, right?" He was right, damn him. And I had about my fill of ribbing for the day.

"Lay off."

"She coming over tonight?" he asked, ignoring me. "Peyton wants to meet her," he added.

To that, I chuckled, rubbing the side of my face. "I don't know if she is quite ready for Peyton yet," I told him.

"She's not that crazy."

"She drives a hearse."

"So?"

"She likes snuff books."

"They're not that bad," he defended her even though I had seen him trying to read one once. And his hardened criminal ass looked a little green.

"And don't think that alien cock story didn't get around to me too," I added, making him smile as he hung his head, knowing he was defeated.

"I don't want the girls to get their hooks into her until I know where things are heading myself," I admitted.

"That's fair enough," he agreed. "But you got about a week before they all get on your ass. So decide shit fast."

A week.

I figured that would work. If we spent time together and didn't get sick of each other, then, yeah, it was fair to say it was heading somewhere. I wasn't talking hearts and rings and shit. But maybe somewhere serious enough that she might be around the club some more. Which would warrant her getting to know the girls club.

My phone buzzed in my hand, something it took her half an hour to get up the nerve to text.

Do you want to come over?

And fuck yes, I did.

TEN

Freddie

The next week was a blur.

But in a good way, not that 'I am too busy and can't even enjoy a moment of my day' kind of blur.

I went from adept enough at handling the often overwhelming input of orders at work to an old hand at it, the pride something pure and unmistakable.

Abby praised me - in her characteristic, offhand sort of way - and then had teased me endlessly about blushing in response to it.

Then I would get home, shower, spend a little time with Thaddeus.

Then Ty would be at my door.

I wasn't sure what I had been expecting after the first night. I guess a part of me had actually figured I would wake up alone.

Not to the sound of voices in the living room.

Thad.

Colson.

Ty.

Then, I figured, maybe all the family squabbling might also be a turn off for him, might send him running. Especially since it wasn't something he was used to. I fought with my brothers practically since the cradle. It was as common as a casual conversation for us. But Ty had never really had a chance for a traditional family. And his arguments with biker brothers likely led to blows, not heartfelt conversations like most of my family fights ended.

Case and point, me and Colson after Ty left.

Thad had handed me a coffee, then walked us both over to the dining table, forcing us each down into seats across from each other, then declared, *"Sort your fucking shit out. I need to go do a full-body shave and lotion*."

With that mental image, he left us alone, full of raw feelings, uncertainty, offense, and more than a pinch of anger on both our sides.

Then, well, we had the hard talk.

Spanning ten years of uncertainty and misunderstandings.

By the end, we had both gotten it all out, all the resentments, hurts, disappointments.

It was all fine.

Until we got to the subject of Ty.

"He's an arms dealer, Winnie."

"I'm aware of that. I'm an ex-con."

"No you're not," he insisted.

"But I am. On paper. According to society. I am."

"But you're not really a criminal, Win. He is."

"You don't even know him and you think we're better than him. That's close-minded."

"It's not close-minded to call a criminal a criminal," he insisted. "We all make choices in life. And we do that knowing people will judge us based on them. Whether you like that, or agree with that, or not. That's how it is. And people who work for a living view people who choose to make a living illegally as less. That's how it is."

"Why is what he does any worse than the gun stores?" I shot back. "And don't bother talking about background checks we both know are a joke. No one blames the gun store when someone takes one of those guns and shoots up a school or does a drive-by or shoots their wife dead in a drunken rage."

"Buying them illegally makes it harder for the cops to do their job," he insisted, losing steam and he knew it.

"Yes. They do a real bang-up job around here," I said with a snort. "There's a street gang in town selling Easy Lay and they aren't doing anything about it. But you know who plans to? The Henchmen. Because maybe they sell guns to people who would *find them regardless*, but they also have morals. They stand up for women. They don't let things get too crazy around here."

"You can't call a vigilante a hero."

"Why the hell not? I don't know what world you are living in, Colson, but the one I have been in has been a lot uglier, I guess. Do you know how many women I was housed with who were molested as kids, raped as young women, beaten by their husbands? And even if they reported it, nothing was done. Do I think it would be *wrong* for someone to deal with those men in a less than legal way? No. No, I don't. Vigilantes exist because the law stumbles and falls flat on its face sometimes. And no one should get away with it just because of a technicality. So, yeah, anyone who sees a wrong and rights it is a hero in my book. Whether they wear a badge or not."

Colson looked away for a long minute, putting his thoughts together, before coming back with, "I can't fucking lose you again, okay? You get that? I know you were inside and that was its own kind of hell. But it wasn't great being out here, knowing you were stuck there, knowing I couldn't protect you, couldn't help you. And it sucked that you couldn't be here. Couldn't come out with Thad and me when he finally came out, have something called a Strictly Dickly *Cock*tail at a gay club a couple towns over. Couldn't celebrate Christmas with us. New Years. Your birthday. That you didn't get to see Jelly as a baby, watch her turn into the sweet little hellion she is now. It sucked for you, but it sucked for us too. And I can't deal with that again. You getting involved with a criminal means there is a chance that you could get wrapped up in something and go away again."

"Fool, did you not hear that fine ass man say that he would never let her go down for his shit?" Thad asked, coming out of the bathroom with a burst of steam, rubbing oil over the top of his head and down his cheeks. It was his anti-aging miracle solution he mixed from four different oils. "My heart went pitter-patter at that shit."

"What he says and what he does are different things. I'm sure Tanner never told you he was going to let you go away for his crimes."

Tanner, I felt, was a sore spot not just because of what he had done to me. But because Colson had met him. Had been charmed by him just like everyone else. Had approved of me dating him.

The betrayal had to have hurt him as well. Filled him with guilt. He didn't want to feel that way again. He didn't want to think that his approval of a guy was a factor in why I dated them, why I may end up in prison because of them.

"I'm not asking you to approve of Ty..."

"Oh, he has a real name. Ty. I like that," Thad butted in, shameless in his eavesdropping as ever.

"But I am asking that you trust me to make my own decisions. I have no intentions of going to prison again for a guy I'm dating. Trust me."

"So... you think this is something?" Colson asked, carefully. "Not just a..."

"Fuck-buddy situation," Thad supplied for him, knowing Colson was not quite as easy talking about his little sister's sex life as he was.

"Yeah, more or less," Colson agreed.

"Honestly? I don't know. In case you forgot, I am new at all of this. And he isn't exactly..."

"A serial dater," Thad supplied.

"Exactly. So this is new for both of us. We don't know what this is or where it is heading yet. But... there's... I feel like there is something here worth exploring."

"You sure that isn't just the orgasms talking, sweet pea?" Thad asked.

"Who invited you into this conversation?" I asked, shooting him small eyes, but smiling. "I felt it before things... escalated," I supplied, feeling more uncomfortable than I ever recalled feeling around them before. "I'm not saying I am going to marry the man and have a dozen future arms-dealing bikers. I'm just... I like him. And it's been a long time since I got a chance to like anything or anyone."

"And she deserves a little happy," Thad added, jabbing Colson in the shoulder with his elbow as he passed.

"Yeah, you do deserve some happy," Colson agreed, giving me a small smile. "I won't keep snapping at him when I see him."

"That is the best he can do," Thad said, sitting down. "Accept it. Now both of you have a hug. Then you gotta go pick up my cute niece from her play date, so we can go to the park."

So we hugged.

And we moved forward.

The next time he saw Ty, he wasn't exactly all warm and fuzzy - but, really, no one would ever call Colson warm and fuzzy unless they saw him with Jelena - but he kept his opinions to himself, didn't grill him, even shared a meal with us.

Which brought me to Ty.

Every time I thought of him, my brain did that cheesy thing that early two-thousands romance movies did, showing him in slow motion, doing basic things like buttoning his shirt or sitting down at his desk, making seemingly banal tasks look incredibly sexy.

I slow-motion thought of his hands sinking into my hips, his lips pressing into my neck, the look of complete satisfaction when he finally got me naked a second time after a long stalling game from Thaddeus who clearly enjoyed the daggers I shot at him as he kept insisting we had to watch just one more episode of some show he liked that I could barely pay attention to because Ty's hands were absentmindedly stroking over my neck and shoulder.

I expected some belated awkwardness as Thad finally went off to sleep and we were alone, but Ty's lips pressed into the spot right under my ear, and he casually asked if I wanted to go to bed too.

As if there was any chance I didn't as my body was pure liquid beside his.

There was no slow teasing. There were no tentative touches, feeling each other out.

The door barely closed before our hands started ripping at clothing, greedy for skin to touch, taste, feel pressed against our own.

I managed to get off his shirt before he reached for mine, pulling it up over my head, but not my arms, yanking it back down, pinning them to my sides as he dragged off my yoga pants, sinking down to his knees before me, yanking up my leg, pushing it over his back, and burying his face between my thighs, driving me up... up... up.

Then stopping, nipping into my inner thigh when I whimpered in disappointment.

Then back he went to my clit, circling, sucking, flicking with his tongue.

Up, up, up.

Then pulling away again, a low chuckle moving through him when my leg sank into his back, trying to pull him closer, make him finish, give me the fireworks he kept denying me.

By the third denial, my poor, confused body was trembling with the need for release.

Then and only then did he slowly get back onto his feet, freeing me of my shirt before discarding the rest of his clothes, lips sealing over mine as he scooted me backward toward my bed.

It wasn't until the backs of my legs touched the side that he ripped his mouth from mine, grabbing me, turning me, folding me forward onto the bed on my hands and knees, ass up in the air toward him.

"Great fucking view," he growled, one of his hands slapping down on my ass, massaging the smart away for a long moment. His other hand slipped forward then down my belly, moving between my thighs, gliding two fingers inside of me, thrusting lazily until my muscles started to tighten again, threaten oblivion.

I had prepared myself for his refusal.

But the denial was no less torturous to my overly sensitive system.

My hands curled into the sheets, my forearms moving down onto the mattress, pressing my ass further out toward him.

A low, rolling growl moved through him, his body half-turning, snagging one of the condoms off the nightstand, protecting us just a second before his hand sank into my hip, holding me still as he shoved inside me with one hard, thick, demanding thrust.

The angle allowed him so deep that there was a foreign, delicious little pinch that I felt myself pushing back against, my hips wiggling in a small circle as his body stilled, taking a deep, steadying breath.

His one hand stayed planted, the other landed another loud whack to my ass, the pain making my body jerk, jolt backward, forcing him even deeper, something that I was sure wasn't possible.

"Work your clit for me," he demanded, voice rough, needy, a sound that made my belly swirl around deliciously, taking away any sense of hesitation, embarrassment as my weight shifted onto one arm, the other slipping down my body, fingers touching his cock where our bodies met before gliding upward, stroking over my clit as he started to thrust.

Hard. Fast.

The bed slamming back against the wall, something that would surely wake up Thad if he had even gotten to sleep yet already.

But I couldn't seem to work up a care as Ty fucked me harder, faster, as my body tensed for another orgasm I wasn't sure it would be allowed to have.

But even as the thought formed, Ty's hand pressed down on top of mine, pushing it harder against my clit - the unexpected contact making the orgasm slam through my system, making my breath catch, my muscles tense, my voice get strangled in my throat, something like a choking noise only managing to come out as the waves crashed and crashed, as Ty kept fucking me through it, dragging it out, before he planted deep, hissing out my name as he came.

His body folded forward with the impact of his climax, his head resting between my shoulder blades as he fought to get his breathing back to normal.

"Didn't think it was possible, but that might have been better than last night," he declared as he slid out of me, my boneless body falling over onto my side, watching as he moved away to the trash bin he knew was on the other side of my nightstand now, then coming back to the bed. "Move over," he demanded with a slow, lazy smile, smacking my ass until I complied, scooting over to leave just enough space for him to climb in behind me on his side, knees under mine, chest to my back, arm over my belly.

Spooning.

It was a silly word.

And one he would probably hate if I murmured about it aloud.

But I let the smile spread, a private little joy, as he sputtered some of my hair out of his mouth before finally settling still, his chin on top of my head.

"Hey Ty?" I called a while later, long enough that I was sure he was asleep, which would have let my long-contemplated question fall on deaf ears.

"Yeah?"

Damnit.

Now I had to ask him.

"What are we supposed to do now?"

There was a short pause. "I was planning on getting some sleep, waking up, fucking you again, then going back to sleep," he declared lazily, completely oblivious to the sparks his words set off through a system that should have been satiated. At least for the night.

"That's not what I meant," I admitted, voice small.

"What'd you mean?"

"Just... in general. What are we supposed to do now?"

"Fuck if I know," he admitted. And, well, his admission of cluelessness somehow managed to comfort me. "But I think we'll be doing a lot of fucking. Maybe getting out of this apartment a bit. Doing shit in the world. Maybe you can come and re-meet some of my brothers eventually. And their women who will be banging down your door in about a week, I am told, if you do not show up and meet them for yourself. And I mean that literally. They will run a check, find out your address, and fucking show up here."

So, it seemed, we just... fell into a swing of things. Into a, dare I even think it, relationship.

My heart, the silly, unpracticed, hopeful little thing it was, swelled at the idea of getting more of this man. Of getting everything.

"We could go to the clubhouse tomorrow instead of here," I suggested, not wanting him to know about my heart and its premature yearnings. "I'm off actually. So... we can go whenever."

"Sounds like a plan. So can I sleep now? I need a good three or four hours if you want me on top. Less if you're willing to ride," he added, giving my belly a squeeze.

I felt it in my chest too.

It was there.

In my bed.

With Ty behind me, falling easily asleep, that I realized I was in too deep. Deeper than I should have been.

"Bitch, you would lose a single minute of being close to that fine ass naked man?" Thad asked an hour later as I sat on the kitchen counter in my panties and Ty's shirt, cradling a cup of tea in my hands. "Is that peppermint?" he asked, sniffing my cup. "Your stomach bothering you?"

"I have feelings for him," I admitted.

"And that is making you sick to your stomach?" he asked, brow raising.

"It's too soon to have feelings."

"It's maybe too soon to want to marry him and give him a litter of babies. But it's never too soon for feelings, boo. I got feelings for that fine ass man at the post office. He could handle my package any-fucking-time."

I snorted at that, taking a sip of peppermint that I hated, but drank whenever my belly felt wobbly. And wobbly was what it felt right about then.

"I meant real feelings, Thad. Like heart fluttery feelings."

"Fred, if your heart ain't fluttering, he wouldn't be worth spending time with at all, right? The heart flutter is what you want at this stage. Down the road is when you can admire his ability to piss *in* the bowl or scrape your windshield in the winter. Right now, it's about the flutter. Down the road is when you start to see a note about being out of TP as a sign of love since he doesn't want you wiping your ass with a coffee filter. That is down-the-road love. Flutters, flutters is fine right now."

"I've known him less than two weeks."

"Did you declare your undying love to him when he rang the bell?"

"What? No."

"Then cut the shit, boo. This is not a big deal. Feel what you feel. No one can tell you it is too soon to feel how you feel if it is *how you feel*. But don't be talking about how you feel for a bit. That's my advice to you. And, honey child, I have a lot more experience with the menfolk than you. So you can trust me. Pour that shit down the drain. You need a glass of wine to make you sleepy," he decided, reaching for the glasses.

So I had wine, got sleepy, and went back to bed only to be woken up two hours later.

But I sure wasn't complaining.

Nor was I complaining when he woke me up early with a cup of coffee made the right way and yet another orgasm.

"You can't still be come-drunk, baby girl. Get up. You got nothing in the house."

"There is plenty in the house," I objected. "The veggie drawers are full. There's fruit on the counter."

"Babe, you're making my point. There's nothing in the house. Let's get lunch. Then head over to the clubhouse. You want me to pack some shit for you?"

"If I let you pack for me, there would be no bra or panties," I objected, begrudgingly sliding my legs off the side of the bed.

"Yeah, well, it's stupid to pack shit you won't need," he agreed, eyes dancing.

"You want me walking around the clubhouse around your buddies without a bra on?" I shot back, watching as the dancing stopped.

"Alright. Bra. But there is no need for panties," he insisted. "Just more layers to peel off."

"I don't mind the peeling," I told him, getting to my feet, grabbing the oversized hobo bag Thad had picked up for me, tossing some clothes inside of it, then going into the bathroom to shower, throw necessary toiletries in it as well, then coming back out to find Ty dressed and ready to go.

We went to lunch, talking about the new menu items Abby was considering. About the changes in the town in general. He gave me a rundown on the organizations and how they interconnected. He told me about the women in the girls club. Which, admittedly, filled me with a feeling of inadequacy. They all sounded like certified badasses who had all sorts of skills or training. And here I was. A short order cook. Ex-con. And... that was about it.

"Got nothing to worry about," he told me, seeming to read my thoughts. "They didn't all start off as what they are now. And there are some who don't really have any skills or shit. Rey and Penny and Kennedy come to mind. Bethany. I mean, they all train now. But it's more of a bonding thing with them now. They don't go out and get their hair and nails done, sip mimosas at brunch. They head up to Hailstorm and try to beat the shit out of each other. Figure it might be why there is almost no in-fighting with them. Any hard feelings get worked out in a physical way. Keeps 'em all happy."

"I wouldn't hate learning some self-defense," I admitted.

It seemed smart, now that I really knew what kind of town I was living in. What threats were around every corner. It would be nice to know I had more than a puny pocketknife to protect myself with.

"They'll be happy to teach you the ropes. You ready?"

To meet a clubhouse full of stone cold sober bikers who all had to be curious about me?

"Not at all," I admitted, sliding out of my booth. "But let's go."

As I expected, Ty must have gotten word back to his friends - likely through Sugar - that he was bringing me over for the night. Because the place was packed whereas he told me it was generally just the single guys who hung around all the time now.

And that list was short.

Roan.

Cam.

And, I guess, West.

I wasn't really sure if they counted him in anything yet until he was out of the prospecting phase.

But he was there. So was Cam, sitting in the living room. West offered me a simple *Hey pretty lady*. Cam opened the lid of a box of donuts, silently - of course - offering me one.

"No thanks. We just had breakfast. It's nice seeing you again, though.

"Alright, who's ready to see the woman who made good old Don't-Give-A-Fuck Virgin give a fuc... shit," another voice trailed off, looking at me guiltily. I knew him from sight.

Roderick.

"I'd apologize, but it's the truth," he admitted, shrugging it off. "You came in here knowing you'd be facing all of us? Brave woman," he decided, reaching for a donut for himself.

"Alright, so you know Roderick, Cam, West. This is..." Ty started, motioning to a man who really needed no introduction.

"Sugar," I cut him off, sending the man a genuine smile. "Ty told me a lot about the trouble you guys got into when you were younger."

"*Ty* did, did *Ty*?" Sugar asked, shooting his friend a raised brow.

I wasn't sure, but I figured maybe Ty giving me his real name, his government name, meant something.

"Your name is Ty?" West asked, almost seeming amused by that fact.

"What's your real name?" I shot back, defensive.

"Apparently, we only give real names to the women we shack up with so they call us it when they come," he told me with a smirk. "So by you asking, I can only assume that Ty here hasn't been performing like you..."

"Easy," Sugar called, making my head snap in his direction, finding him with a palm slammed into Ty's chest, holding him back.

Yes, holding him back.

The most calm, laid-back, didn't-give-a-fuck person I had met had his fists balled, chest puffed, jaw set to stone. Like he was planning on beating the hell out of West for just a comment.

"Who isn't behaving?" yet another voice asked, coming out of the hallway. He was tall, thin, red-haired, tattooed. Attractive. With almost unsettlingly sharp eyes, like he could see right in under your skin. "Dad is here, we need to behave," he added, drawing my attention to the man following him out. Tall, dark, handsome, and a bit, well, terrifying. I didn't have to know to know that was the president. Reign. He carried himself like he owned the place. Because, well, he did.

"The fuck you say now, West?" Reign asked in a sort of resigned father way, the tone he used on a particularly trying, rule-breaking child. "You didn't get enough from Lou earlier?"

Lou.

I rolled through the list of names I had been trying to remember.

Lou wasn't a guy. It was Adler's woman. A bounty hunter.

"I just asked her an innocent question," West insisted, but his lips were twitching.

"You asked her if she liked it when someone used her own cuffs on her in bed," Renny corrected.

"What did he do?" Reign asked, looking at me, then Ty. I was never so thankful for someone to look away from me before. I felt like a little girl facing up the principal. Even though I hadn't done anything wrong.

"Ran his mouth," Ty told his boss.

"Clearly. The fuck never had a mother wash it out with soap as a kid, and it shows. Look, I don't really give a fuck what happened, but you need to remember that you're a prospect, not a brother. You show respect. You bite your fuckin' tongue if what you are about to say insults the patched members. Or their women. Not only do they have a say in your future here, but I'm not protecting your ass from a beating if they get pissed off at you." With that, he turned his attention back to Ty. "Kinda interesting to see you riled up though," he said, shrugging it off. "I'm assuming if you got your girl here, you want off the patrol tonight?"

"I'll cover for him," Sugar offered. "Peyton is going to a - and I quote - Pussy Pleasure Party. Whatever the fuck that is, I don't think I want to be involved. I'll hang back tonight."

"Alright, sounds good. West, doesn't the bathroom need to be re-grouted?" Reign asked.

"Which bathroom?" West asked, dread already in his tone, knowing the answer.

And Reign, yeah, there was pure joy at hearing it.

"You're gonna need a lot of fuckin' grout," he added, moving past him and out into the yard, chuckling a little to himself.

"Don't think he likes me very much," West decided, but sounded completely unbothered by the fact.

"Think he just likes taking you down a peg or two," Roderick supplied. "And, not for nothing, but you kind of need it."

"What? Me? I'm pleasant as fuck. Right, Freddie?"

"Sure. A real delight," I said, only half teasing. He actually did seem nice enough. He ran off at the mouth, didn't think things through, was a shameless flirt, but it all seemed in good humor. Even if maybe Lou and Ty didn't take it that way.

"Yo, West," Sugar called when he went to walk away.

"Yeah?"

"What did Lou do to you?" he asked.

"He got acquainted with those cuffs of hers," Renny supplied. "As she locked him to her wing mirror and made his ass run as she drove across town. He looked ready to drop by the time she got to the yard to unlock him."

I was pretty sure Lou was going to be someone interesting to know.

"Lost five pounds in sweat," West agreed, shaking his head.

"He's a dick," Renny declared, but without malice.

"So are you. Yet here you are," Roderick told him, smiling.

"That's fair enough," Renny agreed. "So, what's your story?"

"None of your business," Ty chimed in immediately.

"It's not like they aren't going to find out if what you said about them running background checks is right."

"It's right," Renny confirmed. "And we always like when someone has the balls to tell us up front."

"I just got out of prison," I supplied, finding the words easier than they would have been just days before.

"No shit?" Sugar asked, making it clear that Ty hadn't been talking about me, about us. I couldn't help but wonder if that was a good or bad thing. "How long?"

"Ten years."

"You were a baby," Roderick said, shaking his head.

"Just turned eighteen."

"What'd you go away for?" Renny probed. That was how it felt, too. Probing. Like an invasion.

"None of your business," Ty declared. "That is for Reign to know if he wants to."

"Alright," Renny agreed, holding up a hand, letting it drop.

"So... we hear you cook," Roderick said.

"She's not here to cook for us," Ty objected.

"I don't mind. If I'm going to be here, the least I can do is cook dinner," I said, tone light, countering Ty's unusual severity.

"See, she doesn't mind," Roderick said with a victorious smile.

"Come on, let's go put your bag down," Ty said suddenly, reaching down to grab my hand, pulling me with him down the hall.

"What's the matter?" I asked once we were out of earshot.

"They're grilling you," he grumbled, pushing open a door, pulling me inside.

"So? I kind of knew that was how it was going to be. They're curious."

"You don't owe them answers about your past."

Why?

Because this was temporary?

If he planned to keep me around in the long term, his friends would all know about my past, right?

"What's this?" Ty asked, moving closer, pressing a finger between my brows where two lines had to have been formed.

"Not..."

"Nope. We're not doing that. Straight answers. That's what we've done so far. Think it's a good system."

"If I am going to be... sticking around for a while, wouldn't they all figure it out eventually?"

"Yeah," he agreed, nodding. "But on your terms. And after you've talked to Reign. The guys - especially Renny who likes to dig too deep into everything - will take that information and twist it before it got to Reign."

And Reign was hard about drugs.

I guess that made sense.

Jumping to conclusions was only going to create undue stress.

"Still didn't explain the frowning," he told me, head ducking low, forcing me to keep eye contact.

"It's nothing. I just... wondered if you didn't want me to tell them because you didn't plan on me being around long enough to."

He was silent for a minute, considering. "Tell you what. If you start wondering about something, ask. Seen too many people get into stupid ass fights over something that could have easily been worked out if they talked about it. I'd prefer not to be those assholes."

I liked that.

He was right.

Fights because people refused to have an adult conversation were ridiculous, unnecessary.

"Speaking of fights," I said, smiling a little. "Were you really planning on getting into one with West?"

"No." My heart sank a little at that, realizing some primitive, cavewoman part of me had thrilled at the idea of him fighting for me. As base as that might have been. "I was going to knock his ass out. There wouldn't have been any fighting," he added with a smirk, like he knew I would like that.

"You don't need to get into fights over my honor. I can handle myself."

"Sure. But I don't mind handling shit too. These are my people. They need to show you respect. I will make sure of that. Well, except the women. Can't make them do shit. You're on your own with them," he added with a head shake.

"I'm kind of excited to meet them," I admitted. "Especially after the handcuff story."

"Just... don't say I didn't warn you," he said ominously, leaving me to wonder what he meant.

About a week to the day later, I would find out.

And he *did*, indeed, warn me.

But nothing could have prepared me.

Nothing.

For a woman with mermaid hair and tattoos.

Named Peyton.

ELEVEN

Freddie

There was a quiet knock on Ty's door at the clubhouse, making my head turn in that direction.

The men were all loud stomps and door slams and raucous laughter.

No way was one of them knocking that softly.

So I guessed it was time.

I was going to finally meet the notorious girls club.

I wasn't entirely sure what had kept them all away up to this point.

Maybe Ty had a conversation with his brothers, asking them to keep them away until I settled in more. Which, admittedly, sounded a lot like him. He had this compulsion to try to shield me, like I was so pure, like I hadn't seen a lot of the rougher sides of life. Maybe I should have told him that it was fine, I could handle it, he didn't have to worry about me. But, quite frankly, I liked it. I liked his need to take care of me, to kind of cocoon me in safety. Maybe that all stemmed from what happened with Tanner, the betrayal, the distrust. It was new, refreshing, sweet to find someone so completely on the other end of the spectrum.

I would tell him eventually.

That I could handle myself.

That he didn't have to tell his friends to shut up when they started talking about some of the brutal things they had been a part of, didn't have to jump in and said no for me when I was offered to go to shooting practice with them.

It had only been a couple weeks.

There was time to show him that I was stronger than he thought.

I moved slowly off the bed, feeling a familiar aching in my thighs that had been letting me know on an almost constant basis lately that regular sex was the best leg workout known to womankind.

Reaching down, I slipped on the jeans Ty had pulled off of me just hours before after we came in from dinner with Thad and Colson and - amazingly - Jelly. I was sure Colson would never let those two interact, but something had passed between the men. Maybe they'd shared words when I had been out of the room at some point or something, but whatever hard feelings that were there softened if Colson was letting Ty meet Jelena.

I grabbed one of Ty's shirts, slipping it on, then going to the door, pulling it open slightly to reveal a small, pretty blonde. Who had a whole pack of dogs sitting in the hall behind her.

Blonde. Animals.

This had to be Rey. Reeve's girl.

"I'm not supposed to be here," she informed me with a glance over her shoulder. Like someone might come and track her down, make her pay for breaking the rules. "But I thought you might want a little notice. The girls are taking you out tonight."

"All of them?" I asked, feeling a bit of dread fill me. Meeting a few, I was sure I could handle that. But all of them at once? That would be more intimidating than I felt prepared for.

"Just a couple of us," she clarified. "Peyton, Lenny, Lou, and Liv. I mean, you never know if someone else might show up, but those are the only ones I know about."

"Do you know where we're going?" I asked, inviting her in as I moved toward my bag, rummaging for something to wear aside from Ty's shirt.

"To Peyton's to pick her up. Then it's, ah, her plan. And we're all in the dark."

Words like *Pussy Party* came to mind.

"I should be scared then, huh?"

"Terrified," Rey agreed. "I hope you're not easily embarrassed," she added, reaching down for one of her dogs - one with a missing eye - holding him to her chest as she stroked his head.

I, unfortunately, was, but I wasn't going to psych myself out of the night before it even happened.

"Should I be expecting them to come charging in with a hood to throw over my head?" I asked from the recently re-grouted bathroom, slipping on a bra and a dusty rose colored off-shoulder peasant top, gliding on some of my lipstick that Thad was right about. It had become my signature look. After trying to make my hair look less recently-rolled-around-the-sheets, then made my way back out to find Rey trying to shoo her dogs out into the hall.

"I wouldn't put it past them," Rey told me with a head shake. "But it is usually a fun time, even if it can be a bit unnerving at first. I hope you don't have problems with female - or male, actually - nudity," she added, moving into the hall.

"I spent the last ten years in a women's prison. I think I have seen all there is to see of the female body," I admitted.

"So Peyton flashing someone isn't going to break your stride," she said with a nod before walking down the hallway into the common room.

Peyton, I knew, was important for me to get along with. Not just because she was part of this girls club I had heard so much about. But because she was Sugar's woman. And Sugar was the closest thing to family that Ty had.

I'd never had much of a chance to build strong female friendships. My aunt hadn't allowed much hanging out after school growing up, so my brothers were the best friends I had. And then it was pointless to try to build those kinds of bonds in prison when people would get out at any point and try to put everything involved with their life behind bars behind them.

Hearing the stories about the girls club - both the older members and the newer ones - filled me with a sense of curiosity, wonder, and maybe hope. That I could fit in with them, get bonds like that myself, have what sounded like an amazing support system.

You needed someone to help watch your kids? Done. Drive you home after drinking too much? Absolutely. Someone to come over and make you soup when you're sick? No hesitation. Just someone to sit and ease your anxiety at the DMV while you're waiting for your new license? They'd be there too.

The stories said it went deeper than that as well. If you got in trouble, the kind of trouble that women in their lifestyles might get into, the girls came together, helped you fix it. By whatever means necessary.

I didn't plan on getting into any kind of trouble.

But that was a fascinating aspect as well.

From a distance.

I took a deep breath, going in Ty's nightstand for a notepad I knew I would find there, something he had used to write down to-go orders, as evidenced by twenty pages I had needed to rip out and get rid of, setting it on the nightstand, and scribbling a note.

I have been kidnapped by the girls club.

Then I waited.

There was no way they could sneak in with Rey's pack of dogs yipping and howling in excitement as, I imagined, the girls showed up.

Figuring there was no reason to stand in my room like I was expecting them, not wanting Rey to get in trouble for warning me, I moved out of the hall.

"They kept waking up the birds," Rey said, voice apologetic. "I figured they would be better off hanging here with the guys to keep them occupied while we're gone."

"I had the same idea," another voice said as I moved into the doorway, seeing a woman with another dog at her side, a bigger, light-colored, Pitbull. "Since Adler is on patrol tonight, Linny would be home alone."

"Well, the surprise is ruined," yet another voice announced, shaking her head. I recognized her from the party. She'd been the one to get behind the bar. Edison's woman. Lenny. "So, you're Freddie."

"I'm Freddie," I agreed with a smile. "And you're the girls club."

"Kinda 2.0," Lou told me. "We wouldn't deign to think we are quite as badass as the OGs are."

"I heard what you did to West. I think you're pretty badass," I told her.

"That little shit," she said, smiling fondly. "I like him," she added. "He just needed a little reminder that we don't take that nonsense. Anyway, I'm Lou. This is Lenny and Liv and Rey. And we are taking you with us tonight."

"Where are we going?" I asked, trying to sound like this was the first I was hearing of it.

"That is up to Peyton," Liv told us. "May God help us all," she added with a smile.

"Ladies," Reign said, walking in from the door beside the bar which I had learned was the garage. I had been given a tour of everything but the gun vault since I had been around. "I want you taking the SUV," he added, tossing the keys at Lenny who snatched them out of the air.

"Something up?"

"Not really. I just... I'd feel better if you took it. And keep an eye on your drinks," he added.

The girls shared a look, one that said they needed to have a talk with their men, that they were pissed that something was being kept from them.

"Not that anyone would fuck with your crazy asses," Reign added. "Where you heading?"

"Peyton is picking."

"Not even gonna fuckin' ease her into it, huh?" Reign asked, giving me a head shake. "Go on. Have fun. I'll make sure the mutts get taken out. Did you bring the rest of the zoo over?" Reign asked, looking at Rey.

"Just the dogs this time. I'm still really sorry about the TV," she added, shaking her head.

"The guys wanted a new one anyway. Don't worry about it, babe," he said, moving over toward the kitchen.

"What happened to the TV?" I asked, brows drawn down.

"Charlie - my cockatoo - ah, broke it."

"How does a bird break a TV?" I asked.

"He tried to eat it," Lou supplied, smiling. "Shattered the screen. He's basically a toddler with a can opener for a beak. You should see the poor furniture at their house."

"But he's sweet, so we love him," Rey said shrugging it off, smiling when her crew of dogs heard rustling coming from the kitchen and darted in that direction to, no doubt, beg Reign for a bit of what he was having.

I didn't know him well, but my money would be on him caving and giving them some.

"So, you ready?" Lenny asked, swinging the keys.

"Yep."

But I wasn't.

I so, so wasn't.

It was a short ride to Peyton's place where I could hear another dog inside, sounding like he was chasing a ball someone had thrown as we came to the door, Lenny fishing in her pocket for her own set of keys, slipping one into the lock, and pushing the door open.

We all got a chance to move inside, to have the door close at our backs.

Before Peyton stepped out of her room.

With a giant double dildo strap-on shooting out of her pelvic region.

"Goddamn, Peyton. How many times do I have to tell you that we are not dildo experimentation type friends?" Lenny demanded, but her voice was amused.

I had yet to get a look at the woman.

How could you look away from a double dildo strap-on?

When one of said dildos was green and *pronged* at the end.

And the other was a rainbow-colored unicorn horn.

"Told you," Rey said near my ear, making me shake off my surprise, my head moving up to see the woman herself.

I could see why Sugar picked her. Everything about her from her mermaid hair to her tattoos to her ridiculously pretty face spoke of an alternative type of woman, someone unique, someone to make a man like Sugar stop and take a second and third and fourth look.

"I gotta ask... what is the purpose of the prong?" Liv asked, brows drawn together.

"Aesthetics? For the dragon kink crowd?" Peyton suggested.

"I don't think we can call the dragon kink people a *crowd*," Lenny said with a smile.

"I could see the unicorn one being interesting," Liv decided, nodding. "Are you writing the blurbs for them or something?"

"Peyton's sister owns the local sex toy store," Rey supplied. "And the manufacturers sometimes send her prototypes. Peyton writes blurbs for them. Or just reviews them."

"Why the strap-on, though?" Liv asked, moving in casually, like this was a common conversation for them to be having. Like seeing Peyton with various sex toys attached to her was nothing out of the ordinary.

"Because I have two dicks, that's why," Peyton declared, taking a step forward, making both dildos wobble hilariously, forcing a snort to escape me at the ridiculous sight. "Oh, you're Freddie," she said, smiling at me. I didn't have a hard time smiling back since she was still approaching me and both cocks were wobble wobble wobbling away.

"I'm Freddie," I agreed.

And then it happened.

The only thing that could make this situation more absurd.

The dog I had heard running around came charging out of nowhere, lunging, and sinking his teeth into the pronged dragon dildo.

"Hannibal!" another voice called, coming out from the hall - a woman with short hair, make-up-free face, and a flannel shirt, grabbing the dog by the collar. "Drop the cock," she demanded, barely able to keep her voice sounding firm as she struggled to make the dog let go.

"Well," Peyton said, shaking her head at her dog. "That is quite the way to come out and tell me you like cock, Hannibal."

"Like mother, like dog-son," Lenny agreed, walking over to help Peyton unstrap herself.

"Who doesn't like cock?" Peyton asked, looking over at her other friend. "Even Jamie likes it. Just not attached to an actual man."

"If you're done making your usual impression," Lou said, dropping down on the couch, patting her lap for the dog to bound up on her. "Where are we heading tonight?"

"We're doing an escape room," she informed everyone, casually tossing the strap-on onto the coffee table, wiggling her hips around. "I have to give lesbians - and the spouses of men who enjoy pegging - credit. Those things get heavy after a while."

"An escape room?" Lou asked, looking suspicious. "That is rather tame for you."

"Wait for it," Jamie murmured.

"Oh, God," Liv grumbled, taking a deep breath. "What is fucked up about the escape room, Peyton?"

"It's just a normal, everyday escape room. Where creepy assholes chase you around and threaten to murder you in horrific ways."

"That is not how a normal, every day escape room works," Lenny told her, shaking her head.

"Oh, who doesn't like getting the shit scared out of them every once in a while?" Peyton asked, and I watched as all the hands rose in unison. "Well, too bad. It was my turn to pick. So we're going. Here..." she said, passing around packages.

"Why do we need earplugs?"

"The chainsaws are loud in close proximity," Peyton declared casually, like it was something we all should have known.

"Chainsaws," Lou repeated.

"I'm pretty sure they don't have the blades on them. What?" she asked, rolling her eyes at everyone's less than enthused faces. "Stop being a bunch of pussies. It's gonna be fun."

It wasn't.

It really, really wasn't.

Well, Peyton had a blast.

She was possibly the only person on the planet who could think clearly while a guy came up behind her with a garrote wire, tightening it around her throat.

The actors may have been fake, but the lines on her neck were not.

"Really, I get enough of crazy shit like that at work," Lou declared as we took up a table at Chaz's after we'd finally - thanks to Peyton's calm head, Lou's knowledge of random torture techniques, and Liv's quick moves - gotten out of all the rooms.

"It was fun," Peyton insisted, cheeks flushed from excitement still.

"Rey had to be escorted out by the owner. Reeve is gonna be pissed at you," Lenny reminded her.

"I called to check on her! She's fine."

"She went home and woke up Charlie to snuggle," Liv shot back.

"Alright, what about you? You've been quiet," Peyton said, pushing a glass of some mixed drink she'd shouted out to the bartender on the way in toward me. "Did you like it?"

"I, ah, just spent ten years locked in a room," I hedged, not wanting to say it was one of the freakiest nights of my life. That having a guy stand behind you threatening you with despicable, terrifying things felt real even if you knew they weren't actually going to do it.

"See? This is why we should be in charge of the nights out," Lou declared.

"You took us to *workout* last time," Peyton objected, grimacing.

"There was a short hike up to the bar," Lou clarified. "No one made you strap icepicks onto your feet then insist on wearing them on a trek up a hill."

"I vote Freddie picks the next outing," Liv decided.

"Oh, no. Don't vote for me. I have no idea what this town is like now. I've really just been working and... hanging out with Ty."

"I still can't get over the fact that his name is Ty," Lou said, shaking her head.

"So, was prison more like *Oz* or *Orange is the New Black*?" Peyton asked.

"Fair warning, she is going to be disappointed if it isn't like *Oz*," Jamie pitched in.

"It's... like neither. I mean... I have only seen trailers for *Orange is the New Black*, so I don't have a lot to reference. But they had more freedom than we did. And all those love stories..." I said, shaking my head.

"Oh, come on. There had to have been some lady loving going on," Peyton insisted.

"There was. But you were lucky if you got three minutes away from a guard or other inmates. So, usually, it was a lot of women priming themselves up then just quickly going at it, hoping they didn't get seen and put into segregation."

"Not hot," Peyton decided, clearly let down. "Why are you watching my drink?" Peyton asked when she turned to say something to the bartender, and everyone zeroed in on the drink her eyes weren't on.

"We don't know," Lenny admitted, clearly annoyed that Edison hadn't told her yet, even if he was under orders not to. "But Reign told us to watch our drinks."

My mouth opened and closed twice. Knowing, perhaps, why Reign was telling us to be careful since Ty had mentioned date-rape drugs being sold on the street. But maybe that was something he wasn't supposed to tell me. Maybe he would get in trouble if it got back to them - by the girls telling their guys that I knew, and were mad that they weren't told.

Unsure what to do, for the moment, I bit my tongue.

"You know... I was at a club last week," Jamie said, brows furrowing with concern. "Cops had to be called twice because two girls went from fine to flat on their asses in minutes."

Lou and Lenny shared a look.

"Why wouldn't they tell us if Forget-Me pills are on the streets around here?" Lenny asked, maybe doubly annoyed because she worked in a bar.

"I don't know. But Adler is right down the street, and I intend to find out," Lou decided, dropping money on the table, moving to stand.

And when there was one determined woman in a group, there was a whole gaggle of them.

Not two minutes later, we were on the street, making our way toward the clubhouse.

"Shite," Adler said, shaking his head as we all walked along the gates.

"Shite is right," Lou agreed. "You're in trouble," she added. "How could..."

She didn't get to finish her sentence though because agitated male voices were approaching from the other end of the street.

Pagan and Sugar flanked a man they each had by the arms, only half-conscious, face bloodied.

"You can punish me later," Adler said, unlocking the gates.

"You guys need to disappear," Pagan declared as we approached. "Reign'll be pissed if any of you get involved in this," he added, shoving the man toward Adler.

"I know it's kinda your default, baby," Sugar said, wiping some blood off his cheek. "But don't be stubborn right now. Go home. We'll call."

I expected them to object, to fight, to demand not to be left out. This group of headstrong women who had been on a mission just a moment before. But to my surprise, they all turned in unison, Peyton slipping her arm through mine, half pulling me away, leading me back down the street where we all shuffled into the car.

Lou, this time in the driver's seat, didn't immediately turn the car over.

"He was Third Street," she said in a small voice after locking the doors. "Right?" she asked, looking to Lenny in the passenger seat for confirmation.

"I didn't get a great look, but I'm pretty sure I've seen him around, yeah."

"And he was on the wrong side of town," Liv agreed.

"What am I missing?" I asked, all of them seeming to have some sort of silent conversation without me.

"This town is territorial," Peyton supplied. "Everyone stays away from the docks but the Grassis. Everyone stays away from Third Street except members of the gang. And everyone stays away from Henchmen turf but Henchmen. Especially if they are dealing drugs."

"And even more so if they are selling date-rape drugs," Lenny added. "It never ends."

"What doesn't?"

"Club drama," Lou explained. "There are periods of peace followed by some kind of situation that has everyone on lockdown or partial lockdown. Or has the men tearing out of town, strapped down. Making all the women worry until they get back."

"Come on," Peyton said, suddenly a voice of reason. "Sean said to get back to my place. Let's move."

Girls night started with a humorous high, hit interesting levels of anxiety, then agitation, then worry.

You could feel it in the air as we got back to Peyton's place, all of us huddled in her living room, episodes of *Angel* playing on the TV, but everyone seemed to be staring through the TV instead of at it.

I couldn't claim to understand their fears, not knowing nearly as much about the town, about the organizations, about how they all interacted, to know what this issue with selling drugs on Henchmen territory meant in the long run.

But the others, well, they seemed to have a lot to think about.

Hours passed.

The knock on the door made us all jolt.

Peyton flew off the couch, knocking the strap-on off the table in the process, clearly excited to see Sugar, to know he was okay.

"Oh," she said, sounding disappointed as she looked through the peephole. "New girl, you're up."

I hopped up, moving into the doorway as Peyton pulled the locks and slid the door open.

There was Ty.

Injury-free from what I could tell.

But there was something in his face that put me on pause, a hard set to his jaw, an uncertainty in his eyes.

"We need to talk."

His hand moved out, grabbing my wrist, pulling me outside with him.

He looked back into the apartment. "Sugar will be here in a minute. If the rest of you want to head back to the clubhouse, you can," he added before turning, his hand slipping down to grab my hand, pulling me along with him.

Ty said nothing as we made our way out of the building, across to the lot, then climbed on his bike.

Uncertainty wobbled in my stomach as we rumbled down the street.

Why did Ty need to speak to me?

Of all people.

Lou and Lenny and Peyton and Liv knew much more about this whole situation than I did.

Maybe he just wanted to explain what I had seen, knowing that I was new to his lifestyle, that - what the records said aside - I knew nothing about crime. He could just want to soothe my nerves, make sure I wasn't freaking out.

That, more than anything, made the most sense.

Maybe his jaw was clenched because he was worried about what my response would be to what I had seen. Maybe his eyes were full of uncertainty because he didn't want me to freak out and leave over this.

And, in all honesty, that made sense.

Because that was how normal, sane people responded to seeing a beaten man dragged into a clubhouse to, as one might imagine, get beaten yet again. Maybe worse.

I should have been horrified.

Were he simply an innocent guy who had done nothing, I would have been.

But I found I had very little pity for a man who was selling drugs that would allow other men to sedate and rape women.

"Ty, what's going on?" I asked as his hand went to my lower back, leading me into the clubhouse where no one was around, save for Reign.

"Go on," Reign said, giving Ty a nod.

"Alright, so you know about this town and their different organizations..." Ty started.

"I know that the man earlier was from Third Street. And that they were on your territory. And that someone has been selling date-rape drugs in town." I left off the part about Ty being the one to tell me all that.

"Can't keep shit from those women," Reign murmured.

"It didn't take too much thinking to put it all together," I informed him with a small smile. "You told all of them about watching their drinks. But... why am I here and not the others?"

"Alright, so this club doesn't tolerate anyone working on our turf," Reign explained since Ty seemed hesitant to go on. "I especially don't put up with someone selling drugs on it. And that goes quad-fuckin'-drupal when it comes to shit like Easy Lay. So we have been keeping an eye out to confirm our suspicions. Tonight, Pagan and Sugar caught someone dealing just half a block away. They brought him in. For *questioning*," he went on, not even trying to make it sound like bloodshed wasn't a part of it.

"Okay..." I said, looking at Ty, eyes questioning. Why the hell were they telling me all this? And not the others?

"We wanted information on the new leader of the gang," Reign went on. "They have changed leadership a lot lately. We didn't know who is running the operation."

"The guy told us that one of the guys who has been in the organization for the past eleven years decided to rise up," Ty pitched in, giving me the feeling that we were getting to the important part if he was the one finally telling it to me. "Someone who started when he was twenty. Had some unique ideas on how to sell the drugs without it being obvious what was going on. Someone with a spiderweb tattoo on the side of his neck."

And there it was.

Ten years charged back to me at once, knocking out my air, giving me the sensations of that day all over again.

The unyielding, cold hood of the police car against my chest and stomach. The tightness of the cuffs around my wrists. The way his face had been utterly blank while my heart went just shy of in attack mode, my belly twisted painfully, my skin breaking out in a sweat, the fear making bile rise up in my throat.

Betrayal.

God, the betrayal.

Nothing would ever feel like that day had.

The day my life as I knew it ended.

"He was here the whole time?" I asked, my voice sounding choked.

The floor felt like it was crumbling underneath me, like the world was trying to suck me into its core.

Ty's hand moved out, grabbing me under the elbow, keeping me steady.

He'd been in town the whole time.

Selling date-rape drugs.

Ruining more lives.

The anger, buried under those things I told myself wouldn't make a difference to my plans for revenge - hope, dreams, happiness, the ideas of a future, a sweet, budding relationship - came back with a vengeance, overtaking me completely.

My hands curled.

My teeth clenched.

My skin started to buzz.

"Breathe, baby girl," Ty demanded. "We're not done," he added. "I know that your plan when you came back was to do something about him. Track him down. Make him pay for what he stole from you. And I figure that revenge of yours had a lot to do with something that might have gotten you locked up again."

"Ah, yeah," I admitted, something that made Ty smile a bit. "What?" I snapped a little, offended that he was amused by the idea.

"Don't underestimate a fucked-over woman," Reign butted in, sounding amused. "They are a force to be reckoned with."

"Anyway, Reign and I figured maybe we could give you what you want, but in a way that won't make you give more of your life away."

Were they offering to... take care of him for me?

Why would they ask? Involve me? When they clearly wanted to handle the situation themselves?

"Why are you running it by me?"

"Because, I figure, it isn't a great way to start something with us by doing something behind your back. And what we have in mind isn't what you had in mind for him."

"What does that mean?"

"It means sometimes the best revenge is giving someone exactly what they gave you," Reign said. "I'm not in a place where I can judge you for wanting him to bleed for this. Trust me, I've been there. But you're free, babe. You don't want to throw that shit away on something as fleeting as revenge. And I don't think you're the sort who could do something like that without regret."

"What is it that you guys have in mind?"

"Reign knows someone in the NBPD who would like nothing better than to stop the date rape drugs on the streets."

"You want to tell them what you know, catch him dealing, and put away for distribution."

"Had Jstorm look into this Tanner fuck. He's been pulled in half a dozen times for possession. But they never caught him with enough on him to really put him away. With that on his record, they will throw the book at him," Reign told me.

Throw the book at him.

Like they'd done to me because of him.

"It's the right revenge," Ty reasoned, seeming to think I was hesitant. "It's the same punishment for the same crime."

"But he might get out in ten years, get right back on the street, doing all this again."

"That's a problem for a decade from now, Freddie," Reign told me. "Don't take on tomorrow's problem right now."

"I didn't want to take your revenge away from you. You give us the go, we'll call Lloyd. You don't think it's good enough, we'll handle it another way."

Another way.

They'd kill Tanner.

For me.

And not just any of them.

It was Ty who would do it.

He would get blood on his hands, take a life, take the risk of getting caught.

For me.

No matter my concerns about the future, Reign was right, that was a problem for then, not now. Now was the issue of Ty.

And I didn't think we could have a future with a body between us. I would never forgive myself for letting him do that for me.

"Call Lloyd," I said, voice not having enough conviction. "You're right. I wouldn't be able to go through with it myself. And I couldn't let you do it either. But he needs to pay for what he has done. Call the NBPD."

"You're sure?" Reign asked.

"I'm sure."

"I might be able to persuade Lloyd to let you get a couple minutes in a room without a camera with the bastard," Reign suggested.

"I'll think about that," I said with a small smile, oddly grateful for his interest in what would make me happiest. "Can I ask something?"

"Sure," Reign agreed.

"Putting Tanner away doesn't really fix the whole problem, does it?"

"We'll see. Maybe someone else will step up and continue this shit. In which case, we'll have to handle it."

"I mean with the date-rape drugs."

"Those will stop," Reign said, voice suddenly fierce. "They can sell what they want to people who use it to ruin their own lives. They aren't going to be selling shit on these streets to ruin others. It's not just us who will have a problem with it either. Mallicks, Grassis, Hailstorm. No one is going to let that keep happening."

"That's good to know," I agreed, giving him a small, grateful smile.

It was half an hour later that Detective Lloyd showed up, casting a knowing look at Reign as I peeked out from the hallway. "So, I'm not going to ask of the fate of the man who gave you this information."

"Not like you'd get a straight answer anyway," Reign agreed.

"So, tell me how to get these drugs off the streets," Lloyd demanded, pretending to completely ignore that he was, essentially, in enemy territory, a place he knew was full of illegal guns, dirty money, and, well, who knew what else.

"Come on," Ty said in a quiet voice, moving in behind me, wrapping an arm around my waist. With that, he led me into his room, dragging me down on the bed with him, tucking me in at his side. "You alright?"

"I'll be better when I know he is not walking the same streets I am," I admitted. "But I'm glad to know it's going to happen soon."

"Lloyd doesn't like working with us. Sometimes, he will look the other way, going after guys who do worse shit than us, but he doesn't like having to sit here and take advice from us. So it shows how hungry he is for this arrest. I imagine this will be done within the next week."

"Hey Ty," I started, voice small after a long silence.

"Yeah?"

"Where's the guy? From earlier," I specified, knowing I probably wasn't supposed to ask questions like that, but not able to stop myself.

"Chained to a bunk bed in the basement," Ty supplied without hesitation. "He will serve us better alive. But he can't go tattling back to his boss. So we will be holding onto him until Lloyd does his job."

I could, oddly, live with that.

It made sense.

And it wasn't like the guy was innocent.

"You think you're gonna wanna have some alone time with him?" Ty asked, voice hesitant.

"I think I would like to lean against the hood of the squad car that will be taking him to county."

"I'll make that happen."

Nine days later, there I was.

With Ty by my side.

It was a day oddly similar to the one ten years before. The sun was out. The weather was warm, but not hot. I even had open-toe sandals on. Just like the ones I'd had on when I'd been arrested.

Ty had gotten the call just half an hour before from Lloyd, telling us it was now or never. So we'd sped across town and got ourselves situated where we needed to be.

Nerves skittered in my stomach, some part of me worried he might do something. But, really, what could he do? Even if he used his calls from county to get in contact with his gang, to try to put some hit out on me or something, there was nothing they could do. Not with the whole of every organization in town watching out for me.

"All you, baby girl," Ty said, pressing a kiss to my temple before moving a few feet away as the door at the side of the station opened.

All the times over the years that I thought on the idea of revenge, none of it compared to seeing Tanner, older, hair thinning, face riddled a bit with acne, far less carefree and attractive than he once had been, being led out of the police station with cuffs in front of him, flanked by a cop in blue and a newly familiar detective in a suit, one who shot me a small smirk as they came into view.

I leaned back a little, wanting to go for casual, not wanting this to appear like what it actually was. A moment I had been anticipating for over a decade.

The moment he got what he deserved.

The moment he knew I was a part of it.

Tanner's head raised, squinting a bit at the bright light after the dark of the building, not seeing me for a long moment.

Then, even after his eyes landed on me, not recognizing for another long few heartbeats.

His lips parted.

His eyes widened.

His feet forgot to keep moving forward.

"Winifred?"

"You took ten years of my life. I hear they're looking to take twenty-five of yours," I said, tone light, teasing even.

"You bitch. You fucking bitch," he hissed, lunging despite his arms being held, his hands being chained.

Ty moved in, closing in at my side. And Tanner's eyes moved over him, taking in his cut, the badge on his chest, realizing who I had aligned myself with. That he would never get revenge on me.

It was an amazing thing to witness a man whose life slipped away right before his eyes.

Humbling almost.

Since I knew that feeling all-too-well.

And even though he deserved it, even though I had earned it, I didn't take the pleasure from it that I thought I would.

"Thanks, Detective Lloyd," I offered before standing up straight, nudging Ty.

"You ready?" he asked.

Looking over, I took a good, hard look at this man. The one who accepted me without question. The one who urged me to heal a rocky relationship with my brother. Who helped me land a job. Who took things at my pace. Who got me an iPod and loaded it down with all the good songs I missed while I was away. Who proudly introduced me to his buddies. Who helped me get a bad man who ruined my life off the streets.

Was I ready to go with him?

To the ends of the Earth.

Through the bowels of hell.

To, possibly, our own unexpected, lovely, happily ever after?

Abso-freaking-lutely.

EPILOGUE

Virgin - 3 weeks

Lou was hanging out on the couch in the living room, a heating pad on her stomach, three blankets on top of her, but one whole leg stubbornly sticking out.

I stood there in the doorway, not knowing if I wanted to head out there. Lou was unpredictable when she didn't feel great.

I was about to turn around when I saw West come out of the kitchen, making a beeline for Lou.

Letting out a sigh, I stayed put, figuring West was about to say the wrong thing to the wrong woman on the wrong day. I was going to be picking up pieces of him later if I didn't stick around to deescalate the situation.

West moved toward the coffee table, dropping down low. Almost like a bow.

A mug of coffee met the surface of the table off a tray he was holding. Then a pile of cookies. A bag of chips. A beer. And a bottle of pills.

The fuck was he doing?

Even as the thought formed, he ducked his head, studying his feet as he slowly backed out of the room, disappearing back into the kitchen as Lou reached toward the table, popping the top off the bottle, tossing some into her mouth, washing it down with the coffee.

The bottle turned, label out.

Midol.

"I can't figure his ass out," Renny said from my side, shaking his head as Lou let out a grumble, tossing over, burying her face in the back pillow cushions. "He picks at the women. Gets inappropriate with them. Gets punished by them. Does it again and again. Then plays nursemaid when it's shark week?"

"Getting rusty, man," I murmured, knowing it would irk him, maybe liking getting under his skin a bit since he liked getting under everyone else's.

"Reign'll get it all out of him," he told me, moving back toward his room which he'd had West cleaning all morning in anticipation of Mina getting back from some job Lo had her on for the past few weeks. It was why he was a bit more of an ass than usual. Word was, before Mina showed up, Renny could be downright intolerable at times. She'd managed to rein him in a bit. But the longer she was away, the more time he had to himself to fuck around and get lost in his head again.

"Stop staring at me," Lou growled, making me shock back into the moment, finding she had turned again, starting to glower at me.

"Eyes on the floor. Eyes on the floor," West's voice demanded quietly. "Back away quietly," he added, moving with me toward the door.

"I'm not a bear," Lou snapped at him.

"Of course not," West agreed in a placating voice as we moved out the front door. "Have some cookies," he added, quietly closing the door.

"You got sisters?" I asked, curious.

"Got one. And a mama. Aunts. Exes. You gotta give them junk food and space. Freddie likes pizza bagels," he added, making my brows shoot up.

"Good to know."

"And an extra sugar in her coffee. But she won't admit to that."

"Seriously, man, who the fuck are you?"

A slow, sly, foxlike smile was the only answer I got.

Yeah, Reign had to figure his ass out.

Freddie - 4 weeks

"Bitch, what is this?" Thad asked, waving a spatula at my jeans and t-shirt.

"An outfit?" I asked, brows drawing together.

"That is a 'I am comfortable in my new relationship' outfit. You better have something sexy on under it."

"Ty wears jeans and a tee every day," I objected. "Why are you cooking? I thought you had a date with Danny? Or was it Allen? Todd? Where are we in the rotation?"

"I'm taking the week off."

"The week off? From what? Being yourself?"

"Maybe you have inspired me to stop being such a slut, and find me a solid man of my own. I mean... they've all been *solid*," he added with a smirk. "But a steady one."

Steady.

I guess that was what we were.

It was hard to believe that it had been less than two months since we met, since I got free, since my life got set on a path I hadn't anticipated. One infinitely better than the one I had planned for myself.

"That's great, Thad," I told him, meaning it, loving the idea of my brothers finding someone steady in their lives. Though, from the sound of things, Colson hadn't even looked at a woman since Jelena came into the world. He might have been a lost cause until she was an adult and moved out. But I would settle for seeing Thaddeus finding love. The kind that came with more than one night in a row. Which, apparently, was against the rules of his rotation. No back-to-backs.

"What's it like?" he asked, head ducked to the side a bit as he watched me.

"What is what like?"

"Having love blooming and shit," he clarified. "And don't try to tell me you aren't falling. You know you are."

He wasn't wrong.

It seemed crazy to think of that word in relation to a man I had known for, objectively, a very short time.

But we had shared a lot. We'd shared everything. All our ups and downs. Almost every single one of our nights - whether at the clubhouse or my and Thad's apartment.

It had been an almost effortless progression of things. And, sure, at the beginning, I was maybe a bit curious if it was all the sex, the endorphins, the love hormones released during an orgasm. But as the weeks moved on and I found myself happy just to sit with him on a couch and watch some biker show on TV and have him tell me all the ways they'd screwed up the facts, or to bake dessert for him while he told me some more of the back stories of his brothers and the girls, I realized it was definitely more than just physical.

And how did it make me feel?

"Upside down," I decided. "I know that sounds weird, but he makes me feel like I am upside down. In the best way possible."

"*Girl*, get your Diana Ross on," Thad said, humming the song.

"That song is about being in love with a man who cheats on you," I reminded him.

"Don't be a killjoy. Alexa! Play "*Upside Down*" by Diana Ross," Thad demanded, cranking up the volume, grabbing my arm, dancing me around the kitchen.

And all I could think as we danced like a bunch of idiots was... I almost threw this all away. I had *planned* to throw it all away.

I was ready to give up beauty days with Thad and Jelena, lunch dates with Colson, nights in bed with Ty, knowing and having fun with the girls club, having a job I enjoyed and a boss I adored, cooking with my loved ones, showing my love like we had always done.

And dancing around the kitchen like a bunch of teenaged girls in their mirrors.

Maybe I had been wrong, after all.

Maybe I never had to be tough.

Just patient. Just open. Just understanding of the way life sometimes threw things at you for a reason, no matter how hard it may have been to see the reasons at the beginning.

There was a knock at the door.

And thinking it was maybe Ty who got back from a run early, I danced my way over, unlocking the door, pulling it open as I did a twirl.

Then nearly whacking my head against the side of the door at who was actually standing there.

Not Ty.

Or Colson and Jelly.

Not any of the girls. Or the guys.

Not even the neighbor down the hall with pre-read magazines.

Nope.

It was a person I was sure I would never see again. And maybe even a person I *hoped* not to see again.

Auntie May.

She didn't show the years on her face. It was still as unlined as it had been the last time I had seen it - telling her I would help her cook dinner on the day my entire life was thrown off its axis. Her hair was different, shorter, thinning just the slightest bit behind her bangs. She seemed thinner, too. But she had the same eyes. Sharp. All-seeing. All-judging.

A box was nestled in her arms, another on the floor at her feet.

"Who is at my door when I am trying to get my *freak* o... well," Thad started then cut off, all the joy seeming to drain from him at once.

There was not a single person I had met who was more accepting of themselves as Thaddeus was. All the good, the bad, the lovely, the not so pretty. He saw all of himself and loved it regardless of what society said. Nothing and no one could make him question himself.

Or so I thought.

I hadn't been around for their fallout. When Thad finally told the world what those closest to him had always known. We hadn't gotten around to discussing it either. And I guess I had been right in assuming it was a sore subject.

Because nothing stole Thad's joy.

Except our aunt.

"Alexa, off," he demanded, grabbing the edge of the door above my head, holding it steady. It was a silent way of saying there was no way in hell he was letting that woman into his home. "Last time I saw you, I believe you said something about how you would show up at my door when hell freezes over."

"I am not here because I want to be," Aunt May declared, voice as intimidating as I remembered it being. It was funny how it still had me wanting to curl my shoulders forward, make myself smaller, shrink away from her. Ten years away where I had become a grown woman. But I still felt like her presence made me small.

"Then you're here because?" Thad asked. His tone sounded unaffected, bored even. Only I knew it was a front.

"I have had these boxes cluttering up my garage for ten years now. I want them out of my house."

Just like she never wanted any of us in her house again.

It shouldn't have, but it still smarted. Not as much as it would have a decade ago, but enough.

"Good. You dropped them off. Go on and head out. You have made it clear you want nothing to do with any of us. What was the phrase again? Something about being *ungrateful* and *an embarrassment*."

"If you're expecting me to say anything different..." Aunt May started to speak.

"Tigers don't change their stripes. Cheetahs don't change their spots. And old, bitter, unhappy women don't change their minds," Thad cut her off.

"I did everything for you," she insisted.

"Except accept us. And love us," Thad shot back.

"How can someone love a rock in their shoe?"

"How da..." Thad started.

"No," I cut him off, shaking my head. "It's not worth the anger. Not anymore. Aunt May, I hope you live a long, healthy life. In your lovely, empty house. And I pray your self-righteousness can keep you warm. And your superiority can be the steadiest of friends. And when you find yourself all alone in that life you built for yourself, I hope you don't know the bitter taste of regret for pushing away your family just because they didn't turn out how you wanted them to."

To that, Aunt May had nothing to say. Really, what was there she could say? She dropped the box down on the other then stormed away, her low heels clicking on the linoleum floor in the same way they had when she had first walked into that child services building the night we met her.

Poetic, that.

"Girl, prison changed you. Made you all wise and shit," Thad said, giving me a small smile as we moved inside, closing the door in what felt like a very final way.

"Wise," I snorted, shaking my head. "This morning, I almost brushed my teeth with triple antibiotic," I told him with a self-deprecating laugh. "When you came out, it was bad, wasn't it?"

"Well, it wasn't all rainbow flags and happy tears, boo. But I didn't expect it to be anything other than what it was. We always knew she was close-minded about this shit."

"Was it as bad for Colson?" I asked since he was in a talking mood.

"Only after he made it clear he wasn't going to put a ring on it. You never met Jelly's mama, but she was a hot mess. Always stepping out on him. Always screaming and throwing shit. He was smart not to shackle himself to that. I mean, you know Colson, he planned to take care of both of 'em. But he had no plans to make it official. Which, clearly, was the right move."

"She hasn't had any contact?" I asked, my heart hurting for Jelena, even though I knew Colson and Thad had done everything in their power to make sure she didn't feel that loss.

"Last Colson heard from her, she was out in California chasing movie stars like she has a chance of getting a sugar daddy or some shit. Not even any birthday cards for Jelly."

"What does she say?"

"Jelly?" Thaddeus clarified. "She doesn't really bring it up. But she told me once that she thinks her daddy needs a mommy to make him happy. Don't get that sad look," he demanded. "You know they are both happy in their lives."

"But they could be happier."

"In a way, everyone could be happier. Except maybe you," he added, giving me a sly look. "You are all glowing and shit. If I knew love would be so good for the complexion, I might have tried it years ago."

Virgin - 2 months

"I'm not scared," Freddie taunted, hopping around on her toes like some stereotypical boxer in a movie, head dipping up and down, hands curled into fists.

A mix of cardio kickboxing classes with her brother and a few trips to Lo and Janie's gym where she'd taken some lessons from Pagan had her get this idea of trying to fight me in her head.

"I'd rather you sparred with the girls," I insisted. "I don't want to hurt you."

"Lo said I'm not going to get better if people treat me with kid gloves."

I imagined Pagan had been careful with her. Not because he objected to going full-force with one of the women, but because he knew I would be pissed if he did with *my* woman.

"And since *someone* sent out some mass text or something about not wanting any of the guys to bruise me, I haven't been allowed to really practice with a guy. How am I going to learn to defend myself against one if no one will practice with me?"

Alright, that was a fair argument.

"You won't need to defend yourself," I shot back. "I got you."

Freddie's arms dropped, her eyes going small.

"Okay. I know it is like... forbidden to even say her name anymore, but from what I hear, there was not a single girl more trained or more protected than Ferryn. She was still taken. Held. Forced to endure who-knows-what. I'm not saying that you can't - for the most part - protect me. But I want to know how to protect myself in case something ever happened when I was at work. Or alone in the apartment. Or walking home after getting my hair or nails done. I don't want to be at someone else's mercy because no one would teach me, Ty. You have to admit that this lifestyle comes with certain risks."

I was painfully aware of that fact.

I had never given the risks a thought before.

It was part of the life. It was part of what drew men to it. The excitement. The unknown. The chance to need to defend yourself at any given moment.

If we weren't - at least in part - adrenaline junkies, we'd have pursued normal jobs.

Accountants.

Electricians.

Physical education teachers.

And it was all well and good when all we had to worry about was our own asses, those of our brothers who also willingly, happily went into the lifestyle.

Everything changed when it was no longer about you and your brothers.

I'd been raised up to be accepting of the fickle hands of fate.

I learned to figuratively and literally roll with the punches.

Very little managed to spark anger.

And the idea of anxiety was a foreign thing.

Until Freddie came along.

Until it wasn't, for the first time, just *my* life who my actions impacted.

Suddenly, all my mind was filled with was these asinine worst-case-scenario fears.

Like what would happen if we were raided and she was in the clubhouse. Guns and illegal money. She could be pulled in and charged. Go to prison again.

I wouldn't be able to fucking live with myself if that happened, if I did to her what her ex had, took more of her life away.

Or what would happen if there was some new, unknown enemy in the shadows, catching me and her walking down the street unaware sometime, popping out of a dark alley with a gun.

What might they do to *her* to make *me* pay?

What if this went where I had a sneaking suspicion this was heading - meaning somewhere serious - and we did the house and the ring and the kid thing. And I caught a bullet like my old man did, leaving her on her own with kids to raise?

It was constant.

And, thus far, uncontrollable.

I wanted to think I could be all she'd need. That I could shield her from anything. But that was my ego speaking. The reality was, she did need to be prepared, trained, capable of defending herself.

She was right.

Aside from some of the women who trained *her*, there was no one more prepared for any situation than Ferryn. Yes, she was still taken, plucked up off the streets like an untold number of women who would never be seen again save for when they were drugged and raped by John after John.

Nothing could stop bad from happening sometimes.

But time spent training for any situation meant you had a chance of surviving it, getting free of it.

Like Ferryn had.

If I was going to pull Freddie into my life, I owed it to her to give her every skill I possibly could.

No matter how much I didn't like the idea of putting my hands on her in a way that would leave marks.

"Okay," I agreed, nodding, watching as her eyes went wide.

"Okay?" she asked, clearly thinking I was going to make her beg.

"Yep. Rule number one..." I started, but then charged at her, grabbing her arm, twisting her around, anchoring an arm around her middle, yanking her up off her feet. "You gotta be prepared for anything," I told her as she kicked her legs straight out. Like most people would do in the same position. "Don't pick up your legs," I told her, dropping her down so her soles touched the ground again. "Use all your momentum to kick off the ground, shoot yourself upward. If you do it soon enough and with enough force, you can break a man's hold. Then it is an elbow to the midsection," I told her, waiting for her to twist to demonstrate. "And, finally, a couple hard-as-fuck closed fists to the cock. Then you haul ass away."

This was stuff the girls would teach her once she was fully adopted in. She'd be dragged up to Hailstorm, be put in every possible situation. Grab from behind. Chokehold. Hair grab. Wrist grab. Rape position.

Then once she managed to break away from whoever was teaching her, someone else would step up. Then another.

And another. Until she bested them all. Then and only then was she deemed trained.

And by then, there would likely be another new girl in the club to train.

An hour later, her tee was damp with sweat, her breathing harsh, hard, her eyes frustrated, but determined, as I slammed her back against the floor in the rec room - or whatever the fuck Reign wanted to call the room that was supposed to house all the prospects that we had co-opted to use for this session - trying not to wince at the crack of her body on the hard floor.

My hands circled her wrists, pinned up above her head on the floor, my upper body curved over hers, the only part of us touching being my pelvis crushing hers down.

The move was simple.

She'd done it a dozen times already with varying levels of success.

She needed to pull up her legs, knees to chest, press her feet into my hipbones with force, enough to shoot pain through my system, make me let her wrists go, allow her more range of motion to keep hitting, kicking, get me down so she could get up and run.

Her feet lifted up off the floor.

But paused, lifted up too high, wrapping around my lower back, clamping tight as her hips lifted up, doing a roll, grinding up against me.

Surprised, caught off-guard, my hands loosened.

Just enough for her hands to slide out.

It happened too fast for me even to react.

Her hands free, she cocked her arm, catching me in the jaw with her elbow with enough force to make me rear back, the crack sending off sparks of pain through my jaw, mouth, teeth. Using the opportunity, her foot finally found my hipbone, cracking in hard, knocking me off, onto my ass.

She was up in a blink, shoving her hands into my shoulders as her hips slammed down on mine, pinning me to the ground.

On top of me as pain ricocheted off my nerve endings, her face victorious, proud, beaming, she was the sexiest fucking thing I had ever seen.

"You're supposed to run," I reminded her, my hands settling in at her hips.

Her smile went slow, sly, as her body folded forward to press against mine, her lips pressing into the spot below my ear as her hips ground down into me.

"You want me to run?" she asked, voice low, teasing.

It was right then that I realized two things.

Training turned her on.

And I suddenly had absolutely no objection to it.

Freddie - 1 year

Okay.

I was being picky.

I will admit that.

And, judging by Ty's defeated look, I didn't even have to.

We'd been looking at places.

As in to move into.

Together.

It was time. We'd spent pretty much every night - save for when he was on a run - together since we had started officially dating. But it was always at the clubhouse where there was next to no privacy, or Thad's apartment that felt a lot more crowded lately since he finally found his upside-down-feeling person.

Had you told me that a tall, skinny, cardigan-wearing, glasses-clad, economics professor would be the one to steal his huge - albeit carefully guarded - heart, I would have laughed in your face.

But Olwen Doyle had been his first back-to-back.

Then his first week-ender.

Then his first meet-the-family-at-a-formal-introduction guy.

Until, finally, four months into dating, they decided it was time to move in together. And since Olwen's place was a shoebox in a crummy area a long drive away from the college, it made sense for them to shack up at Thad's apartment. Where they promptly adopted a bright orange flat-faced cat with unsettling yellow eyes named Odette who silently judged everything you did.

After a couple months of awkward 'we heard you having sex last night' morning interactions, Ty had been the one to suggest it was time to get our own place.

Then probably just as promptly regretted it.

I'd dragged us to eighteen places in seven days.

Some were great, but too far from the clubhouse and my job.

Some were just around the corner, but had noisy neighbors or terrible light or too small of a backyard.

See, my mind was on things other than a house where we could have sex without being overheard.

There needed to be at least two bedrooms.

And a yard to play in.

Because, well, while I hadn't taken a test yet, I was late. And I was never late. You could set national calendars based on the regularity of my schedule. First, the craving for sweeter coffee. Then pizza, always settling for pizza bagels instead of ordering in. The telltale soreness. The cramps. Then finally, the big event.

It never mattered what was going on in life, it came as expected since I was fifteen-years-old.

I was going on three weeks late.

I didn't want to settle for a smaller space, only to have to upgrade with a baby or toddler in a year or two.

"Just this last one today, I promise," I consoled him. "Then I will make you something to eat."

"Two courses," he demanded, rolling his neck as we climbed back into my car which I had proudly bought with my own money after six months of working. Sure, it was three-times used. The back seat had stains that no upholstery cleaner could fix. And the radio came and went. But it was mine. I bought it. I took care of it. Took it for its oil changes. At Repo's garage. Because he, apparently, got butt-hurt if you paid for it at another place.

If Ty thought it was weird that I insisted on the car instead of the bike all the time, he didn't mention it.

We would get there.

I just wanted to be sure first.

"Done," I agreed, thinking of what was in the fridge and cabinets as we drove two blocks over. Still walking distance from the clubhouse. In fact, it was just one street behind where a bunch of the other club members bought houses, nearly owning their entire neighborhood.

It was a quiet street of starter homes - nothing with a second floor, everything with quaint fifth of an acre lots.

The one we were going to see was the last, on the corner that butted up to the back of a soccer field where there used to be little league games when I was growing up. I imagined there still were every weekend. It was a craftsman style painted a sweet gray-blue color with all white trim. I knew from the online advertisement that it was just shy of twelve-hundred square feet with three bedrooms, one oversized bath, and a basement that could easily be converted into more living space.

I knew before we even got out of the car.

"This is it, huh?" Ty asked, moving to stand next to me at the side of the car, looking at the small front porch where I could see us standing in the morning, waiting for our son or daughter to get on the school bus, waving to us from the window.

"This is it," I agreed.

"Alright. Let me go find the realtor."

I went to laugh at that.

It wasn't that easy.

There could be other offers.

There was the matter of loans and mortgage affordability quotes.

But, as it turned out, when someone was willing to pay cash at ten grand over the asking price, it really was that easy.

His arms wrapped around me when the tears - hormonal, they had to be hormonal, right? - Welled up in my eyes. "I love you," I told his chest, feeling it to a depth I never knew existed before.

"Love you too, babe," he said, kissing the top of my hair, his hands moving comfortingly over my back for a long minute before sinking into my ass playfully, making me laugh as I pulled away.

"Gonna have to put a swing set up," Ty told me as we climbed back in the car, making my head whip over, my surprise clear on my face. "I'm a lot of things, babe, dense isn't one of them. Haven't touched the pizza bagels. Eased up on the coffee. Won't ride on my bike anymore. Being picky as fuck about the house 'cause you know we need extra room and a yard. When were you planning on telling me?"

"When I knew for sure," I told him, shrugging it away.

"Well, let's stop on the way home," he suggested. "Let's get sure."

That night after eating pork chops with sides of mashed potatoes and green beans, while waiting for the banana bread to bake, we both huddled in the bathroom, me on the toilet lid, Ty on the edge of the tub, waiting for the timer.

According to the box, one meant nothing.

And life could go on as usual

Two meant we were about to be three.

Sure enough, life as we knew it was about to change.

The next morning, I rolled over to find Ty in bed.

With a diamond ring.

Virgin - 2 years

Roan came flying up the stairs, not even remembering to close the front door on the way out in his hurry.

It seemed the storm he had been waiting for had finally blown into town.

Virgin - 3 years

If there was one person I never expected to see walking into The Henchmen clubhouse, it was my brother-in-law.

Not Thad.

He always showed up when some big event was going on.

But Colson.

The man who approved of my love of his sister, of the life we had started, the family we were building.

But never my lifestyle.

"Colson, everything alright?" I asked, getting to my feet as Sugar sent me a lowered brow look.

"Can we talk?" he asked, voice weighted. It was then I noticed the tension. In his jaw. His shoulders. His hands were clenched down by his sides. "In private?" he added, looking around at Sugar, West, Cam, and Edison.

"Sure. Let's take a walk out back," I agreed. "What's going on?" I asked as soon as we were halfway into the backyard.

"I don't have anywhere else to turn."

"What's wrong?"

Both his hands rose, scraping up his forehead, over the top of his head.

"I lost my job."

He lost *another* job.

He used to have the security job at a club at night, but the owner had gone belly-up, closing without a warning, holding their last paychecks hostage.

That had been less than a month ago.

And I knew that he must have already been hurting financially.

Neither job paid that much. He paid a lot in rent to live in a nice area of town so he could send Jelly to a good school. He had her dance classes. And lately, karate. Freddie had suggested it, had wanted to give it to her niece as a gift, but Colson was a man with a lot of pride. He had insisted on paying for it himself. He also had a savings he put away for her college.

So losing one of the jobs had to have made him hurt.

Losing the second one must have been devastating.

"Downsizing?"

"Someone fucking accused me of stealing," he told me, his breath a savage hiss. "Me. Been there forever. Never even took a ketchup packet home. But they are sure it was me. Fired just like that. No reference. And, to be perfectly honest - and it fucking kills me to admit this - I was already hurting."

"That's fucked, man," I told him, shaking my head. "I'm sorry to hear that."

"Don't make me beg," he demanded.

Beg?

My head twisted to look at him. Seeing the desperation, the uncertainty, but also the determination.

And I understood.

I had once told Freddie that if he ever needed a better-paying job, more security for him and his daughter, to get in touch with me.

This man, who so completely disapproved of my lifestyle, wanted to sign up.

"I'll talk to Reign," I assured him, clapping a hand on his shoulder. "My word will go a long way. So as long as you don't change your mind, I figure you will have a weight off in a few days."

The numbers of the club were decent.

Reign didn't want to get much bigger.

But he would do this as a favor for me so long as Colson got through an interview and prospecting.

"I won't change my mind," he assured me with absolute certainty.

He didn't either.

I could see it the moment Reign handed him the cut.

The weight that got lifted from his shoulders, a weight he had been shouldering for years. Near poverty and single parenthood full of uncertainty and stress.

He wouldn't have to worry about money again.

About taking care of Jelly.

About not being able to get out of work when she was sick or off from school.

He was set.

Because he was now a Henchmen.

Freddie - 10 years

"Ronan, get your turtle off your plate."

Motherhood, it seemed, consisted of sleepless nights, endless worries, annoying cartoons on obnoxious repeat, and saying a bunch of phrases you never could have imagined yourself saying before.

Especially, I imagined, when you chose to raise a small litter.

We were on four.

Ronan, our oldest, a wildlife lover who spent most of his free time over at Rey's place, playing with animals. And, apparently, bringing some of them home too.

Then there were the twin girls. Aged five. Zora and Jovie. Who I swear loved their Uncle Thaddeus more than me.

Then, finally, two-year-old Carver. Who still loved me best. Bless his heart.

"He's hungry too," Ronan insisted.

"He can eat in his tank."

"He's part of the family too."

"Let me get the kid a dog," Ty whispered to me as he passed. "It would stop all the little critters."

He'd had them all.

Hamsters of the dwarf and full-size varieties.

Guinea pigs.

Hermit crabs.

Mice.

"The cage cleaning is worse than the upkeep of a dog," he added.

He wasn't wrong about that. I spent a couple hours every week cleaning out cages and tanks and making specialized meals for all his creatures.

I had been worried about a dog knocking over Carver who was still a little unsteady on his feet. I figured it would be something to look into in another year or two.

But maybe it wasn't fair to Ronan to deny him something he would absolutely get a lot of joy out of because of his brother.

"Something small," I specified. "And don't say anything until Rey finds something. Otherwise, we'll never hear the end of it."

"Knock knock," Thad's voice called, cutting off whatever Ty was about to say.

"Uncle Thad!" Zora and Jovie said in unison, hopping off their chairs it had taken me twenty minutes to make them sit down in for breakfast.

"And Uncle Olly," Thad added, moving inside. "And someone else."

Honestly, I expected their cat.

Who they brought everywhere.

I never thought it was possible for Thad to keep a secret. He was far too into attention, in being the center of every conversation.

He couldn't keep it to himself when he got a wax, or when he and Olwen tried a new sex position, or when he had a really fantastic brunch somewhere.

But, apparently, he could keep some things secret.

Big things.

Like the baby hopped up on his hip.

It all came back to me at once. The way Thad had been more distant lately. The way the guest room door at their apartment was stubbornly closed when it was always empty. The extra classes Thad was taking on at the gym, earning money I didn't think he truly needed for anything. And, of course, their mini-vacation they took last weekend.

It wasn't a vacation at all.

It was a trip to pick up a little girl with huge brown eyes in a doll-like face.

"Oh, my God," I gasped, settling Carver on the floor, forgetting all about cutting up apples and pears to go with the oatmeal I was supposed to be making. "Why didn't you tell us?"

"Like you told us?" Thad shot back, still a little salty about the fact that we hadn't told anyone the news until we were almost five months along.

"That was different," I insisted, moving close, leaning down to give the baby a smile which she returned easily, without hesitation.

"Mmhmm," Thad said, rolling his eyes. "Anyway, this is Bea. Her birth mother named her Beatrice," he clarified. "But we like Bea better."

"She's beautiful."

"She sure is," he agreed, leaning into Olwen who automatically put an arm around his husband, rubbing the side of his face against Thad's.

"You're going to be an amazing daddy," I told him, meaning it from somewhere deep.

"I've had a lot of practice," he brushed the praise off. Something the Thad he had been a decade ago never would have said.

A decade.

I had hardly even noticed the passing of it.

The same span of time that I had lost inside a prison.

It was amazing how much had changed.

Thad had shaken off his singleness, had found the man of his dreams, had started his own family.

Colson had become a Henchmen. He had found a woman who made his family complete. Jelena went from the cutest little girl to the most beautiful young woman. Who could dance like a swan. Or kick your ass if you looked at her wrong.

I had a strong, amazing, unexpected support system of fantastic female friends who could seem to sense when I was at my wits end being shacked up with all the kids, and show up at my door with coffee, with new craft projects to keep the kids busy, and would sit with me, having adult conversation that solidified the brain that started to go to mush when all it had to think about was diapers and laundry and if the new show the twins were into was mildly sexist or bully-promoting or not.

There were the men too, a whole new, giant group of brothers. The kind who would change the oil in my car without having to be asked. Who all showed up on the day when a giant swing set arrived, ready to get it all together. Who all happily watched the kids when the girls all wanted to go train at Hailstorm.

And, of course, then there was the best of all the men.

At least in my little opinion.

Ty.

It was hard to believe it had been a decade. It felt like last month when we had been cuddled in bed after our first night together, eating brownies right out of the baking tray. Just last week that we shopped for houses and watched a stick tell us our lives would never be the same.

He'd been right there in the room, letting me nearly break his hand as we welcomed Ronan into the world.

He'd dried my cheeks after an epic meltdown when, suddenly, at just three months, Ronan refused to breastfeed any longer, and we needed to switch to bottles.

He'd wrangled Jovie in front of him while I worked on Zora, both of us carefully styling their hair as quickly as possible.

He would sit up with me after we put all the kids to bed, exhausted, but not ready for sleep, wanting some adult time to just exist.

In the mornings, we would take our coffee out to the front porch while Carver played in the gated living room, waving as the bus took Ronan, Zora, and Jovie to school.

We'd created a life from what had felt like - at the time - impossible odds.

We'd become the couple I never thought I could have.

We'd become the parents the world had denied us.

He'd been the man I hadn't even let myself dream about.

And more.

So much had changed.

And I was so incredibly thankful.

"Bitch," Thaddeus said in a low voice, hip free of his new daughter, "what in the actual fuck are you wearing?"

Well, some things stayed exactly the same.

And for them, I was thankful as well.

XX

DON'T FORGET!

Dear Reader,

Thank you for taking time out of your life to read this book. If you loved this book, I would really appreciate it if you could hop onto Goodreads or Amazon and tell me your favorite parts. You can also spread the word by recommending the book to friends or sending digital copies that can be received via kindle or kindle app on any device.

ALSO BY JESSICA GADZIALA

If you liked this book, check out these other series and titles in the NAVESINK BANK UNIVERSE:

The Henchmen MC
Reign
Cash
Wolf
Repo
Duke
Renny
Lazarus
Pagan
Cyrus
Edison
Reeve
Sugar
The Fall of V
Adler
Roderick

The Savages
Monster

VIRGIN

Killer
Savior

Mallick Brothers
For A Good Time, Call
Shane
Ryan
Mark
Eli
Charlie & Helen: Back to the Beginning

Investigators
367 Days
14 Weeks

Dark
Dark Mysteries
Dark Secrets
Dark Horse

Professionals
The Fixer
The Ghost
The Messenger
The General

STANDALONES WITHIN NAVESINK BANK:
Vigilante
Grudge Match

OTHER SERIES AND STANDALONES:

Stars Landing
What The Heart Needs
What The Heart Wants
What The Heart Finds
What The Heart Knows
The Stars Landing Deviant
What The Heart Learns

Surrogate
The Sex Surrogate
Dr. Chase Hudson

The Green Series
Into the Green
Escape from the Green

DEBT
Dissent
Stuffed: A Thanksgiving Romance
Unwrapped
Peace, Love, & Macarons
A Navesink Bank Christmas
Don't Come
Fix It Up
N.Y.E.

ABOUT THE AUTHOR

Jessica Gadziala is a full-time writer, parrot enthusiast, and coffee drinker from New Jersey. She enjoys short rides to the book store, sad songs, and cold weather.

She is very active on Goodreads, Facebook, as well as her personal groups on those sites. Join in. She's friendly.

STALK HER!

Connect with Jessica:

Facebook: https://www.facebook.com/JessicaGadziala/
Facebook Group: https://www.facebook.com/groups/314540025563403/

Goodreads: https://www.goodreads.com/author/show/13800950.Jessica_Gadziala
Goodreads Group: https://www.goodreads.com/group/show/177944-jessica-gadziala-books-and-bullsh

Twitter: @JessicaGadziala

JessicaGadziala.com

<3/ Jessica

<<<>>>>

Made in the USA
Monee, IL
16 April 2022

94754177R10142